DESERT HEAT

ELIZABETH REYES

ATRIA PAPERBACK

New York   London   Toronto   Sydney   New Delhi

ATRIA PAPERBACK

A Division of Simon & Schuster, Inc.
1230 Avenue of the Americas
New York, NY 10020

First Atria Paperback edition May 2014

ATRIA PAPERBACK and colophon are trademarks of Simon & Schuster, Inc.

For information about special discounts for bulk purchases,
please contact Simon & Schuster Special Sales at 1-866-506-1949
or business@simonandschuster.com.

The Simon & Schuster Speakers Bureau can bring authors to your live event. For more information or to book an event, contact the Simon & Schuster Speakers Bureau at 1-866-248-3049 or visit our website at www.simonspeakers.com.

Interior design by Kyoko Watanabe

Manufactured in the United States of America

10 9 8 7 6 5 4 3 2 1

Library of Congress Cataloging-in-Publication Data

Reyes, Elizabeth.
  Desert heat : a novel / Elizabeth Reyes.
     pages cm
  Summary: "Between running from her past, working three jobs, and worrying about her family, the only thing that could further complicate singer Bethany Amaya's life is falling in love. But after serendipitously attending a speed dating event and meeting the intense and sexy detective Damian Santiago, that's exactly what happens. In the blink of an eye, Bethany is caught up in a passionate affair with the most irresistible man she's ever met. As their romance heats up, Damian's skills of detecting and reading body language begin to raise his suspicions. Bethany is keeping something from him. But Bethany refuses to get Damian caught up in her troubles. She feels that some things are better left unsaid. With everything suddenly working against her, the race is on to fix her life before the truth is revealed and Damian finds out it's even worse than he imagines. Steamy and addictive, *Desert Heat* is the story of a fiery whirlwind romance threatened at every turn by a dark secret."— Provided by publisher.
  1. Love stories. I. Title.
  PS3618.E9383D47 2014
  813'.6—dc23
                              2014008278

ISBN 978-1-4767-3458-3
ISBN 978-1-4767-3459-0 (ebook)

DESERT
HEAT

To Mark.
There's no way I could do this without you, and without
you none of this would mean anything. I love you!

ACKNOWLEDGMENTS

I *need* to thank my family, who continue to love and support my art. I'm eternally grateful for your patience with me while I'm lost in writing, or when I go on and on about an idea that's brewing. I know I can be *bad* sometimes, but I love you for "getting it" and just going with it.

To my beta readers, Dawn Winter, Judy DeVries, Emily Lamphear, Theresa Wegand, and my *commadre* Inez Sandoval—you're all just an amazing group of women, and I feel so blessed to have you all on my team. I thank you for continued dedication and for not having gotten tired of my endless questions. I look forward to working with you on *all* my other projects!

My dear friend Tracey Garvis-Graves, I'm so honored that you took the time out of your very busy schedule to read my novel and give me your feedback. It really means the world to me. Thank you so very much!

To my agent, Jane Dystel, I feel so blessed to have you in my corner, thank you for all your insight and guidance throughout this entire project, and I look forward to having you there for many more.

To my editor at Atria/Simon & Schuster, Johanna Castillo,

thank you for seeing something in my writing and deciding to take a chance on it. I'm extremely grateful for this awesome opportunity. I only hope I make you proud! As you know this experience is a very first for me. I thank you for your patience and thorough explanation while holding my hand through it all.

I'd also like to thank the many bloggers out there who have supported me, reviewed, and participated with my cover reveals and announcements. You guys have been a HUGE part of my success, and I thank every single one of you from the bottom of my heart!

I want to give a special shout-out to "my FP girls," my very special group of incredibly talented and superstar authors. Without you, I think I'd be insane by now. You really are the only ones who truly, *truly* get it. Thank you for the support, love, and *always* being there, ready to say the perfect thing when I need to hear it most. I hope to be including you all in my acknowledgments even when I'm on my eightieth book! I love you all!

And, of course, my incredibly awesome readers! Thank you so much for your continued support, emails, messages, and comments, which always seem to come at the most perfect time, making me smile and sometimes even tear up. I've had the enormous pleasure of meeting and chatting with many of you, and I really hope to meet you *all* one day! I love you guys, and I can't wait to get the next one out to you! I wish there were more ways I could show you all my appreciation. I hope to have a few surprises for you guys in 2014 just to show you that I really am listening and reading ALL your messages and comments!

Desert Heat

PROLOGUE

Drowning in the reality of this impossible nightmare, Damian stared at her, the words coming out of her mouth nothing more than a droning buzz. Only one thing mattered right now: Could this really be true? He'd convinced himself for weeks that this was all in his head, that there was no way it could be true. As he stood there after hearing that it was even worse than he'd suspected, his heart still held out hope that there was some kind of explanation.

Taking her abruptly by both arms, because his heart couldn't take even a second more of this, he stared into her tearful eyes, his own vision beginning to blur now, too. "Just tell me one thing. One fucking thing, Bethany. It's all I need to know. Is it true?"

Her pinched brows over her pained and flooding eyes said it all. The very weak nod was the final confirmation. Just like everything else that had happened between him and Bethany—at lightning-fast speed—the lava in his veins was instantly frozen, and the murderous rage he had felt just moments ago was replaced by something so numbing he could barely breathe. His heart was still fighting it, but there was no way around this. No reasonable explanation. Not anymore.

Damian had no choice but to accept it now. The relationship he'd dived into so impulsively, never imagining he'd fall as profoundly in love as he had so quickly, had been viciously pulled from under him like a rug flipping him over on his back and knocking the wind completely out of him.

CHAPTER 1

Speed dating—The day they met
9 weeks earlier

Why the hell had he agreed to this? Damian drummed the Speed Ticket, a booklet they were all given in which to take notes when they got to the hotel banquet room. The whole thing was such a joke. Damian's eyes bounced around from one desperate sap to another, all sitting there with their badge numbers on their shirts. He glanced down at his and nudged Jerry. "Hey, man. I changed my mind. I can't do this."

"Why?" Jerry leaned toward Damian.

"This is so stupid. Look at these losers."

The guy with the thick glasses next to Damian sat up straight and fidgeted with his tie.

Jerry elbowed Damian and whispered, "Just give it a shot." He frowned before reminding him, "You promised, Damian. Besides, you owe me."

Damian sank back in his seat. The door to the waiting room opened, and the same woman who had assigned them their badges and given them their Speed Tickets walked in, once again overdoing the smile.

"Okay, guys, we're ready for you." She winked. "If you follow me, the ladies are anxious to meet you."

Damian turned to Jerry as they all stood up. Jerry gave him an optimistic smile, but Damian could tell he was nervous as shit. Glancing back at the exit, he knew this was his last chance to make a mad dash out of there, but obviously knowing Damian too well, Jerry shoved him forward.

They were herded along with all the others into the large banquet room with tables set up all around. All the tables were numbered, and there was a woman sitting at each one. Damian did everything he could to avoid eye contact with any of them. So far the only one he'd glanced at looked to be in her early to mid-thirties, and her hair was shorter than his.

The hostess stood at the front of the room as they all finished filing in. "I'll explain how this works quickly, and we'll get started," she began. "As you've noticed, I'm sure, all the tables where these lovely ladies are sitting are numbered. Gentlemen, your badges all have numbers on them. If your badge number has a number one, you will start at table number one. If it's a two, then you sit at table two, and so on. After four minutes I will ring a bell, and you'll be given a few minutes to take notes on your Speed Tickets." She held one up for everyone to see, and again she was back at it with the overdone smile.

Damian easily tuned her out. He glanced around the room as she went on. None of the girls were what he considered attractive. There was something a bit odd about each of them. He took in one that might pass for cute, but just the fact that she was here, doing *this*, was enough to turn him off. They all looked older than he was, too. Damian was twenty-seven, but for his dating taste, they had to be at least a few years younger than he was. The older ones were just too set in their ways or carrying a load of baggage he didn't have the patience to deal with.

His patience was already running thin, and the damn thing hadn't even started yet. This was ridiculous. If Jerry weren't his best friend and hadn't helped him out of so many jams, Damian would be at J.T.'s right now, having a cold one and watching the game.

Well, being here was one thing. He didn't have to take it seriously, and he certainly didn't plan to. Jerry had told him to give it a chance and that he might actually meet someone worthwhile, but the more he looked around, the older each chick looked. No, thanks.

Jerry, on the other hand, liked them older. He said the younger ones were too wild and unpredictable. Damian never understood his taste in women or why he liked trying all these goofy dating things.

"C'mon," Jerry said, snapping Damian out of his thoughts.

The hostess was done talking, and all the guys were making their way to their respective tables. Damian hadn't even bothered looking at the number on his badge. Jerry pointed at it. "You're number eight. Over there." He motioned to the table with the big eight on it. The girl sitting at it was a mousy little thing. She had shoulder-length, light-brown hair that was straight and parted in the middle.

As soon as Damian sat down, he noticed two things: her big, chapped lips and her nails, which were chewed down to the raw nub.

"Okay, everyone," the hostess announced. "Your time starts now."

Damian glanced over to Jerry. He was sitting with a blonde two tables down from him. Damian looked back at the girl at his table, and she smiled.

"Hi," she said sheepishly.

"Hey." Damian tapped his Speed Ticket.

"I'm Carey Drummond." She held out her hand.

"Damian." He shook her hand and cleared his throat. "Damian Santiago."

"Well, first off," she started, "I'm thirty-two, never been married, no kids, but I have two cats. Mitzy and Mr. Grump. They're my babies . . ."

Damian *despised* cats. He spent what seemed like an eternity nodding and trying not to stare at the dry skin on her lips.

The bell finally rang, and the hostess asked everyone to take a moment and make a few notes about the date. Everyone started writing furiously, Carey included. She looked up for a moment and smiled, stretching the cracks in her lips so far, Damian thought they would bleed.

He smiled back and brought the notepad to his leg where she couldn't see. There was a whole section marked Date Number One. He wrote two words. *Hell no!*

Several agonizing tables later, it was break time. He headed straight to Jerry.

"Can we get out of here?"

"What?" Jerry took a quick look around and gestured for Damian to lower his voice. "We're not done yet."

Damian let his head fall back and took a deep breath. "How can you *stand* this?"

"Give it a chance, will you? I met two very nice ladies so far."

Damian's jaw dropped open. "Are you kidding me? Ray Charles would flinch at this bunch!"

Well, the ones Damian had met so far, anyway. But he'd seen what was coming up at the next table.

Jerry shook his head. "It's not all about looks, Damian. You gotta give their personalities a chance."

"It's four minutes. How do you get to know someone in that short a time?"

Damian started to walk away, but Jerry grabbed hold of his arm. "Dude, please. We're almost done. I'd do it for you."

Damn him. Yeah, he would. He'd pretty much do anything short of murder for Damian—if he asked real nice. With his shoulders slumping, he grudgingly conceded. "All right."

"It's not so bad; there are a few cute ones in there. Did you see the one coming up next table?"

"Yeah, you mean the one with the big fucking bow on her head and all the gaudy makeup?"

"Well . . . yeah," Jerry gestured for Damian to lower his voice again and whispered, "but she's cute."

The bell rang, and they all walked back into the room.

Damian trudged over to the table. The girl wasn't back yet. For a moment he hoped she'd felt the same as he did and decided to leave. Jerry was looking at him from his table with a worried expression. Damian smirked, giving him the thumbs up, and pointed at the empty seat across from him.

"Did you make a connection already?" The girl in the bow asked, then glanced over at Jerry before taking the seat in front of Damian and smiling.

Her fragrance and the slight accent were the only things subtle about her. Most people probably wouldn't have picked up on the accent, it was so faint, but since it was his job to make note of the tiniest of details in people, he hadn't just picked up on it, his trained ear could even pinpoint what kind of accent—a Hispanic accent. She was also a bit younger than the others. Her eyes might actually be pretty. They were big, and darker than any he'd ever seen. But they were lost under the heavy glittery turquoise eye shadow she wore just on the lids. It matched the bow on her head and her oversized dangling earrings. She wore a fresh coat of heavy gloss on what could've been attractive pouty lips.

"No, uh, that's my friend."

"Oh, how nice, you two decided to do this together." Her dark eyes brightened.

Damian tried but couldn't hold back a sarcastic chuckle. "Actually, this is all *his* idea. He wanted me to come with him. I'm not really into this kind of shit."

She raised an eyebrow. "And what kind of *shit* is this?"

"Okay, everyone," the hostess announced, "your time begins now."

He glanced at the clock and smiled. "I just mean, you know, this isn't really for me."

"Dating?" Her bracelets jingled as she placed her hands on the table and leaned forward, revealing a perfectly manicured set of clear polished nails—a complete contrast to the rest of her loud outfit and makeup.

"Well, no. I'm into dating. Just not like this." He leaned over to her and lowered his voice. "This is kind of stupid. Don't you think? How are you supposed to get to know anyone in just four minutes?"

There was something sexy about the way her lips curved up slowly into a smile. "I think I know a lot about you already."

Damian choked back a laugh, but before he could say anything, their eyes locked. Her heavy eyelashes narrowed in around her charcoal eyes, wiping the smirk off his face instantly and making him gulp in reaction.

"You're in your mid- to late twenties, you've never been married, possibly never even been in a serious relationship." She turned slightly in Jerry's direction. "That's probably one of your last single friends," she paused, "*and* you're hoping he doesn't meet anyone tonight."

She sat back in her seat, never once breaking eye contact.

Shaking off what her eyes had done to him, Damian feigned a weak laugh. "You're way off!"

Her dry chuckle confirmed she knew he was full of it. He glanced at the bow on her head, reminding himself how gaudy he had thought it—*she*—was just moments ago.

"So you're not single?" she pressed.

"I'm single."

"Are you in your mid-twenties?"

He smiled, trying not to look as uncomfortable as he was beginning to feel. "Twenty-seven."

"Is that your last single friend?"

That's where she was way off. Most of his friends were single, but Jerry *was* his closest friend. Unlike most of Damian's other friends, Jerry was a bit old-fashioned, and, just three years older than Damian, he was already showing signs of panicking about his single status. Damian wasn't panicking about it. In fact, he was in no hurry at all to get sucked into that again. He had plenty of time to sow his wild oats and too many things to accomplish before thinking about settling down.

"Actually, no, I have lots of other single friends."

She smiled, this time showing a perfect set of white teeth, and the corners of her eyes crinkled. She shifted her weight from one arm of the chair to the other. Her blouse moved slightly, allowing just a glimpse of the top of her breast.

Damian's eyes darted back to her face. "So . . ."

The bell rang, and the hostess reminded everyone to make notes. Damian glanced down at his Speed Ticket. All his dates so far had the same two words on them. He realized then he hadn't even gotten her name.

Glancing up quickly, he noticed she wasn't writing anything down. "Oh, hey, I didn't even get your name."

A lazy smile spread across her lips. The dark lashes that

seemed to slow down midblink had his unwavering full attention. "You won't need it."

"All right, please make your way to the next table, gentlemen," the hostess said.

Damian sat there stunned for a few moments before realizing he had to move over to the next table. The following tables were an annoying blur. He caught himself continually glancing at her table. Having had a closer look at her now, he knew she had to be in her early twenties, but that eighties garbage she was wearing didn't do a thing for her. It irritated him, the way she sat there talking and laughing, then jotting things down on her Speed Ticket after every date. He couldn't get her words out of his head. *You've never been married, possibly never even been in a serious relationship.* What did she know anyway? Of course he'd had some serious relationships. He'd been in a very serious one just last year, and he had plenty of others that had come close.

———

It was beginning to drizzle as they got out of Jerry's car and walked toward J.T.'s. Damian needed a beer bad. His thoughts were still on the eighties chick. *You won't need it.* He knew what *she* needed! He'd thought about going up to her after it was all over, but she was busy chatting with some fat loser. Damian wondered if she'd end up with him or any of those losers. What did it matter anyway? At least he'd never have to see her again.

He came back to earth when Jerry punched his arm. "What?"

"I said thanks for doing this for me."

"Oh, yeah, that wasn't too bad."

"I told you it wouldn't be. I got a few email addresses out of it. Some of those girls were real characters. Janis was shy but cute, and Lydia was funny, but I think Bethany was the one I found most intriguing. Not to mention the hottest."

Damian refrained from rolling his eyes. Not *one* of the chicks there was what he would consider *hot*. Okay, maybe one was . . . *memorable*, but her taste in clothes and makeup was hideous. Jerry's taste in women had always been way out there. They went inside and sat down at the bar. Jerry bought the first round. Out of curiosity, Damian asked, "Which one was Bethany?"

Damian had ribbed Jerry enough over the years about his taste in women. He was sure Jerry knew what he was thinking.

Jerry took a swig of his beer and shrugged. "The one with the big fucking bow on her head."

CHAPTER 2

"Places, everyone!"

Bethany rushed to take her place on the stage. Her lines were the last thing on her mind. Her article for the paper where she was doing her internship was what occupied her thoughts today. It was due in just a few days, and she was nowhere near finishing. It was just one of the many things she'd been trying not to stress about these last couple of days. Every break the producer had them take during rehearsal, she worked on it on her laptop, instead of memorizing her lines.

"Okay, so we take it from when Iona walks in."

Bethany's secondary role as Iona in the stage version of *Pretty in Pink* was a far cry from her previous roles in Hollywood. But then this second-rate theater in old downtown Las Vegas was also nothing compared to the theaters in Tinseltown where she'd previously graced the stage.

She didn't care. Bethany could at least hold her head up high knowing that she was not only still doing what she loved for a living but also paying her debts—all of them, without the help of anyone else. Yawning, she frowned. If only this job alone were enough to pay it all. She'd recently landed a more impressive gig at another small theater, but it still wasn't enough. It was in the less prestigious part of town, but she reminded herself that's how it needed to be for now. Between that, her internship, research, and her other part-time job, sleep was a luxury she indulged in less and less these days.

They took it from the top. Bethany fumbled her lines a few times but finally made it through the rehearsal. She gathered her things and rushed out.

Her life had become one big scuttle after another. From rehearsals to her internship to her other job, and the shows took up most of her evenings. Her understudy took Bethany's place as Iona only twice a week. That was when Bethany put in most of her hours for her internship.

Often Bethany was forced to leave the shows in such a hurry she left in costume, as she had the night of the speed date. She was writing an article on the complexities of dating in this day and age. She needed to research at least five different types of acceptable socializing congregations. Two of them could not involve the Internet. What a joke that had been.

Bethany thought of one of the guys she'd met that night. The only one whose name she didn't even get. She actually agreed with him when he said it was stupid. If he hadn't been so damn cocky, she might have told him so and gotten his name, if not more.

At first she'd been surprised to see someone as good-looking as him there. And to say he was good-looking was putting it mildly. She'd noticed him from the moment he walked in, and she wasn't the only one, either. Some of the women there were so loud and obvious she almost felt sorry for them. *Almost.* The woman at the table next to her who actually gasped when he walked into the room was just obnoxious. She even thanked the sweet baby Jesus as if he had anything to do with bringing a man that attractive there that night. Bethany had to wonder if he told the other woman how stupid he thought the whole speed dating thing was, too. Had he sat there and told each of them how he felt about being there or was she the only one?

Admittedly she'd been excited when she saw it was her turn to sit with him. Up close he was even better-looking than when she'd first seen him across the room. His dark eyes had a playfulness combined with a sultry gaze she'd had a hard time looking away from. The man even had a perfectly sexy cleft chin to complete his already handsome face. Problem was he obviously knew it. He hadn't even bothered to shave, and he still pulled off the look better than any man she'd ever seen. He oozed self-confidence. She wasn't at all surprised when he told her he was just there for his friend. A man like that probably had women knocking down his door. The last thing she needed was a smooth-talking, womanizing man in her life. In fact the *last* thing she needed was a man, period. Bethany could barely keep up with her schedule as it was. There was no room for dating. But most important, her life was already too damn complicated. Getting involved with anyone would not only complicate things further, it had the potential to wreak havoc.

In spite of all that, here she was thinking about him. *Again.* She frowned as she walked up the stairs to her small apartment. Lugging her heavy bag of groceries, she huffed up the two flights of stairs. The elevator was permanently broken, and the landlord offered no apologies.

She had to remind herself that though not all her troubles were in the clear, some of the most important ones were, like her aunt's health. She was better now, and though everything else was still a mess, she should be grateful. She was. But did the grocery bag have to weigh so damn much?

Dropping the bag on her counter, she rolled her sore shoulder and proceeded to put the orange juice, yogurt, and cold cuts in the fridge.

The loud knocking on her door made her jump. Only one person she knew would knock on her door that way. The rent was due, and Mr. Hadley was here to collect the moment he saw her get home.

She walked over to the pantry where she kept her secret stash of cash, in a locked box inside an empty cereal box, and unlocked it, pulling out the envelope with the amount for her rent. Mr. Hadley knocked again. "I'm coming!" she called out as she hid the smaller box in the cereal box again.

The stench of cigarette mixed with alcohol and sweat hit her nose immediately as she opened the door. The usual un-shaven, filthy-T-shirt-wearing Mr. Hadley peered at her, then suspiciously over her shoulder. "You got company?"

"No," she said, unable to keep her hand from automatically covering her nose as casually as she could.

"Rent's due." His beady eyes were back on her, and he held his hand out.

She handed him the envelope, and he counted the bills. Then, as he always did, he pulled out the prefilled receipt from his grimy back pocket. "Here's your receipt." He handed her the damp piece of paper. She tried not to grimace as she opened it with her fingertips to make sure everything was correct. "And let me know if you see anyone snooping around here looking suspicious."

Immediately she forgot about the nasty receipt and looked at him, the alarm instantly at her gut. "Why? There's been someone snooping?"

Mr. Hadley shrugged, already starting to walk away. "Maybe, maybe not. You know Myrtle from the third floor. Seems the pilot light in that woman's head is snuffed out half the time, but she swears she's seen a man snooping 'round here. Said she even thought she saw someone looking in her window." He cackled loudly walking away. "Like that old hag has to worry about sexual predators peeping in *her* window." He cackled even louder as he turned the corner toward the stairs.

Bethany stood there frozen for a moment, her stomach plunging. "There's no way," she whispered to herself in an attempt to calm her nerves.

Hurrying back into her apartment, she closed and locked the door. With the panic beginning to simmer, she rushed to her book bag, knelt, and pulled out her cell phone. No texts or messages.

The rule was they only messaged or called each other during the week if it was an emergency. She chewed her fingernail, wondering if she should alarm them for no real reason. Myrtle *was* pretty wacky. The woman told stories of being abducted by aliens when she was a young girl, for crying out loud. Still, her gut told her she should at least check whether anyone had heard anything.

She dialed and held her breath waiting. "Beth?"

The sweet voice on the other end made Bethany smile and let out a breath. "Yes, it's me."

"I think I'm starting to get used to this phone."

Bethany exhaled softly, already relieved by how calm Stella sounded. "Good. I told you, you would."

"So why are you calling? Something wrong?"

Bethany walked over to the sofa and sat down. "No, but my landlord said another tenant in the building saw someone snooping around here suspiciously. It made me nervous. I wanted to check and see if anything's up. Have you heard anything?"

Bethany heard the heavy sigh on the other end and braced herself. "No. Things have actually been pretty quiet."

"Hmm." Bethany chewed her fingernail again. "Nothing new or unusual?"

"No. Nothing at all."

Bethany held her breath before asking the next question, as she always did. "Has the bank called?"

She heard her sister exhale, "Yes, twice, but I didn't answer."

"Good." Bethany let out a sigh of relief. "I'll have some of the money soon. I promise."

"Bethany, they said they won't take just part of it. They want it all."

"No, don't worry. I asked around. As long as we in good faith try to pay at least part of it, they have to accept it. Okay? You promise me you won't, you know . . . freak out?"

"I promise."

"Good. I'll call you this weekend. I love you."

"I love you, too."

She hung up and sat there on the sofa letting her head rest on the back pillow, looking up just in time to see the small roach crawl across the ceiling. "Eeeuw!" She cringed, jumping off the sofa to go look for the broom.

After swatting at the gross bug and squealing when it fell, then jumping and stomping on it a few times, she heard the banging from the downstairs apartment. Of course her apartment would be right above Mr. Hadley's. As exasperated and grossed out as she had felt a few minutes ago, she couldn't help giggling now when the memory of how Trinity had explained it suddenly came to her. Trinity was her tall, blond voluptuous neighbor with the southern drawl from across the hall. Her occupation had been somewhat of a mystery until just recently. Though Bethany had pretty much figured that one out on her own.

The first day she'd met Trinity was the day Bethany moved

in the few things she owned. Trinity came over to introduce herself. She was really nice and gave Bethany a few tips about the building, like who to stay away from and never to go into the laundry room after dark.

"The light bulb in there is permanently broken, and it's not safe to get caught in that dungeon at night," she'd warned.

Trinity was also the one who warned her about getting a lockbox to keep her valuables in and hiding it somewhere no one like a snoopy landlord would think to look. Trinity told her not only did Mr. Hadley smell badly, she'd sooner trust a politician than trust that creepy old man not to go through her apartment when she wasn't home. She said she even hid her unmentionables for fear he might go into her apartment when she wasn't there and sniff them.

Bethany giggled again remembering how Trinity had literally shivered when she told her. At the time Bethany was hardly laughing; instead the dread of what her reality had become had sunk in fast. She actually cried those first few nights she slept in this apartment. But she forced herself to snap out of it, and after living here for months now she'd decided it wasn't *too* bad.

She'd never get used to the roaches, but she was getting used to her neighbors. None were without their quirks, but so far they had been harmless. And she didn't judge Trinity for doing what she did for a living. However, Bethany did draw the line there. Several times, after seeing Bethany drag her tired ass up those stairs and talk about having a ton of homework to finish, Trinity had tried talking her into quitting all her jobs and taking up her line of work. Even though Trinity didn't stand on a street corner, and, she argued, being an escort wasn't the same as being a prostitute, Bethany knew firsthand that it was *exactly* the same. Trinity insisted that Bethany's adorable yet "curvaceously sexy" body would drive the men crazy, and it was so much more money working far fewer hours. Trinity even assured Bethany that if she wanted to she could stipulate she wouldn't do anything sexual before she was fixed up with these men.

"Some are just old, arrogant fools who'll pay a good fold to have you hang on their arm as they make their way through the high-roller lounge at these fancy casinos."

Bethany didn't need to get into the specifics of why there was no way she'd even consider it. "No, thanks" had been her only response.

She'd break her back and work herself to the ground the good old-fashioned and self-respecting way before she'd stoop to that level. Desperation had already driven her to do things she was not proud of, but even her aunt insisted it was for good reason. It might be unethical, illegal even, but at least she could still look into the mirror with her dignity intact. Well almost intact, but at least she'd had the sense each time when it counted most to walk away. Desperate or not, she stuck to her guns and held on to what was left of her self-respect even when she knew how much it would cost her.

The knock on the door startled her. She froze in place, waiting for the sign that she didn't have to panic. Then it came. The most pathetic little whistle she'd ever heard. She was so relieved she laughed as she hopped off the sofa and walked over to the door. Before Trinity, she'd never even heard of a person who couldn't whistle, but her neighbor was adamant. Bethany suggested that with all the weirdos in the building, they should have a signal when they came to each other's door. Since Bethany had laughed so much at Trinity's first attempts at whistling, now Trinity was determined to get it right.

Peeking through the peephole just to be sure, she smiled

when she saw Trinity standing there, all done up as usual, holding a bag of what was probably food.

"Hey!" she said, stepping back as Trinity walked right in as if she lived there. "Your whistling is getting so much better."

As pathetic as it still sounded, it was actually better than her very first attempts.

"I told ya it would," she said, holding her head up proudly. "Ain't nothin' I've ever put my mind to that I didn't get right eventually. I broughtcha Chinese," she announced as she marched into the small kitchen. "And not that fast-food kind either. Mr. Bloomington *loves* P. F. Chang's, and I ordered stuff to go."

Bethany's mouth practically watered from the smell of the food Trinity began unloading from the bags. "Oh, my God, that smells so good." Bethany picked up one of the boxes and opened it, immediately digging in with a fork. "Thank you so much." She barely got the words out, her mouth was so full. Then she laughed and had to cover her mouth before she spat anything out.

"I knew you'd be starving. Girl, I'm telling you, all you need is a couple of Mr. Bloomingtons lined up a few nights a week, and you'd be making more than you do now with them three jobs of yours. *Gawd*, I don't know how you do it." Trinity leaned dramatically over the crowded little counter.

Mr. Bloomington was one of Trinity's regulars. She said he was just a lonely old man willing to pay her to keep him company and to join him for dinner. Unlike some of her other, richer clients, he could only afford her twice a month, and their time together consisted mainly of a movie and then dinner out. "You poor girl," she pouted, standing up straight again. "You must be so exhausted. You know Carl," she drawled, crunching up her nose. "He doesn't want me callin' him Mr. Bloomington no more. Me and him only hold hands on our dates, and I just peck him a little itty bitty kiss when we say hello and again when we say good-bye. I'm sure you can live with that."

Bethany continued to inhale her food, nodding without even thinking.

"You can?" Trinity smiled excited.

Stopping mid-chew, Bethany shook her head, wiping her mouth. "*No!* No. I *couldn't.*" She wouldn't make Trinity feel bad by telling her how she already knew that was something she couldn't do, no matter what the amount of money. "That's just not me," she offered after seeing Trinity frown. "You're just much more social than I am. I'm a little shy, I guess."

That couldn't be further from the truth. Bethany lived for the spotlight, and she could act, dance, and perform like nobody's business, but no amount of acting could cover up how she'd feel about being fondled or even touched by someone she didn't want touching her. That's exactly why she was living the life she was now. No matter how exhausting her life was, she'd take it any day over giving up the self-respect she'd sacrificed so much to hold on to.

Shaking her head, Trinity walked toward the door. "Aren't you gonna eat?" Bethany asked, glancing down at the other two unopened boxes of Chinese food.

"No, honey bee, that's all for you." Trinity placed her hand on her flat stomach. "I've already had dinner, and I really need to start watching what I eat. Maybe I'll drop by that Zumba class of yours one of these days."

"You should." Bethany smiled. "I can get you free passes. It's fun. I promise."

Trinity made a pained face. "I'll let you know."

Bethany thanked her again for the food, and after locking the door, grabbed her book bag off the floor. She had that article to finish.

After firing up her laptop, she sat there still eating out of her Chinese food container and went through her emails quickly. She had a few from some of the guys she had met at the speed date. There was another one from Jerry, bringing her mind back to his friend. Last week Jerry had asked if she wanted to get together this Friday night for drinks. She'd told him the truth: She was working late. When he'd asked where she worked, she told him about the place where she'd just recently started her new gig, leaving out what her role exactly was in it, but she did mention he might enjoy the show. He told her he'd have to check it out sometime, but that was it.

This time his email was a short follow-up just to say he hoped she'd had a good week and to let him know when she'd be free to get together.

"Never," she grumbled, closing out her email and not even responding.

Sitting back visualizing Jerry's friend again, she sighed deeply. It sucked that because of her crappy circumstances she wasn't free to socialize like the rest of the girls she knew in school and even in her theater gig. She was always over-hearing them talk about going out dancing and hanging out at the casinos. But Bethany had to stay focused. Things could very easily fall apart. Already she was going to have to figure out how to get more hours waitressing. She needed more money fast. She couldn't let anything screw up her carefully laid plans. Especially a sexy stud who no doubt would be interested in only one thing. As much as he protested that the speed date was a dumb way to meet someone to *date*, she'd caught his eyes wandering to the only thing he *did* seem interested in that night—her cleavage. No, thanks.

CHAPTER 3

⎯⎯

The past two weeks had been grueling. Three homicides in the last five days alone. Damian was sure the world was going to shit. He'd spent so much time examining corpses, interviewing witnesses, and interrogating suspects. His social life had been pretty much nonexistent for the last few months. Not that it was anything new to him. Working six- to seven-day weeks was far too common for him lately.

These days he welcomed the hectic schedule. Since his last relationship, about a year ago, he had had nothing but one-nighters. By choice, of course. There was no shortage of women ready to settle in with him. He just didn't have time for that right now. Being the youngest detective in his department and knowing that some of the older veterans resented him for moving up so fast, he was determined to prove he belonged there. He'd earned it, damn it. Putting his career first and working his ass off for years hadn't come without a price. He'd given up a social life and in the process lost the only girl he'd ever gotten serious with. So at the very least, he'd make damn sure it had been worth it.

As caught up as he'd been in trying to prove himself, he hadn't even been too broken up about the split. He was certain now that relationships and love were overrated. Not that he actually thought he'd ever been in love with Lana. In fact, the moment she admitted she'd turned to her ex-boyfriend to vent about how lonely she was, he knew he wasn't in love, because it didn't hurt. She assured him she hadn't done anything physical, had just needed someone to talk to, but it didn't matter. As far as he was concerned, this was just as bad, if not worse. Emotional affairs could be more damaging to a relationship than the physical ones. Though he'd never put up with either. Regardless, it should've hurt.

He'd been pissed, and his ego took a blow, but there was no pain. None. After that he couldn't get her out of his house fast enough. With everything he was dealing with at work, the last thing he needed was to get home and wonder if she'd been talking to or texting her ex all day.

He could admit now it was weird at first not having anyone to come home to. Still it hadn't taken long to get used to being on his own again. He enjoyed being his own man. Not having to answer to anyone about anything. Including having to work late . . . again. The older he got, the more he was beginning to think he'd be on his own forever. And that was fine by him. That's why he didn't understand why Jerry was so hell-bent on finding a soul mate.

He hadn't talked to Jerry since the night of the speed date until earlier today. Their talk that night had been brief, and even today's talk had been a rushed one. Jerry never finished telling him about the girls he'd met the night of the speed date, because Mason, their latest friend to fall victim to the relationship pit, showed up at J.T's with his fiancée. Jerry didn't want anyone else to know about the speed date, so the subject had been canned.

Glad the day was finally over, Damian threw his coat in the backseat and jumped into his Camaro—a '69. A true classic. Damian couldn't help smiling as the engine roared to a start.

He finally had a night off, and where was he headed? To meet Jerry at some dive downtown, where one of the girls he'd met worked. Apparently, the girl had mentioned to Jer that the dinner show that Friday was supposed to be a good one. And of course Jerry took that as an invite.

The only reason Damian agreed to go was that the girl was working there tonight, so Jerry wasn't meeting her for an actual date. Damian wouldn't be a third wheel. That, and Jerry had mentioned some heavy stuff going on with his teenage daughter, Ashlynn. He'd been pretty stressed out about her in the past few months. Damian had heard it in his voice, over the phone. Things were getting worse.

Considering all the times Jerry had been there for him, Damian figured the least he owed him was to sit and listen, while throwing back a few. Damian was almost there when Jerry called.

"Damian, I'm running late." The agitation in his voice was unmistakable. "Ashlynn kept me on the phone so much today I fell behind on my work. But I'm outta here now. Get a table for us and order me a steak—well done. I'm starving. I spent my whole lunch on the phone with her. I've already reserved a table. Just give the hostess my name."

"You got it, man." Damian smiled feeling for his friend. "I'll order you a shot, too. Sounds like you need one."

Jerry didn't respond, and for a moment Damian thought maybe they'd been cut off. "Jer?"

"Uh, they don't sell alcohol there."

"What?" Damian asked, already feeling this night beginning to tank.

"They have beer and wine," Jerry added quickly. "But their liquor license was pulled for the hard stuff recently, so no shots. She said they're working on getting it back, though."

Damian shook his head and frowned. Tonight was a total exception he'd made for Jerry's sake. Normally, he would never venture to that side of town for social reasons. He had zero intention of ever returning to the place, so their working on getting their liquor license was no consolation. The only times he'd ever been in that area at all were back in his patrol days, when they were called out there constantly. The whole area was trouble.

More than having to drive out to this dive, the fact that he'd have to settle for beer was a pisser. After the week he'd had, he was looking forward to having a stiff drink or two.

Hearing Damian's lack of response, Jerry continued. "Don't sweat it," Jerry assured him. "We'll eat and hang for a bit, then we're out of there. We'll get that bourbon on the rocks I know you're wanting somewhere else."

Minutes after getting off the phone with Jerry, Damian drove up to the small theater in old downtown Vegas. "City Lights." He read the old sign out loud. Several of the bulbs were missing, it was so old.

He'd never actually been in the place, but he had been called out several times to deal with drunken fights in the very lot he was now parking his car in. Back then he was sure this was a strip bar, and seeing that they were using the same name he now wondered about the girl Jerry was coming to see tonight. Jerry had called it a dinner show, so Damian had to assume it was a different kind of show now, and the new owners had just been too cheap to invest in a new sign.

Walking into the place, his assumption was immediately confirmed. The posters on the wall of the different performances ranged from jazz bands to piano soloist, even a magic act. Then he saw the poster for tonight's show. A glamorous singer in front of a vintage mic who looked like a forties Hollywood starlet in a long, red, shimmery dress with curves that had to be Photoshopped. Even the long, perfect leg, which was exposed by the slit in the dress that went all the way up to the top of her thigh, was too perfect. A thick shiny sheath of black hair fell over one eye, and the photo's dramatic shading was such that the only part of her face he could make out was her luscious, heart-shaped, blood-red lips.

He chuckled inwardly, because aside from the fact that she was not a redhead, it was very Jessica Rabbitish. She even wore the long satin gloves all the way past her elbows. No doubt the show would be as cheesy as the photo. He wondered if the stunning girl in the photo was the actual performer or if they'd hired a model for it. From the looks of the place, it could very well be a stock photo. There was no way someone who looked like that would be working in a dump like this place.

He read the top of the poster:

VINTAGE SOUL
One woman
One night
One unforgettable experience

Before he could read the entire poster, the hostess informed him she could show him to his table. He'd already given her Jerry's name, and she'd told him they were just getting the final touches done on the table. Damian had wondered what that meant but didn't ask.

As they reached the table, Damian stared at her for a moment. Jerry *had* to be kidding. She set the menus down on the table, and that confirmed it. Jerry had in fact reserved the table front-row center. They would literally be having dinner just feet away from where the vintage mic, like the one in the poster, stood. And the final touches she'd mentioned included a bottle of wine on ice and some long-stemmed roses lying across the table.

What the hell?

Jerry was too much. Shaking his head as he took a seat, Damian actually felt a little embarrassed as a few people at the other tables glanced at him. It would only get worse when Jerry walked in and sat with him. They'd then know this incredibly romantic setup was for the two of them, and since Damian had arrived first, they'd assume the whole thing was his idea, roses and all. Great.

Instead of taking the hostess up on her offer to pour him a glass of wine, he ordered a beer. He'd man this shit up, one way or another. He also put in their dinner orders, so they could start moving things along as fast as possible. The second they were done eating, whether the show was over or not, he was insisting they get the hell out of there. The hostess smiled, telling him she'd put his order in and that she'd send the waitress back with his drink.

Now that he'd gotten a better look at the hostess, he decided she was way too young to be the girl Jerry was here to see, and he didn't recognize her at all as any of the girls from the speed date. The waitress who brought his drink was cute and had a beautiful smile, but he didn't remember there being any African-American women at the speed date, so that ruled her out as well.

Three beers later, Jerry wasn't there yet. Even though they'd dimmed the lights, their food hadn't been brought out yet, so Jerry still had time to get there. In Damian's experience, dinner shows normally didn't get started until everyone's dinner had been served. Just as he began to scrutinize the young, blond girl with a guitar setting up on one corner of the small stage, his phone buzzed. He flinched and snatched it out of his pocket—Jerry.

"You almost here?"

"I hate to do this to you, man." Jerry sounded even more agitated than earlier. "But I'm not gonna make it."

Damian let his head fall back, refraining from cussing. "You're kidding me, right?"

"I'm sorry—"

"You're *serious*? I'm already here, and I already ordered. Oh, and by the way, you mind telling me what's with all this romantic shit? Wasn't it enough that I agreed to come with you to a cheesy dinner show, you have me sitting just feet away from the damn mic. Then you set the table up with chilled wine and long-stemmed—"

"Ashlynn ran away."

For a moment it didn't register. Damian blinked repeatedly, squeezing the phone. "What?"

Jerry sighed. "Shannon just called. She and Ashlynn got into it again today, pretty bad, and Ashlynn took off. But she's done that before and come back after a few hours. This time she didn't. Shannon checked her room and noticed her suitcase along with a lot of her clothes and laptop were gone."

Damian felt like a jerk for starting to go off on him. "Where do you think she went? Have you reported it?"

Damian wasn't even sure if he could do much, since Ashlynn lived in California, completely out of his jurisdiction, but he'd stop at nothing to help Jerry.

"No, but I'm pretty sure I know where she's headed if she's not already there—my place. If she left just after noon, she should be there already. I didn't tell Shannon, but she's threatened to run away and show up here before."

"You need me to do anything, call anyone?"

"Actually, yeah, I don't want to call Beth at work, can you let her know I'm not gonna make it?"

"Beth?" Damian looked around again, spotting a different waitress a few tables down. "Which one is she, I don't recognize any of the waitresses."

"That's 'cause she's not a waitress," Jerry informed him. "She's *in* the show."

"What?"

Damian brought his attention to the girl with the guitar who was now sitting on a stool strumming the strings softly. Just then his dinner arrived. The waitress set down the plate in front of him along with a fresh basket of bread and butter. Damian mouthed the words thank you, but she seemed to be waiting for something.

"Hold on, Jer. The food just arrived."

Pulling the phone away from his ear, he gave the waitress his attention.

"I'm sorry, I didn't mean to interrupt your call. I just want to let you know that the other steak will be out shortly. It's just taking a bit longer because you asked for it well done."

"It's okay." Damian smiled. "Actually, can you just make that one to go? The person I was meeting just canceled." He pointed at the phone. Her face immediately went all sympathetic, making him feel even stupider about this big elaborate setup now that he'd apparently been stood up. "No," he shook his head, smiling. "I was meeting a guy friend." Her eyes expanded widely, and she nodded quickly, her face tingeing ever so slightly. Now Damian's head moved quickly also, only he shook his. "*He* did all this, not me. You see, I didn't even know about it and now . . ." Seeing how she continued to nod and seemed a little uncomfortable even, he gave up. "Never mind." He exhaled, feeling completely annoyed with Jerry again. "Just . . . just make the other one to go."

The lights began to dim even more as she walked away, and he brought the phone back to his ear. Jerry was chuckling on the other end. "Yeah, laugh it up, you ass. It wasn't bad enough that she was thinking what a pathetic loser I am for setting up all this crap only to get stood up. She now thinks I got stood up by my *boyfriend*."

Jerry laughed even more now. "Well, your food's there now, and I've already paid for everything upfront. Dinner's included, so just eat and enjoy the show; it's supposed to be good. Then you can leave at intermission. But can you just do that one thing for me?"

Feeling exasperated that Jerry was not only expecting him to hang around, he still had the nerve to ask him to hunt down this girl. Damian turned back to scrutinize the blonde onstage. "Does she play the guitar?"

Damian hoped Jerry would say she did. He was already having visions of walking up to the girl with the guitar, delivering Jerry's message, then letting his waitress know something had come up so he could get the hell out of there.

"I don't know. Bethany was pretty vague. Just said she was in the show."

The second he heard the name he stopped staring at the blonde, and his attention was brought to the curtain at the back of the stage. The silhouette of a women behind the curtain looked as perfectly curved as the girl in the poster.

"Bethany?"

"Yeah, she's who the roses were for. You remember which one I'm talking about, right? The one with the bow?"

Damian gulped. "Yeah." He gripped the phone now as the guitar's mic was turned on suddenly, because it was much louder now. "I remember. I'll let her know. The show's starting. I gotta go."

Jerry began thanking him and apologizing again, but Damian clicked End before his friend could finish and turned the phone off. With the place completely dark now, except for the spotlight behind the girl onstage allowing for an incredible silhouette, the only other lighting in the room was the candles on the dinner tables. Damian reasoned that the fact that she was *in* the show didn't mean she was the girl behind the now-opening curtain. That Bethany, the girl who had dismissed him so unceremoniously, couldn't possibly be the bombshell on the poster—the girl with the perfect hourglass shape beginning a slow sway of those hips in his direction.

Squeezing his beer bottle, Damian tried not to think about the fact that in just a few seconds she'd be standing but two feet away from him. With the light's changing, now he could see that her dress *was* the same red shimmering one he'd seen on the poster. Her incredible curves and cleavage had not been Photoshopped. The only thing he was yet to make out was her face, because the lights were moving slowly up her body, pausing at her neckline—teasing.

As she finally made it to the microphone, she was so close to his table he could smell her intoxicating fragrance. There was no doubt about it. This was the same girl from the speed date—Bethany. As different as she looked now, with her impeccably elegant makeup, as opposed to the overdone gaudy crap she'd worn when he first met her, there was no mistaking it was her. He saw it in those eyes, which even under all that makeup, he'd been so drawn to that first day.

As she glanced around the room slowly, her lips gave way to a very self-indulgent smile. He still couldn't get over the fact that someone who looked this perfect would be working in a dive like this. Even if she had participated in the goofy speed date, remembering her self-assured demeanor from the moment she'd sat down and seeing that sinful smile now, *clearly* she knew she was too good for this place. The only thing he could think of was that she couldn't be very good.

That thought hadn't even finished sinking in when the lights suddenly shut down, and the guitar went silent. After a few dramatic seconds of nothing, the guitar began strumming a slow song he didn't recognize. He braced himself, almost nervous for her, afraid that she'd be really bad or would sing something painfully cheesy. The spotlight was on her face again. Her skin actually sparkled. The lighting did something to the makeup around her eyes and her lips. Moments ago with the different lighting he hadn't seen it, but now under this light it appeared as if her eyes and lips were surrounded by glitter. It was mesmerizing, and he felt like a mosquito being drawn into a light. Then out from those lips poured a song he now recognized, but only because of the famous lyrics, because the spin her sultry vocal put on it made it completely different from the original. It was still the same song, but she added such an essence of poignant sensuality to it, he hadn't even realized he'd been rendered immobile.

Sitting there staring at her, with her eyes locked on him the entire time, it felt as if she were singing the song to him.

Will you still love me tomorrow?

He'd been way off about her not being good. Her voice was silky smooth—soulful, with such a unique richness about it that he sat there glued to his seat *feeling* every word profoundly. It wasn't until after the third or fourth song that he began to wonder just how much Jerry had paid for that table. The owners of this place *had* to have told her to pay special attention to whoever sat in it, because nearly the entire time she'd sung to *him,* her eyes reaching deep into his; he felt her words touch his soul. What he was feeling was so fucking ridiculous he almost had to laugh! But he wasn't laughing, and no amount of rationalizing that this was just a performance could snap him out of it.

A few times she'd sashayed away to sing in the direction of another member of the audience, leaving him sitting on the edge of his seat in almost childlike anticipation of her return. Each time he'd feel an illogical but very real heat begin to build inside him at the sight of her singing to another guy. Then she'd spin slowly and come right back to him, turning his heated insides instantly into putty. It was insane, and he continually had to remind his delusional and way too easily convinced heart that she *had* to come back. Right? The mic stand was right in front of him, but the way she gazed deep into his eyes as she belted out the songs left him completely breathless.

Then, to his surprise and utter annoyance, especially because the poster out in the lobby did read *one woman*, a guy joined her onstage to do another soulful, unique rendition of a song he didn't even recognize at first, because he was so caught up watching how the guy played with her hand as he held it.

Fortunately, the guy was only onstage with her for the one infuriating song. But he did kiss her. It was one of those seemingly platonic kisses that, even though she'd turned her head, caused the guy to come way too close to her mouth. That's how closely Damian watched them, clenching his jaw and feeling a heat he had no business feeling.

Not only was her show anything but cheesy, but as the show continued, each song she sang was unexpected. Because of her attire and because of the looks of the place, he'd anticipated a shoddy, forties, cabaret-type show, with mediocre singing at best. She'd gone from opening with a classic sixties song to eighties classics to a Celine–Bocelli duet to Beatles songs and ended it with a Joss Stone song, all of which she made completely her own. Most were arrangements that sounded even better than the originals.

It'd been intermission now for a few minutes, and Damian still sat there awestruck. He hadn't even touched his dinner. He couldn't during the show. It would've meant taking his eyes off her, and from the moment she walked out from behind that curtain that had been impossible. And now he couldn't even think of eating, he was still so lost in thoughts of Bethany and her phenomenal performance. But he knew better. It was more than her performance. It's what her performance had done to him, and that was what had him still so rapt.

Needing to get some air—snap himself out of the unreasonable stupor he still couldn't get out of—he got up and walked to the crowded lobby.

CHAPTER 4

"I'm fine," Bethany insisted, taking a seat in her dressing room before Simon or Amos could notice just how light-headed she really was. "I'm just a little winded, but I'll be okay, really."

Amos shook his head adamantly. "I knew it. I knew it!" Amos turned to Simon with a scowl. "Didn't I tell you this was going to be too much for her?"

"No! It's not too much for me." She sat up, immediately feeling the dizzy spell, and had to grab hold of the chair's arm. If only she'd had time to grab something, *anything* to eat before the show. But she'd barely made it there on time as it was. "I just need a little water and a breather, and I'll be good to go back on for the second half of the show."

"Not happening," Amos said, crossing his arms.

Michele, one of the other performers at the theater, walked in the dressing room at that most opportune moment. "Anything I can do for you, Bethany?" she asked sweetly.

Bethany didn't even get a chance to respond before Amos was already ordering Michele to get something together and finish out Bethany's show for her. "But Amos—"

"But nothing," he said, cutting Bethany off with uncompromising finality. "Michele's finishing the show, and you're going home and getting some rest."

"It really is for the best, Bethany," Simon agreed with a reassuring smile. "You've been working yourself into the ground without a break all week."

Amos didn't have to ask Michele twice. "Sure thing, Amos." She nodded at Bethany and flashed her one of the fakest sympathetic smiles she'd ever seen. "Feel better, Bethany." She practically flew out the door and squealed just outside of it, then she giggled, apologizing to someone profusely.

Amos stuck his head out the door; his already cross expression went even more dire. "You there." He called out to someone in the hallway. "What are you doing back here? No one but performers or employees are supposed to be back here."

Bethany slumped into the chair as whoever it was began to explain himself. The disappointment was sinking in fast at not getting the chance to go back out and continue her love affair with the guy in the front row. Even if it was imaginary, it had been incredibly thrilling. Sure it was a little irresponsible of her to lay it on so thick and send out the wrong signal, but that was the best part. She'd been drawn to him the moment she laid eyes on him and could swear she knew him from somewhere. At first she'd been a little nervous, thinking maybe it was someone from back home. But as the show went on, the more her concentration became focused on him, the more convinced she was that he posed no danger to her. She couldn't explain it, but there was just something about him, and that's exactly why that had been the best part about being able to behave the way she had. As alarmingly drawn to him as she'd felt, she could always blame the show for how uncharacteristically she responded to him. It was all just part of her act.

"I just need to relay something to Bethany," she heard the guy in the hallway say.

Immediately she sat up a bit. Simon was now at the door as well, and they exchanged curious glances. Amos was already being his usual cantankerous self, letting the guy know he couldn't just walk back there to meet the star of the show.

"But I did," the guy argued. "There was no one watching the door. *Anybody* can just walk back here. You really should consider getting a security guard or at the very least a door that locks."

His voice rang familiar, but just as with the guy in the front row, she couldn't place it. Just as she leaned over to try to steal a peek, her eyes met his. He was doing the same thing she was, stretching his neck to peek into her room. She realized it *was* the guy in the front row, and her heart suddenly fluttered. Especially because he was holding the roses that had sat on his table the whole time she sang to him. All through her performance, she'd wondered how long it would be before whoever he had bought the roses for would join him at that table—forcing her to tone down the titillating act she'd been enjoying so much.

"Hey," he said with a sweet smile, squeezing in between Amos and Simon.

A single word from him, and the seductress in her vanished. That one word and the smile attached to it coupled with the twinkle in his eyes had her melting already. "Hey," she responded, not sure if she should feel alarmed about her insides going wild so quickly.

Amos stepped in front of him, blocking their eye contact. "She's not feeling well, and I already told you, you can't just—"

"Amos," she said, worried that her grumpy boss might succeed in chasing away this guy she was now dying to talk to. "It's okay. I know him."

Simon turned to her, his brows pinched ever so slightly. "You do?"

All three men were staring at her now. "Yes," she said, hoping she wouldn't be asked what the guy's name was.

"Yeah." The guy stepped forward with the roses and held them out to her. "These are for you. You were incredible out there, by the way. The audience was completely captivated by your performance."

She smiled, feeling like a giddy schoolgirl suddenly, as if she'd never been complimented on her performance. Trying not to let her excitement bubble over, she reached out for the flowers. Both Simon and Amos stepped grudgingly out of the way.

"I'm gonna get you more water," Simon said, lifting a brow again as he took her visitor in from top to bottom.

"Make it fast," Amos instructed as Simon walked past him. "I'm gonna need you onstage with Michele for the second half of the show. The audience won't be too happy that Bethany won't be back out. Maybe if they see you out there again it'll lighten them up some."

Simon nodded but kept walking, without saying more. Amos turned to Damian now with his ever-present puckered brow. "You make it fast, too. She needs to get home."

The guy nodded, then reached his hand out to her. "I'm Damian, by the way."

"I thought you said you knew him," Amos said with a scowl.

Bethany took Damian's big, strong hand in hers and shook it, peering into those breathtaking bedroom eyes of his. "I do. From somewhere . . ."

His smile brightened and, oh, what a smile it was. Having gazed into his seriously penetrating eyes for nearly an hour during her show, the way his eyes now shone brightly at her made her insides liquid. "The speed date," he said.

Tilting her head a bit, she continued to peer at him, confused, then it hit her. Sitting up straighter now, she had to smile. "*That's* where I remember you from."

Her eyes went immediately to the cleft in his chin. She'd been so enthralled by the relentlessness of his gaze that his eyes had her complete attention during the show, and she hadn't even noticed the sexy cleft, a surefire sign that would've given him away. But there was something else different about him now. He was clean-shaven and in a button-down, long-sleeved shirt and slacks, unlike the carefree look he'd worn to the speed date. The look that said the very thing he'd confirmed that night—he *did not* need to be there.

She gave Amos a reassuring look as someone out in the hall called out for him. Giving her one last chastising look and doing another suspicious once-over of Damian, he walked away grudgingly.

As soon as he was gone, Bethany dug her teeth into her bottom lip to keep herself from smiling as hugely as she really wanted to. Had Damian really sought her out and come here tonight to see her? "I remember now," she said with a playful arch of her brow. "You were the one who didn't seem too interested in making a connection with anyone that night."

Leaning his big shoulder against the door frame now, Damian crossed his arms, a sexy smirk replacing his smile. "No, I believe I said I didn't think four minutes was long enough to get to know someone. Not that I wasn't interested in making a connection."

She eyed him, remembering the riveting connection she'd felt with him during the show, and surprisingly feeling even more playful now. "Hmm, so is that why you're here now, Damian? To make a connection?"

Just like that, his smirk was gone. "Actually those," he pointed at the roses in her hands, "are from Jerry."

Looking down at the roses and feeling stupid now for jumping to conclusions too quickly, not to mention incredibly disappointed, Bethany thought about it. "Jerry?"

"My friend, you met him at the speed date," he offered. "He's why I'm here. He asked me to come with him tonight to see your show, but just before it started he called to say something came up and had to cancel. He wanted me to let you know he was sorry." Uncrossing his arms, he ran one hand through his hair, looking a little unsure now. "You *did* know he was coming, right?"

Bethany brought her hand to her mouth, her eyes going wide. "Yes, yes, Jerry. Well," she said, pausing and feeling terrible that her mind had been so wrapped up in Damian that she'd completely forgotten his friend Jerry. "Not exactly. I mean he mentioned he'd have to check out the show sometime, but he never confirmed a date or anything."

Damian seemed put off for a moment, maybe even annoyed by that. "Why doesn't that surprise me," he muttered, so low she wasn't sure she heard him right.

"What was that?"

Before Damian could answer, Simon walked in with a bottle of water. He handed it to her, glancing at Damian, then turned to her again. "You really should go home and get some rest."

"I plan to," she assured him, taking the water and thanking him.

"Well then get moving," Amos said, walking into the room. "I gave you the rest of the night off so you can go refuel, not so you can socialize."

Bethany took a drink of the water, trying not to roll her eyes.

"I gotta stay for the rest of the show," Simon reminded her. "How you getting home?"

Finishing up her long drink of the much-needed water, she exhaled slowly. "I'm walking."

"What?" All three men said at once.

Both Simon and Amos turned to Damian, then back to her. "I've done it before. I'm only a few blocks away from here."

"Yeah, but it's dark out now," Simon insisted. "You can't walk home in the dark. This neighborhood's dangerous."

"Sure I can," she countered. "It's not a big deal, really. I've walked farther."

With a frown, Amos shook his head. "Don't be ridiculous. I'll throw you over my shoulder and stick you in a cab before I let you—"

"I'll drive her home," Damian said to Amos.

Simon and Amos both turned to him suspiciously. Damian pulled his wallet out of his back pocket, opening it and showing it to them. "I'm Damian Santiago, a detective for LVPD. That's my badge number and ID. You can write it down if you want. I'll make sure she gets home okay."

Amos took it from him, examined it closely, then looked at Damian with a suddenly big, goofy smile. "Well I'll be. You should've said something, son. I wouldn't have hassled you like that." He handed the wallet back to Damian, patting him on the back, then turned to Bethany. "Looks like you got a ride home with one of Vegas's finest."

There was no way. No way she was going with him. He was a cop, for Christ's sake! "But—"

"Take the ride," Simon agreed, though he didn't seem nearly as impressed with Damian as Amos was.

Not wanting to make her panic too obvious, Bethany looked at Simon, then back at Damian, who gave her a playful smile, lifting his eyebrows with a shrug.

Slumping back in her chair, realizing she wasn't going to

be given a choice, she conceded. "Okay," she finally said. "Just give me a minute to change."

The relief she felt in the room at that moment was almost a tangible thing. She forced a laugh to mask the dread she was suddenly feeling as they all filed out of the room. Amos placed his hand on Damian's arm, already telling him about the recent vandalism they'd had at the theater.

Even while her head screamed that letting anyone in law enforcement into her life was a very bad idea, before the door even closed behind them her insides were bubbling with a very inappropriate excitement. She got up, reminding herself that Damian was there tonight only because of Jerry. So why was the girl looking back at her in the mirror grinning like the Cheshire cat?

No matter how crazy one word from this man had made her heart, she had to remind herself the last thing she had time for was romance, especially with a cop. She'd nearly passed out from exhaustion, because she was working so much she'd hardly made time to eat lately.

Besides, even if she did have time and even if they did get past the fact that she was his friend's interest, not his, getting involved with *anyone* right now was out of the question.

Changing quickly into a pair of jeans and a simple cotton top, Bethany also decided the amount of makeup she wore for the show looked ridiculous now that she was dressed down, so she washed it off. She forced her heart to slow as she took deep breaths, pulling her hair up into a clip.

As she gathered her things, her heart began to race again, but for an altogether different reason. The text indicator light on her phone was blinking. *Shit!*

Putting everything down on the dresser, she pulled her phone out of her bag just as someone knocked on her door. "You coming out any time soon?" Simon asked. "I'll need to be onstage in a few minutes and I was hoping to say good-bye to you before you left."

"I'll be just a little bit longer," Bethany said, clicking on the envelope. She could already see who it was from, and she braced herself for it.

"Don't forget your ride is waiting for you, too," Simon added.

Within seconds she heard the sound of Damian's voice near the door. "Take your time, Bethany. I'm in no hurry."

She thanked him and let him know she'd be out soon, as she read the text.

I know you're probably working right now and I know I'm supposed to wait for the weekend to contact you but you've been so stressed about the money I wanted to give you SOME good news. We got the paperwork in today. I'll fax it to you tomorrow! Love you!

The news made Bethany nearly choke up. This was really happening. *Finally*. Knowing she'd already made Damian wait long enough and she didn't have time for what she knew would be a long conversation, she texted back quickly that she'd be calling later tonight.

She threw the phone into her bag, looked back in the mirror at her freshly washed face, and headed out to meet Damian in a much better mood than she had been just moments before.

"Wow, is this your ride?" Bethany asked, her eyes staring at the rear of his Camaro as they walked up behind it.

Damian smiled, with a nod, surprised that his older-model car would excite her. Even though it was a classic, typically, in his experience anyway, most girls wouldn't know that.

"Let me guess," she said, turning back to the car. "Sixty-eight—no, wait." As she got closer she seemed to be studying the taillights; then she turned to Damian with a smug smile. "Sixty-nine, right?"

"Yeah." Damian smiled, impressed. "How'd you know that?"

She walked alongside the car, her finger tracing the curved edge of hood. "My uncle was a classic-car enthusiast. He got me into classic cars. He was in a classic-car club—let me ride along with them and everything. He even took me to a lot of car shows. He was saving up to buy an old car and rebuild it himself and promised to let me help him."

Damian had never seen someone go from hot to cold as quickly and as often as she did. When he'd walked out of her dressing room earlier so that she could change, she had looked very drained, and despite the playful conversation they'd been having he noticed a change in her suddenly—a distinct unease. Then she walked out smiling brightly. Damian had been happy Simon was onstage by the time she came out, because he got the annoying impression that Simon was waiting to give Bethany another too-near-the-lips kiss good-bye. Her bright smile had turned into excitement about his car, and now she was suddenly looking solemn again.

"My aunt said the car clubs my uncle was part of might as well have been gangs, because they acted a lot like them. They even had turf wars. My uncle wasn't violent or anything. He didn't even own a gun, but . . ." She shrugged, running her finger over the hood of the Camaro. "He was just at the wrong place at the wrong time and was shot by a stray bullet during one of the arguments his club was having with a rival club." Her eyes finally met Damian's again. "He was only twenty-one."

"I'm sorry" was all Damian could think of to say.

She smiled softly, glancing into the car. "That was a while

back, but my fascination with these classic cars didn't die when he did. I still follow a lot of car blogs and stuff online and watch the restoration shows on TV whenever I can."

That got Damian's attention. "Do you now?"

"Yeah," she said, smiling a bit more genuinely. "They fill a void, I guess."

Damian got into the car, feeling a strange excitement. This could be a good thing. He leaned over and unlocked the passenger door.

Bethany's fragrance filled Damian's car almost as soon as she sat down. She began putting her seat belt on. Damian had a million questions, but he stopped cold when he saw her pulling the clip out of her hair, and she shook her head gently so the long lush strands of hair fell over her shoulders.

"Beautiful," she said, taking the words right out of his mouth, but she was talking about something entirely different from what he was thinking. Her hands caressed the dash of his car as if it were a work of art.

Damian couldn't agree more, but then it had been restored and detailed by the very best. Still, his eyes had only been on the dash and her fingers caressing the metal and wooden details for a moment before they were on her loosened hair again. She smiled when she looked away from the dash and saw he was looking at her in as much awe as she had been looking at the dash. He cleared his throat and straightened out in his seat, turning on the ignition.

"So what's the deal with your boss cutting your show short?" Damian pulled out of the parking space and onto the street.

With a sigh, she turned and looked out the window. "I tend to get dizzy spells when I go too long without eating. Between my other two jobs this morning and then finishing up an article for my internship at the *Desert Informer*, I didn't have time to grab anything to eat before my show. So after the show I got a little lightheaded and sort of lost my footing as I made it back to the dressing room. Amos had to help me the rest of the way there." She shrugged, glancing back at him. "I've known Amos and Simon for some time now, and they both know how I run myself ragged. Amos has always thought I work too much. So when I pitched him the idea of my show, he was against it for that very reason. Said he didn't wanna add to my already packed schedule and be responsible for me collapsing from exhaustion or anything. Simon had already told him about some of the things that've happened to me because of my lack of rest."

Curious, and a little concerned now himself, Damian peered at her inquiringly. "Like what?"

To his surprise, she laughed so sweetly it made him smile. "I got locked in the school library a few months ago." As they came to a stop sign, he turned to her in time to see her bring her hand to her mouth and laugh some more. "I laugh now, but it was pretty embarrassing, not to mention I missed my internship that day. I fell asleep while trying to get my notes caught up at the community college library since their Wi-Fi is one of the best in my area. Which," she laughed even more now, "*wasn't* the first time that's happened, by the way. But normally they don't close the library up during the day. That day the staff had something going on somewhere else in the school, so they closed up and locked the library and didn't notice I was still in there. It was so embarrassing when they all finally got back, and I had to explain what I was doing in there."

From the moment Damian had gotten past Amos and was able to get a glimpse into her dressing room, he'd had a hard time keeping his smile toned down. By now the smile on his face was beginning to feel like a permanent fixture. Just hearing her laugh and seeing that genuinely cheerful smile had him smiling again from ear to ear. Then something else hit him. "So, wait. You haven't eaten anything yet?"

She abruptly stopped smiling and thought about it, pinching her brows together, concentrating so hard for a moment even *that* made him smile. "No, I guess I haven't."

Remembering his intact dinner plate at intermission that he never went back to, his smile grew wider. "I hardly touched my dinner, so I'm actually pretty hungry, too. You wanna grab something before I drop you off?" Before she could say no, he added, "You really should get something if you say going without makes you dizzy." He glanced at his watch. "It *is* almost eight."

The bright eyes were back suddenly. "You like *pupusas*?"

Damian thought about it. "I don't think I've ever actually had one."

"Oh, they are so good. My best friend when I was growing up was Salvadoran, and her mom made the best *pupusas* ever. Think corn tortilla only thicker and stuffed with cheese, beans, or meat. My favorite is the *chicharrón* and cheese. Oh, my God." She sat up straighter, laughing. "My mouth just watered thinking about it. I guess I *am* starving. There's a *pupusería* not too far from here, and they're by far the best I've ever had next to my friend's mom's."

Seeing her excitement over a *pupusa* and knowing he'd be spending a little more time with her tonight than he expected, the damn smile was plastered on his face again. "Tell me which way. Now you made *me* even hungrier."

The place she led him to was exactly what he expected in this part of town, but he was so enthused about it, he didn't want to knock it. The food was actually really good and the place was clean enough, it was just the location it was in that was questionable. And obviously a small mom-and-pop *pupusería* on this side of town was not going to be anything fancy.

The whole time he sat there, as she went on and on about the other Salvadoran dishes her childhood best friend's mom made for her over the years, Damian couldn't get over one thing: what a difference a few hours had made. Not too long ago, he'd been utterly awestruck by this young girl. At moments her seductive eyes almost felt as if she might be toying with him, and even with that in mind, he'd been sucked into it completely.

Now she sat here fresh-faced, looking younger than either the time at the speed date or when she'd been onstage tonight. That same deliciously sensual woman who'd sung to him in such a carnal way that it left him thunderstruck, even after she'd left the stage, was now sitting across from him laughing and having a completely down-to-earth conversation with him.

As much as he hated for their dinner to end, after getting caught up in her beautiful, playful eyes too many times, he did have to admit they were looking noticeably tired. Wrapping things up, they headed back to his car.

"So are you a fan now?" she asked as she placed her seat belt on.

"Of you? Absolutely."

He turned to her in time to catch her timid smile—a first for her. So far he'd seen the slow, seductive smile and the adorable, infectious one. This was different. Had he actually embarrassed her?

"I meant the Salvadoran food, but thanks," she said, fiddling with a strand of hair in what he knew was a sure sign she was embarrassed.

Smiling smugly, he pulled out of the parking lot. "Yeah, I am. I'll have to come back and try the other dishes you talked about. You sold me on them."

They passed a building where there were a few patrol cars

out front. Damian noticed how Bethany stared at them. "Would that be you if you weren't off today?"

"I wasn't off today," he explained. "I actually drove down here when I got off work. And no, that wouldn't be me. I stopped patrolling over a year ago. I'm a homicide detective now."

He turned to her, curious about what expression she'd indulge him in now. "Really?" her wide-eyed stare didn't disappoint. "Wow. You actually get to see murdered people and stuff?"

"Yeah." Damian frowned now. Talking about his job was usually pretty interesting until they got to the gruesomeness of it. And Bethany had jumped right to it. She must've mistaken his agitation for sadness, because she reached over and touched his leg. That simple touch was enough to make him smile again.

"I'm sorry. I didn't mean to be so blunt."

Surprised, he allowed an unexpected laugh to escape him, and Damian shook his head. It amused him how easily she could go from being adorably playful to being genuinely compassionate.

"Nah, that's okay. I'm used to my job." He smiled at the crinkle between her eyes; clearly she was still feeling very sorry. "Relax, this may sound a bit disturbing, but there are many aspects of my job I actually *enjoy*."

The curiosity in her eyes intensified at that. She officially reminded him of his four-year-old niece, Carey. Carey listened to any story he told her with such intensity, taking in every detail, sometimes forgetting to blink, like someone who would be tested on it later. Bethany was now staring at him just like that.

"Really? What do you like about it?"

With a quick lift and drop of his shoulder, he stared

straight ahead. "I like catching the bad guys. Sometimes it takes a while, and it can be extremely frustrating, but in the end there's nothing like knowing all the hard work paid off and the bad guy is behind bars."

She turned to make herself more comfortable as he continued, making him glance at her. Throughout their *pupusa* dinner, he'd picked up on a few of her habits. Like the way she licked her lips clean after every bite or drink she took. And how she'd sink her teeth into her bottom lip when she was really listening, as she was now, but it was distracting as hell. She didn't speak or respond to what he'd just said, as if she was waiting for him to go on.

"So it's, uh, very rewarding when we get to tell the families of the victims that the suspects have been caught, and they can sleep better at night now. A feeling I'll never get tired of. Makes it all worth it, you know?" He tilted his head. "Does that make sense?"

He watched her curiously as that last question sank in, sure that like his father she wouldn't get it either—wouldn't understand how he could be so devoted to putting countless hours into a job where his life was constantly at risk. Of course his father had an even harder time understanding this, since in his eyes Damian was just being stubborn. He could very easily give up his dangerous job and join the family business. Either that or live off the investments he'd made in the last few years.

"Nothing like doing what you enjoy for a living, huh?" Her eyes went a little solemn again, as they had earlier when she spoke of her uncle.

"It's what most people dream of," he maintained.

Bethany took a very deep breath, looking back at him. "You're preaching to the choir, Damian. It's what I dream to be doing full-time someday. So it makes perfect sense to me."

Feeling more relieved than he expected, he now wanted to know what her dream job was, but before he could ask, her expression eased up suddenly and her big eyes brightened again. "I almost interviewed a cop once."

Seeing the sudden excitement in her big eyes and her quick change in mood again, he smiled. "Interviewed?"

"Yeah, for the paper," she said, then gestured for him to switch lanes. "You're gonna turn right at the next light."

Damian turned on the street as she had asked him. She pointed at an old building with a couple of questionable-looking guys standing outside smoking. "This is it."

Having worked this area quite a bit, Damian knew this entire neighborhood was a cesspool. Not a positive thing could be said about it. Nothing but crackheads, prostitutes, and drug dealers. What was a nice girl like Bethany doing living in an area like this? Surely she had to have some family she could stay with anywhere else but here.

"You live alone?" He pulled in and parked right in front of her building. The guys in front of the building were staring at them now, and he glared back.

"Yeah, I live alone." She turned in the direction he was glaring and smirked. "You don't have to do that, you know, *detective*. They're my neighbors."

"Just 'cause they're your neighbors doesn't mean they're not trouble," Damian informed her, for a moment distracted by those playful eyes of hers, before looking back at the guys, who'd since stopped staring. "I've been spotting trouble for years, and, trust me, these guys are trouble."

"They don't scare me," she said with that same defiance he'd heard in her voice when she tried to argue she'd be okay walking home. "I've lived here for months, and they've never given me *any* trouble." Looking back at her, he caught the way she eyed his chin, then quickly brought her eyes back to his.

Damian couldn't help frowning. "They don't scare you? They look like thugs, and believe me when I say I *know* thugs. They *should* scare you. So you haven't been out here long?" Another worrisome factor; obviously she wasn't aware how bad this area really was.

Once again she did an about-face in a split second. "Almost eight months," she said, reaching for the door handle as if she were suddenly in a hurry.

"I'll walk you in," Damian said, already opening his own door.

She started to protest, but he was out of the car before she could finish. By the time Damian reached her side, she was out, too. He caught his breath when he saw her standing before him. It was as if he were seeing her for the first time again. No eighties makeup, no seductive cabaret singer. Just a fresh-faced, sweet-looking girl in jeans and a tank, and he couldn't decide which look he liked more.

"Well, thanks for the ride, Damian." She saluted him with a small smile, their eyes meeting in that special way they had throughout her entire show, for just a moment. Then she looked away. "Maybe I'll see you around."

Damian stood there even after she'd walked into the building and closed the door behind her. He wasn't sure what he was waiting for, but he didn't feel comfortable until he was reasonably sure she was safely in her apartment.

The guys out front gave him a once-over as he walked around his car to the driver's side. About to get in, he heard something up above. A window in Bethany's building opened, and her head popped out. Her big, dazzling smile was back.

"Hey, Damian, I never finished telling you about my almost interview with the cop."

The guys out front were all looking up now, too, and already there were chuckles. Damian wasn't at all thrilled that they all now knew which window was the one to her apartment. Did she really plan on telling him about the interview now, from up there?

"Yeah, I know. We got off-track."

"It was a few months ago. I never got through it." She started giggling again. Apparently she *was* going to tell him from the window. "I made a joke about him not trying to sell me tickets to the highway patrolmen's ball."

She laughed harder now and got Damian going even though he had no idea why she was laughing. Her head disappeared back in the window, and it popped out again, but this time she put her head on her arm.

"Then he said," and she couldn't finish, bringing her hand to her mouth, her laughter hitting a higher pitch. God, she was adorable. Every little detail about her was slowly drawing him more to want to get to know her better.

She tried again. "He said highway patrolmen don't have balls!"

The guys downstairs started laughing, and her head disappeared back in the window. Damian laughed at the thought of her rolling around on her floor. Was she not coming back out? He waited a few more minutes. Her head popped out again. She'd regained her composure but lost it again as soon as she looked at him, shaking her head and burying her face in her hand in apparent embarrassment over her silliness. He was lucky she was way up there, or he probably would've had to fight the urge to grab her and kiss her.

"Is that the whole story?" That sweet laugh was something he could very easily get addicted to.

She nodded, wiping tears away from her eyes. "Yeah, as you could imagine, I never got through the interview."

"Oh, yeah," Damian couldn't even remember the last time someone made him smile so much. "I can imagine."

CHAPTER 5

Damian hadn't been able to get hold of Jerry that night, and for the following few days, they either texted or played phone tag. Jerry had his hands full with Ashlynn and her mother, and Damian had been immersed in work. He texted Jerry, explaining briefly how he'd spoken to Bethany and that he'd given her a ride home. The following day, Damian woke to an overapologetic voicemail from Jerry about leaving him hanging that night and how grateful he was, saying he owed Damian one.

By the end of the week, Damian's mind had been completely preoccupied with thoughts of Bethany. He reasoned that his unease about the area she was living in all by herself was because of his job, and it was in his nature to feel concern. He'd seen enough happen on that side of town to know he wasn't exaggerating. But even with the cases in which he was involved, he could always detach himself from the possible victims. This felt a little too personal for someone he knew so little about, and *that* he didn't quite understand.

He worked through most of the weekend, as he was pretty much accustomed to. So Sunday afternoon he took advantage of the time off and decided to give his car a much-needed wash. Like playing his guitar, waxing and detailing his cars was also therapeutic for Damian. He could lose himself in the fine lines and curves of the rims—waxing and polishing the intricate details of the moldings, headlights, and grille. He'd been out there for almost an hour and was about to get started on the inside when he opened the passenger door and something fell out. It hit his foot and bounced under the car.

"Damn it." He got down on one knee and leaned all the way down. It was a weird shape, and he couldn't make it out. Reaching for it, he knew what it was the second he touched it. By the time he pulled it out, he was smiling like a fat kid at an all-you-can-eat pizza joint. A woman's hair clip— Bethany's. It had to be. There'd been no other women in this car in at least a month, and he cleaned most of his cars at least once every other week.

Deciding to skip the inside detailing of the car, Damian jumped into the shower instead. He had a delivery to make. Would she be performing today? He'd find out soon enough, and if she wasn't, he knew where to find her.

———

Thinking it'd be best if he dressed down, Damian threw on a pair of cargo shorts and a tank. It *was* his day off, after all, and besides, it was hotter than hell out. He wasn't going to be in the audience again if she was performing, just making a delivery that he hoped would get him her number this time. He smiled as he slapped some aftershave on, remembering Bethany's sweet laugh and bright eyes. Glancing at his shoulders and arms, he smirked. He'd bulked up before he'd even joined the force, but over the years he'd picked up a pretty impressive amount more. Figuring it wouldn't hurt to show a little of what he'd worked so hard for, his choice of a muscle-revealing shirt was a good one.

Just as he was about to walk out, his phone rang. He frowned, staring at the caller ID—Jerry. For a second, Damian considered just sending it to voicemail, but his conscience won out and he answered.

"Hey, Jer, what's up?"

"Damian! There he is!" Damian was glad to hear his friend sound upbeat. "Finally no tag, you're it. What are you up to, man?"

"Not much, just getting ready to run some errands."

"Errands? Really, on a Sunday?"

"Well, yeah, I need to pick up a few things and then maybe stop at the market." He winced, because he felt like a jerk lying to Jerry like that, but what was he supposed to do? Tell him he was driving all the way downtown to take Bethany her fifty-cent hair clip? If anyone would see right through that, it would be Jerry. He started out the back door, slipping his wallet in his side pocket and pulling his sunglasses on.

"What are *you* up to?" Damian asked, in an effort to get off the subject of his *errands*.

"I got a date with my speed date girl."

Damian stopped in his tracks. Jerry was going out with Bethany? Damn, he knew he should've said something sooner. "Really? Wow, so she's giving you another shot?"

"What?"

"Bethany, right?" With his voice suddenly sounding a bit hoarse, Damian cleared his throat.

"Oh, no. No, no, no, this is one of the other girls I met that night." Damian heard what sounded like a chuckle. "I'm a stud, dude. I got 'em coming at me from every direction."

Damian thought about how it took Bethany a few seconds to remember Jerry and smiled. But this was too close and way too unsettling. Though the amount of time he'd spent thinking about her all week was bordering on the obsessive, he'd come to the same conclusion each time. Moving in on someone his best friend was actively pursuing was out of the question. And since he hadn't had a chance to talk to Jerry all week, Damian wasn't sure how serious his friend really was about it. He'd even begun to prepare himself for the possibility that he just might have to be around her with Jerry. Since nothing had actually happened between them, except the unspoken incredible *thing* he was certain she'd also felt during her show, he figured he could live with it if he had to. That it wouldn't be so bad seeing her with Jerry. Each time he thought this, he ignored the memories of his insides warming when she'd sung to someone else and when he had to watch her sing with Simon. It wasn't until he heard Jerry say he was going on a date with his speed date girl that he finally admitted this was *bad*.

No girl had ever inundated his thoughts like this. And certainly never this quickly. He'd convinced himself that it was just temporary infatuation—nothing but physical attraction. But judging by how overwhelmingly relieved he was to hear Jerry wasn't going out with Bethany tonight, he knew it was more than just a physical thing.

Obviously things between her and Jerry weren't serious *yet*. As far as Damian knew, Jerry hadn't even seen her again since the speed date. Filled with a sudden urgency, he gripped the phone and bit the bullet. He had to before it was too late. "Listen, Jer, so you and Bethany haven't gotten real close, have you?"

Jerry was quiet, then he spoke up. "Uh, no, why? Did she say we had?"

"*No!* I mean," Damian backpedaled from his overzealous answer, but the last thing he wanted was for Jerry to get the idea she was interested. "I didn't ask her, and she didn't mention anything. I was just wondering."

"No, I haven't had a chance to even chat with her. We've only emailed. That night was going to be my first chance. And, well, you know what happened."

Not about to give him a chance to say he was still interested in trying, Damian went in for the kill. This was the last thing he thought he'd be doing when he got up that morning, or five minutes ago, for that matter, but he had to now even if it meant embellishing a bit. "'Cause, uh, I think she and I hit it off that night." He paused, holding his breath for a moment, but Jerry didn't say anything. "So I was thinking since you're obviously still shopping around, that it might not be a big deal if I asked her out."

His friend's continued silence unnerved him. But moments later, hearing Jerry's sudden laughter had him letting out a heavy sigh of relief. "You dog, you! Hit it off? Really? Knowing you, that could mean anything." He laughed some more, and Damian rolled his eyes. "Yeah, sure, I'm cool with it on one condition."

"What's that?" Damian asked, getting into his car and knowing that at this point there'd be nothing he'd object to so long as he and Jerry were cool about this, and he wasn't breaking that unspoken bro code between them.

"You gotta tell me exactly what you *hit* and don't leave any of the gory details out." Jerry laughed again. "And you said that speed date thing was stupid."

"It *was* stupid," Damian insisted, slipping on his earpiece and switching the call over before starting the ignition. "And I didn't *hit* anything. What kind of friend do you think I am to try anything before checking with you first?" Damian decided he'd keep his hair clip delivery trip all the way downtown to himself. "All I did was give her a ride home, and we stopped to grab something to eat. She hadn't eaten all day." He made sure to add that last part since he was supposed to have been eating the steak Jerry paid for, but he wasn't about to admit why he hadn't. "She just seems like someone who might be cool to hang out with, that's all."

"I told you she was intriguing," Jerry reminded him, sounding a little too smug. "And I don't care what you say, that speed date landed us both future wife prospects. I was thinking about emailing Bethany again, but after talking to Janis for over an hour last night, I'm really excited about hanging out with her in person now. She may be the one— my soul mate."

Damian couldn't help but shake his head as he hopped onto the freeway. *The one? Soul mate?* After just one call? And *future wife prospects*? Damian didn't know about all that. All he had said *and* was thinking was that it might be cool to hang out with Bethany. As usual, Jerry was way ahead of himself. "Easy now," Damian said, smiling. "I'm just looking to hang out with her, not marry her."

"Well, you know what they say." Damian could hear the silly smile in Jerry's voice already. "Love strikes when you're least expecting it. When are you asking her out?"

Having just come up with the idea of taking Bethany her hair clip, Damian hadn't thought this through, but since he did make it sound as if they *hit it off,* he couldn't tell Jerry he didn't even have her number yet. "Not sure, sometime in the next few weeks maybe."

Maybe sooner if things went his way today. He wasn't like Jerry. He'd feel her out for a while. Get to know her before deciding if he was ready to plunge into anything at all.

"Well, let me know if you go back to where she works. You may not like dinner shows, but I do."

"Yeah, I'll let you know."

Like hell he would. His second encounter with Bethany had gone a hell of a lot better than his first, but the fact remained she'd hit the big fat Reject button on his ass at the speed date. She'd at least given Jerry her email and the possibility of another date. Damian hadn't even been able to get a name out of her that first night. And while this time around she'd been far more amicable, neither one of them had addressed the connection he felt during her performance. He hated to even think it, but there was still the very real possibility that she did that at every show.

The last thing he needed was to go back with Jerry and for her to put on a similar show for him. Jerry might not be a ladykiller, and no one would be getting rich putting out sexy insurance salesmen calendars anytime soon, but he was a nice guy with a kind of charm some women might be into, including Bethany. Damian would pass on bringing Jerry around Bethany until he was sure he'd gotten past the Reject button.

"So anyway," Jerry said. "I was calling to tell you it looks like I'm gonna be a dad."

"What?"

"A full-time dad, that is." Jerry exhaled loudly, then explained about Ashlynn hating Shannon's boyfriend, who had just moved in a few weeks ago. She'd also been getting bullied at her current school. "She's really miserable, so Shannon and I agreed she can move in with me and go to school out here until she goes away to college."

Damian didn't know whether to laugh or head straight to Jerry's place and try to knock some sense into him. "You have any idea how hard it's going to be to raise a sixteen-year-old *girl* all on your own, Jerry?"

"I won't be totally on my own. My mom and my sister are already excited and have agreed to help out with the girl talk and shopping and all that. She's already spending the night at my mom's house tonight. They're having girl movie night with my sister." Jerry paused for a second before continuing with a sigh. "I gotta do it, man. In sixteen years this'll be the first time I'd be stepping up to the plate and being a real dad."

"It wasn't your fault you couldn't all this time, Jer," Damian reminded him.

"I know. But it wasn't her fault either, and I guess now that we have the chance to bond, I think it's the right thing to do."

"Yeah, I guess it is." Damian smiled. "Let me know if you need me to help out in any way. Not that I know the first thing about raising teens, but remember I do own guns. Uncle Damian would be more than happy to come over and clean them at your place if she ever invites a boy home to meet you."

Jerry laughed. "I'll keep that in mind."

"I'm serious, Jer."

"I know you are, man. Don't worry, Uncle Damian and his guns will be the first to greet any boys sniffing around her."

After getting off the phone with Jerry, Damian did his best not to let his nerves get worked up. He'd drop off the hair clip with Bethany, make some small talk, and perhaps get her number. He still didn't know a whole lot about her except that she had the ability to make him visualize taking her every which way he could think of one minute, and in the next minute have him grinning silly, feeling all kinds of craziness only twelve-year-old *girls* were supposed to feel in their stomachs. Most important, and it surprised him that he'd even be thinking so much about this—she was single and looking to make a connection with someone.

Damian thought about it for a moment as he pulled off the freeway, taking the exit toward the dive she worked at. Was *he* looking for a connection with her? He'd told Jerry she seemed like someone who would be fun. But clearly there was more to it. There were plenty of girls he could have fun with. And he hadn't made time for anything more than just the sexual kind in a while. Damian wasn't sure what he was looking to have happen with her. All he knew was that only a week after *really* meeting her for the first time, he was already craving to hear her laughter and get caught in those eyes that could go from lustful to bright and sweet in an instant. But *soul mate—the one*? That was going a bit too far, even for Jerry, but especially for himself.

He parked his car in the same spot he'd parked it in the last time he'd been to this dive. Glancing around, he noticed there were a lot fewer cars here than last Friday. Maybe Vintage Soul was only on Fridays and for obvious reasons was more popular than any of the other shows he'd seen posted on the walls. The thought of guys lining up to be the one at the front table had him clenching his jaw already.

He walked in and immediately knew she was most likely not there, because he could hear the classical piano music coming from the showroom. The hostess smiled at him. "What can I do for you?"

"I'm looking for Bethany. Is she working today?"

Amos walked out from the back hallway and smiled when he saw him. "Detective Santiago. Are you here to enjoy another show?"

"Actually, no." Damian smiled at the heavyset man. "I was hoping to catch Bethany here."

Amos's forehead pinched. "She didn't tell you?"

Feeling a little alarmed, Damian shook his head. "Tell me what?"

"Her show will be on hiatus for a while."

"Why?" Damian asked, suddenly feeling concerned. "Did something happen?"

Amos peered at him. "You and Bethany close?"

"Yeah," Damian said, stretching the truth.

"Then how come she hasn't told you herself?"

"I haven't talked to her in a few days," Damian countered immediately. "I've been out of town," he added. Technically he hadn't been on this side of town all week. "Is she okay?"

Amos stared at him for a few more annoying seconds before responding. "She's fine. She just won't be coming in to work for a few weeks. But you'll have to get the rest from her. I'm sorry." He shook his head. "But I'm not at liberty to be giving out her business, son."

"Thanks." Damian rushed out, feeling an agitation he didn't understand. He knew so little about Bethany, and yet here he was jumping into his car and skidding out of there as if he needed to save her *now*. He squeezed the steering wheel, reminding himself that Amos had said she was fine. Instinct, however, told him otherwise.

He didn't even realize how fast he'd been driving until he had to swerve to miss hitting the car that swung into the lane in front of him. *Fuck!*

Turning onto the street she lived on, he looked up as he neared her apartment building. The window she'd popped her head out of when he'd dropped her off was wide open. With his air conditioner on, he couldn't feel the Vegas desert heat, but the temperature display on his phone read 103 degrees. He seriously doubted any of the air conditioners in her run-down building were in working order either, so her open window was a good indication she was home.

Feeling a little relief seep in, he parked across the street from her building and got out of his car.

CHAPTER 6

Even sitting on the sofa with a sheet over it, in thin running shorts and an even thinner tank top with the fan pointed right at her, Bethany still felt the sweat trickle down between her breasts. This was torture. Of course the ancient air conditioner in her apartment and every other apartment in the building was out of order, and *of course* Mr. Hadley had cackled loudly when she asked if he was going to have someone come out and fix it.

Putting her laptop aside, she got up to grab another bottle of water from the icebox. It was the only part of that old refrigerator that kept anything as cold as she liked it. Bethany grabbed the coldest bottle, opened the top, and took a long swig, then ran the water in the sink and splashed a generous amount on her face, neck, and cleavage area. She went and stood in front of the fan, feeling the tiniest bit of relief as the fan blew on her wet upper body.

Just as she took a deep breath, the knock at the door made her stop dead and hold it in. Waiting for Trinity's whistle, she didn't move an inch. No whistle, but another knock—this one a little louder. With her heart speeding up and, in her panic, looking around for anything to use as a weapon, the water bottle in her hand hit the fan, knocking it over. "Shit!" she muttered as it fell loudly to the floor.

There was an even louder, more demanding knock on the door this time. "Bethany? Are you okay in there?"

Bethany held her breath again, deliberating whether that was who she thought it was.

"Bethany! It's Damian, from last week. Are you all right? Do you need me to call someone for you?"

Gasping in relief and ignoring the other unacceptable emotions she was now feeling as her excited heart began beating, Bethany exhaled before responding. "I'm fine. Just give me a sec."

She picked up the fan, frowning when she noticed a part of the cage around it had broken off. Luckily it turned on when she plugged it back into the socket where the cord had pulled out with the fall. With a harsh huff, she headed to the door. She peeked out the window just to be sure, chastising her already fluttering heart from just the sight of him.

Another alarming thought suddenly hit her. Had he possibly looked into her? Could he be here because he knew something? She shook her head with a frown. She was being paranoid.

Running her fingers through her hair, she opened the door. "Hey." She smiled cautiously.

"Everything okay?" he asked, glancing behind her, looking a little too concerned.

"Yeah, yeah. The, uh," she motioned behind her, "the fan just tipped over."

As concerned as he first appeared, Bethany didn't miss the way his eyes did a quick scan of her body from top to bottom. It reminded her that she was wearing shorts she'd only ever wear indoors, because they were *that* short. The tank top she wore was almost soaked through, and it'd been too hot for a bra. She moved over so the door covered half her body, beginning to feel paranoid. "What brings you around these parts?"

He held his hand up to her. "This." She glanced down at it. To her relief, he held a hair clip in his hands. "This is yours, right? I was cleaning my car out and found it in there, and since I was in the area today, I thought I'd bring it by for you."

Bethany smiled, reaching out for it. "Thanks." She took it, her hand brushing his warm fingers as she did.

"I stopped at the theater, and Amos said your show's on a hiatus for a while. But you were so good."

Bethany sighed, leaning her head against the door. "Yeah. Well, I'm on a mandatory leave for a few weeks."

"Why?" Damian asked, his brows furrowing, bringing Bethany's attention to those dark, penetrating eyes she'd been so drawn to since day one at the speed date, but even more so after spending time with him last week. "Did something happen?"

She lifted her shoulder, wondering how much she should tell this cop whom she barely knew. "He worries too much, is what happened. He thought I needed the time off—says I work too much."

With his brows still furrowed, Damian stared at her as if he was waiting for more. Deciding it was no big deal if she told him, she went on. "The day you were there, I was just a little lightheaded, but then a few days later I almost passed out. With my jobs keeping me busy all day and then the articles for my internship keeping me up most the night, I was running on very little sleep and a couple of Red Bulls. He'd warned me when he first gave me the opportunity to do my show that at the first sign of burnout I'd be out, so when I nearly passed out, he said he wasn't canceling the show indefinitely, but I did have to take a few weeks off."

The concern on Damian's face went even more severe now.

In an attempt to escape the intensity of his gaze, Bethany glanced away and took in his big hard shoulders and arms. Even under his work shirt and slacks last time and the shirt he'd worn to the speed date, she had had an idea of the kind of muscle he was probably packing, but this surpassed all of her expectations.

Was it possible he got better-looking every time she saw him? He'd gone from the understandably smug best-looking guy at the speed date to even sexier when cleaned up in his dress-up shirt and slacks to near perfection now that she could see what was under those layers of clothes. With the re-alization that she'd been taking in every inch of his hard body when her eyes finally made it back to his eyes, she felt her face warm. His previous severely concerned expression was now a playful grin. "Amos is a good guy." This time he took her in from top to bottom unabashed, and how could she protest? She'd just shamelessly swallowed him up whole with her eyes. "How you feeling now? The time off doing you good?"

She shrugged. "I guess, but I was so used to constantly being on the move, I almost don't know what to do with the extra time now."

"So you have a free day today?"

She cleared her throat, standing up a little straighter and hiding a bit more of her body behind the door. "Yes, today's just one of the several semifree days I have coming in the next weeks. It's gonna take some time to get used to. I hope by then Amos will let me come back." Because God knew she needed the extra money *bad*.

The smoldering bedroom eyes she'd gotten caught up in during her show and even a few times when they had dinner later made an appearance once again. "Well, if you have some time, I've got something I'd like to show you." Her jaw nearly dropped, but before she could beg his pardon he added, "It's a place I think you'd really like to see. In fact, I'd be willing to bet you'd more than like it, you'd be thrilled."

"What place?"

The curiosity suddenly replaced the scandalous thoughts that had shamefully crossed her mind when he said he had something to *show* her. He knew nothing about her; how could he possibly be so sure she'd be *thrilled*?

"Let me surprise you," he said, the smolder in his eyes becoming a bit more vulnerable. "It's not too far from here. Maybe twenty minutes."

Secretly delighted already that he would even *want* to surprise her—*thrill* her—she held back the enormous grin that threatened to splash itself across her face. Instead she continued to study him curiously. "Well, I'm not totally free. I *do* have this article I *have* to get written today." She bit her lip, trying to decide if she should do this. "Twenty minutes?"

The relieved but nervous smile on this man, who had every reason to emanate confidence, began making her insides feel all kinds of craziness. Was it possible *she* made *him* nervous? Had he really been in the area and happened to drop off the hair clip or did he drive there just to see her again and invite her somewhere and try to *thrill* her? She wanted to scold herself—remind herself that she had neither the time nor the room for any of this in her convoluted life. But her heart pounded away, beating out all the forewarnings.

"I might be able to do twenty minutes," she said, biting her lip again in a desperate attempt to keep the smile restrained.

He lifted a mischievous brow that made her heart beat even faster. "I said it's twenty minutes from here, but once you get there, I'm pretty sure you're gonna wanna hang around for a while."

That piqued her curiosity, and the enormous smile broke through. "Can you give me a hint?"

Exhaling a bit exaggeratedly, he crossed his big arms and squinted as if to think of a good hint. "Let's just say you've probably already seen it but not in person."

That could be a lot of places in Vegas. Maybe since she was a performer, he had easily figured out she loved the theater. Could he be taking her to a show? "Do I need to dress up?"

Damian obviously took the question as an invitation to look her up and down again, because he did so with a very satisfied grin. "I know it's hot, but you may wanna throw a little more on, and no, no need to dress up. Just wear something comfortable."

With that Bethany stepped back, opening the door wider for him. "It'll only take me a few minutes, but you're welcome to come in and wait if you'd like." As she'd expected, there was no need to insist; he was already making his way into her small front room. "Would you like some cold water? Sorry I don't have much else to offer you."

She turned from her refrigerator in time to catch him just as his gazing eyes darted away from her body where they'd been focused.

"Sure, I'll take one," he said, glancing around the very small apartment. For a cop he wasn't the slickest, and it was unlike her not to be annoyed by his ogling. Normally that's exactly how she'd feel: *annoyed*. Maybe it was that she hadn't allowed herself to even consider being attracted or excited by any man in so long, and there was something so undeniably exciting about a guy like Damian being attracted to her. The thrill of it stomped away any annoyance she should've felt.

As she handed him the bottle of water, their eyes met once again, warming her insides instantly. What the hell was with her? She'd *never* been one of those girls who were easily taken by a man's good looks. She was not about to start now. With that thought in mind, she broke out of the spell-like gaze and spun around. "I'll only be a couple of minutes. Have a seat if you'd like."

After closing her bedroom door behind her, she stripped off her clothes and rushed into the shower, rinsing off in record time. She'd already showered that morning, but there was no way she was getting into his car after sitting in her ovenlike apartment for hours, feeling the sweat drip through all her body crevices. Fortunately, she was used to living in a rush; jumping out of the shower and getting dressed in under five minutes was the norm for her. Within minutes she was pulling her hair into a ponytail, powdering her face, and smacking her glossed lips in the mirror.

With a deep breath, she reflected on the fact that in the eight months she'd been living here, this was one of the very few times she wasn't leaving her apartment for work, her internship, errands, or research. She was actually leaving for pleasure—and with one of the sexiest men she'd ever laid eyes on. The very thing she knew she *should not* be doing.

Refusing to let her conscience ruin this for her, she reminded herself how hard she'd worked to get where she was at now and that soon it would all be over anyway. She deserved to enjoy herself a little, and with things moving along now, maybe she finally could.

———

The apartment was very sparsely decorated, something Damian always made note of when searching suspects' properties. Was it really their home, or was it a hideout—a temporary residence while they finished whatever premeditated crime they had been planning for months?

She did have a few plants on the kitchen windowsill and

a corkboard with help-wanted ads tacked onto it along with some grocery and fast-food coupons. There were a couple of photos on the outdated TV console of herself, a younger girl, and an even younger-looking boy in a baseball cap, possibly siblings, if he had to go by the resemblance. Then there was the one he couldn't help pick up. She and Simon stood in front of a stage, but not the one at the City Lights Theater. Simon had his arm around her shoulder and, in this case, the big, beautiful smile she wore didn't make him smile. Instead he found himself examining the exact placement of Simon's hand on her shoulder as his jaw worked. Though in the end, Simon had agreed she should take the ride, Damian wouldn't be forgetting how the guy had also kissed her onstage and then seemed anxious to *say good-bye* to her before she left.

Hearing the doorknob of her bedroom door jiggle, Damian quickly put the photo down. She walked out, and he held his breath, reminding himself not to be so damn obvious. He and his brothers had always laughed at the idiots who practically let their tongues hang out in the presence of a good-looking woman, and here he'd been close to doing just that more than once today.

The worst thing was she'd caught him each time. He already knew he was physically attracted to her, but that wasn't why he was here, and that's not the impression he wanted to make. He knew plenty of physically attractive women. But none had even come close to having such an effect on him. With the stress of continually having to prove himself to all the condescending old pricks at work and all the depressing shit he'd seen in the past two weeks alone, the very short time he'd spent with Bethany had been a breath of fresh air. He wasn't even sure how to explain it, but just thinking about her smile and that easygoing, adorable laugh of hers made him smile as he hadn't in too long.

Seeing her again was confirmation that she was exactly the kind of distraction he needed in his life right now. But he hadn't been prepared to see her in those mouthwatering little shorts and the wet tank clinging to her perfectly plump breasts that had him twitching in his pants instantly. It was a wonder he hadn't made more of an ass of himself. As hard as he'd tried, it was nearly impossible to keep his eyes from wandering. When she'd turned to get the water out of the fridge, he'd been surprised his legs hadn't buckled at the sight of her tight, round ass, especially since the tiny shorts she'd worn left little to the imagination.

Sexy and sensual were two words that would easily describe her. Her dark, cold, but smoldering expressions at the speed date. Those lips she so slowly curved in such a breath-taking, teasing smile. The unforgettable way she'd worked him into a complete frenzy during her show, then left him stunned. Even the way she'd let her hair down in his car had been pant-tightening exciting, but today took the fucking cake. Now he'd have an all-too-clear visual of the places he'd love to get his hands on and the things he'd do to her if he ever did. The image of the swell of that perfect ass peeking out of the bottom of her tiny shorts would torment him now. Why did his eyes always have to go *there*? Even after she'd caught him, the second she turned away his eyes had gone right back there.

Now she'd changed into a pair of denim shorts that were a bit longer than the ones she wore earlier, but even her curve-hugging, simple, cotton T-shirt had him letting out a slow breath. He recognized the writing of the word "Wicked" on her T-shirt to be from the Broadway stage show, but the way the word was sprawled across the curves of her breasts, enhancing what didn't need any more enhancing, gave the word a whole new meaning.

Taking a swig from his bottle of water in an effort to bring his attention to something else, he cleared his throat. "You ready?"

"Yep," she said, walking over to the sofa and pulling out a small wallet from her book bag. "Need more water?"

Damian gulped down what was left of his water before walking over and dumping it in the small wastebasket in the kitchen. "Nope. I'm good."

After locking her door, they walked down the flight of stairs to the first floor, Bethany first. The heat alone as soon as they'd stepped out into the sun was enough to make him feel clammy all over, but the added need to take the stairs only furthered the uncomfortable heat. "How long has that elevator been out of order?"

Bethany smirked, looking back at him with a roll of her eyes. "It was out of order when I moved in, but my neighbor said it's been at least a year now."

"Can't you ask your landlord to do something about it?" Damian asked, reaching his hand out for hers as they stepped off the curb to cross the street. She looked at him, then at his hand, a little weirdly, without extending hers. Damian let out a quick laugh, bringing his hand back to his side. "Sorry. Instinct. I have a little niece."

His flub came with instant gratification, because her sweet laugh had him grinning already. "I was gonna say, I've crossed this street plenty of times on my own. I'm pretty sure I got this."

"Yeah, well you never can be too safe." He smiled, enjoying the fact that just like last time, being around her felt very natural. He hardly knew her and yet, even hearing her laugh at his expense, he felt as if they'd been doing this forever.

He came around and opened the door for her, waiting until she was all the way in before closing it. As he climbed in on his side, he decided he'd take advantage of the drive out to her surprise to get to know her a little better. There were a few things he was curious about, though some he decided to hold off asking about until later. "So you mentioned you haven't been living out here too long. Where'd you move out here from?"

He started the car but didn't miss how she straightened awkwardly. When he glanced at her, she immediately looked away. A big part of his training included studying body language, and Damian was one of the best at it. He was usually spot-on when it came to figuring out whether someone he was interrogating was telling the truth or full of shit. This was a simple enough question with no motive behind it, other than that he was curious, but already he could tell this was a subject she was uncomfortable discussing.

CHAPTER 7

⁓

This was *not* something she'd been anticipating talking about so soon, but she reasoned that just as with everyone else she'd met here so far, this was the first thing she should expect to be asked. It shouldn't feel any different with Damian than when anybody else asked—but already it did.

Clearing her throat, she decided that, regardless of how it felt, she'd stick to her usual spiel. "I'm from the southern tip of Arizona—Nogales."

"Hmm." He glanced at her, then his eyes were back on the road. "So what brought you out here?"

"The internship," she responded, maybe a little too quickly, then added, "Interning at the *Desert Informer* was a really good opportunity. And since I knew the potential to get jobs in theater out here, I decided why not take a few months off school, maybe a year, and do this instead."

She hoped with all her might he didn't know too much about *DI*. There was *nothing* exceptional about this particular paper. In fact it was rather inferior, compared to most other papers she would've preferred.

"Journalism, huh?" Damian asked still staring ahead at the road. "Is that the dream job you were talking about the other day when you mentioned doing what you love for a living?"

"Sort of."

Bethany glanced away and out the window before she could get too caught up staring at his profile. He'd obviously been off work for at least a day, because the five-o'clock shadow she remembered from the speed date was back. She couldn't make up her mind which look was sexier on him: the clean-shaven one like when he'd shown up at her show or this one. One thing was for sure, this way had her visualizing herself cradling that strong, scruffy jaw in her hands, maybe even leaning in to lick his lips. *Stop it.*

"What does that mean? Sort of?"

Gulping away the completely unexpected and danger-ously vivid visuals, she glanced back at him. Since they were at a stop now, he was staring at her.

"I'm sorry. What was that?"

He smiled but seemed to be studying her face. "You moved all the way out here for the journalism internship at *DI*, but it's only *sort of* your dream job?"

"Oh, yeah, well it's sort of a backup plan. My real passion is in entertainment. Not just singing either. Anything in the field. I've always loved singing, dancing, acting, being on-stage, period. My aunt always said it was in my blood. There were a lot of entertainers in my family. Mostly in Mexico, but still they were big in their own right."

That sexy brow lifted as he turned to her, and for a mo-ment she was tempted to brag about her success in none other than Hollywood, the capital of the entertainment world. If you could make it there you could make it anywhere, and she nearly had. But she knew she shouldn't tell him—couldn't.

"Really, wow." His smile was sweet now, genuinely im-pressed, not at all sensual like some of the times he'd smiled at her before. "So that's why you came out to Vegas? Have you done any of the bigger theaters? You're good enough to, you know."

"I have, actually." She sat up suddenly, swelling with pride. This hardly compared to her gigs back in Hollywood, but at least she could talk about it openly. "I've had a few gigs singing in some of the bigger casino lounges."

His continued sincere smile made her smile, too, and her insides were all warm again even in the comfort of his air-conditioned car. She even giggled when he nearly missed that the light had turned green, he'd been so engrossed in listening to her. But she continued telling him about her Vegas successes as he drove. "I was an understudy for the lead role in *Imagine* at the Crown."

He turned to her, his eyes wide now. "*Really?* That's a huge one. Did you ever get to stand in for her?"

Her smile growing even sillier now, Bethany nodded enthusiastically. Oh, if she could only tell him about some of the roles she'd had before she moved here. Never in her life had she felt the need to impress anyone outside of the directors she auditioned for, and now she wanted to very badly. "I did. It was mostly during the week and in the day shows, but the girl that plays the lead had to go away to New York a few months ago, and I took on the role for the entire weekend."

"How'd you do?" He turned to her, his smile as big as her own smile felt.

"I nailed it." The laughter escaped her, and she was suddenly giddy. She hadn't been able to brag about this to anyone but Simon and Amos, who were happy enough for her, but the ones who really mattered she didn't dare tell, since she knew they'd be worried. Trinity, bless her heart, hadn't even heard of *Imagine* but did pretend to be excited. "One of the biggest critics at the *Sun News* said I was better than

Holly, who still has the lead." She stopped smiling suddenly and shook her head. "Ever since then, Holly hasn't missed a show."

"Of course not," Damian said as they drove onto the highway. "I've seen and felt firsthand the effect you have on an audience. I completely understand why any other performer would be intimidated by you."

"Really?" Bethany tilted her head, giving up trying to calm her insides. Everything he said to her now, every time he looked at her, made her insides a little crazier. It was bordering on the absurd, but at the same time she was enjoying it. "Intimidated?"

He turned to her with a confused expression. "You really don't see it?"

"No." She shook her head, staring at him. "I mean I don't think I'm an intimidating person."

"You probably think you're not, but trust me, you can be." That eyebrow went up again with a smirk. "You have this aura of self-confidence about you. But not in a conceited way," he added quickly. "There's just nothing about you that says you're not nervous or even scared, like the night of the speed date." He laughed softly, making her feel guilty about how cold she'd been to him that night. But before she could even begin to try to explain, he went on. "And when you said those thugs outside your apartment didn't scare you. Maybe in instances like that, you're a little *too* sure of yourself—dangerously so. At any rate, that kind of self-confidence can be intimidating, since most people are just the opposite." The smirk turned into an all-out smile, though his gaze seemed to seep deeper into her each time he looked at her, as he did now. "Although I think it's sexy as hell."

As sure of herself as he seemed to think she was, her insides were officially a hot mess. Unable to look into those concentrated eyes anymore, she gulped, glancing out into the dirt and Joshua tree–lined highway. They were getting farther away from the city and driving deeper into the desert. She should be concerned. Here she was letting this near stranger drive her out to God knows where in the middle of the desert. Instead she felt strangely safe being with him. Add to that an inappropriate amount of exhilaration she was feeling because he'd just said she was sexy as hell, and she knew she should be scolding herself, not basking in the pleasure of it.

"Well," she finally responded, but wouldn't touch the *sexy as hell* comment. "I don't mean to come across as overconfident, but in the entertainment industry you have to have swagger."

"Swagger," he said, nodding in agreement. "That's *exactly* what you have."

"But I'm also an actress," she reminded him. "Not all of it is real."

"Interesting," he said as he pulled off the highway onto a paved but lonely desert road that seemed to lead out to nowhere. "It'll be fun getting to know the two sides of Bethany."

Getting to know? She'd let the comment simmer for a moment. She should be dismissing the comment. When she'd agreed to come out here with him, she had no intention of letting this become anything more than just a break from her monotonous routine. The excitement of suddenly realizing this man wanted to get to know her better was unreal. Deciding it'd be safer if she didn't mention it, she changed the subject. "Should I be worried?"

"About what?" His eyes focused on her now.

"About this," she said, pointing out onto the lonesome desert road. "Here I am with a guy I hardly know who claims he's a cop, but for all I know he could be a serial killer, driving me out to the middle of nowhere."

His expression eased into an understanding smile. "No, but I'm glad you are." He motioned to the glove compartment with his chin, and for a moment Bethany was distracted by the crazy, sexy, hard chin with that perfect cleft. "Open it."

Looking away before he caught her gawking, she glanced back at the glove compartment and did as she was asked to.

"Don't touch the gun," he warned gently. Seeing the gun in the holster should've scared her, but instead it excited her. It was big, daunting, and, dare she say it? It was sexy—just like Damian. "Grab my wallet."

She hadn't even noticed the black leather wallet just inches from the gun. She took it and began to hand it to him.

"No, open it," he said very seriously. "Amos and Simon saw it, but I forgot you didn't actually get to see it. It's a good thing you'd question whether I'm actually a cop. You'd be surprised how many guys try passing themselves off as one. I'm glad you're being cautious. Examine it."

For a moment she hesitated, feeling kind of bad now. She didn't actually think he might be lying. She was just trying to change the subject. But since he was glad she had, she once again did as she was told. On one side of the wallet was a heavy, star-shaped, shiny metal badge with the word "Detective" at the very top and the words "Las Vegas" at the top of the metal ring in the center of the star. Nevada was just under that, then at the bottom of the ring was the word "Police." With a big gulp she traced with her finger the cold metal along the wording before bringing her attention to the ID card on the other side with a headshot of Damian. This was a hardcore reminder that she was playing with fire, allowing herself to be here in this car with him. But even with that reminder she couldn't help smiling at the hardened look on his face in the photo, since her impression of him was hardly that of a hard-ass man. Sure he seemed a no-nonsense kind of guy and she had no doubt a man with his build and stature could kick some ass. And while she had seen a bit of his concerned, protective side, she liked to think of him as more of a sexy sweetheart than a hard-ass. But even in the photo, he *was* all kinds of sexy.

After reading the very official-looking State of Nevada stuff and his title, she got to his name. "Detective Damian Nicholas Santiago." She turned to Damian at the sound of his muffled laugh and saw him smirking but staring straight ahead. His hands opened, then gripped the wheel again, bringing her attention to just how much muscle he had on his suddenly flexing arm muscles. "What?"

He shook his head, still not looking her way. "Nothing, I just . . ."

"I just what?"

"I just don't think I've ever heard my name sound as good as when you say it."

Swagger. She had to remember she had swagger. Simple compliments like these should not be making her feel like swooning. She needed to get hold of herself, but she was already smiling like an idiot. It couldn't be helped; everything he said to her rang positively genuine. These were no lines.

"Most people wouldn't pick up on it, it's so subtle, but I did the moment I first heard you speak—your accent. Were you born here or in Mexico?"

The smile was instantly axed. She had no idea anyone could still catch the accent. Nobody, not Simon or Amos or Trinity or anyone she'd met out here, until now, had mentioned it. "I was born here," she said, trying not to sound defensive, but she closed the wallet and put it back in the glove compartment, shutting it a little harder than she should have. "I just had a lot of family on the other side—Nogales, over the border—so I spent a lot of time over there. Not to mention my parents always spoke Spanish."

"*Okay,*" he said, glancing at her, obviously picking up on more than just her accent. Bethany wasn't sure she liked that he was a detective so much anymore. This was just another reminder that she was playing with fire. He was a little *too* perceptive. "I didn't mean anything by it, you know? I'm rather fond of it, actually."

"I just didn't think it was still noticeable."

"Like I said, Bethany, to the untrained ear—and that's most people—it's probably barely discernible, if at all. But I've been training for many years to pick up on even the tiniest things that set one person apart from another. It's important in my line of work."

She turned to him, after refusing to look at him for a few moments, and peered at him now. "How is picking up on an accent important in your line of work?"

He lifted and dropped a very muscular and distracting shoulder as he turned into an even-more-abandoned-looking dirt road. "If a suspect is described as having a certain accent, it's likely he'll try to mask it if ever questioned. It's as important as being able to tell if someone is a true blond or if he dyed his hair to disguise himself. Just like the color of your hair, an accent can distinguish you from someone else." With a smile that nearly melted her, he turned to her and their eyes locked once again. "But unless you're trying to disguise who you are, I don't see why someone picking up on your accent would bother you."

Refusing to give him a single thing more to "detect," she looked away quickly. She *needed* to change the subject again, and fast. "Okay, so now I'm starting to worry," she said, staring ahead at nothing but dirt, desert, and a rock mountain ahead. "Where exactly are you taking me out here in the middle of nowhere that's supposed to *thrill* me? I'm beginning to have flashbacks of Brad Pitt holding a gun to Kevin Spacey's head out in the desert."

Damian laughed, nodding. "Oh, yeah, I guess this is a bit reminiscent of that. I can't wait for you to see, Bethany. I really can't. It's really going to be something," he said, sounding as creepy as the serial killer in that movie.

Bethany stared at him until the corner of his lips tugged, then laughed. "Oh, my God!" She couldn't help laughing now herself. "Did you really just remember that word for word, or do I need to start freaking out because this whole thing is a setup?"

His sexy laugh did things to her, and she prayed she really hadn't been coerced here by this incredibly hot but possibly demented guy. "Relax. Obviously I'm a fan of movies that involve detective work. But I promise I'm perfectly harmless. I think you'll understand when we turn the corner of that mountain up ahead."

Bethany wasn't so sure about him being harmless. A man like Damian could easily crush her heart. The tension that had built from his previous comment was replaced now with utter curiosity. What in the world could be out here that he thought would thrill her? She wasn't much of a nature fanatic. Even a hot spring or waterfall wouldn't be all that exciting. Of course it might be a little romantic. Frustratingly, *that* excited her when she knew it shouldn't.

As they came to the mountain and began to turn the corner, she was literally at the edge of her seat. At first she didn't get it—a huge gated warehouse completely hidden out here behind the mountains.

They drove closer, and then she saw the familiar sign

and logo. That's when it began to make sense. *Santiago.* She turned to Damian, immediately seeing the resemblance, and her mouth fell open. "Are you related to . . .?"

"Yep, my dad and younger brother run this place." Damian nodded, smiling at her, obviously happy to see this was more than thrilling to her. She turned back to the warehouse, reading the words that ran across the top.

Vintage Desert Heat

Staring at it now, she had to keep her mouth from falling open. It hadn't happened often in her life, but it was happening now. She'd been rendered speechless.

CHAPTER 8

Priceless—the look on Bethany's face when she realized where they were and what this place was had exceeded any expectations Damian had of not only impressing her but exciting her as well. Once again controlling how hugely he smiled was proving to be impossible.

After they got past the security fence, with her hands still at her mouth, Bethany glanced around wide-eyed, then looked back at Damian as he drove through the warehouse lot slowly. "Mace Santiago is your dad? And Dimitri is . . ." she paused, shaking her head as if she still couldn't believe it.

"Is my kid brother," Damian finished for her.

He didn't think it possible, but those beautiful eyes of hers got even bigger. "So that makes Diego from the Desert Ratz your brother, too?"

"Yep," Damian nodded with a smile.

Just when he thought her reaction couldn't get any better, they came around the corner of the first building to the giant open warehouse doors of the second building.

"*No!* The shop!" she said lifting her hands from her mouth to the sides of her face. "Do you have any idea how many times I've watched your father and brother restore classic cars in that very shop?"

"And go at it like junkyard dogs fighting for a bone?"

Bethany laughed, but unlike her usual genuine laughter, this seemed nervous. As impressed as he was by her *swagger,* he could get used to this vulnerable side of her. "Are they really that high-strung?" she asked in a voice so low he had to laugh.

"Oh, yeah," he assured her. "It still amazes me that of all my siblings, Dimitri would be the one to hang around and wanna run this place with him. He and Mace are exactly alike. Sometimes I think his fuse is shorter than Mace's. That's why they butt heads so much. My sister works the back end, but she's smart enough to stay far away from the shop."

"I didn't even realize Dimitri had any siblings aside from Diego."

Damian smiled, pulling into the parking space, and turned off the car. "There are five of us."

"Five?" her eyes were wide and once again the bewilderment in her expression reminded him of his niece.

"Yep." He reached for the door handle and opened it. "My sister Fina is the oldest. Then it's me. Then Diego, and there's Dominic who lives in New York, and finally the youngest, Dimitri."

Once out of the car, he looked over the hood at Bethany, who was looking at him, her eyes full of questions, as he had known they would be. Everyone was when they found out he was related to *the* Santiagos of *Vintage Desert Heat,* one of the most popular reality shows on television for the past three years. Not to mention Diego's band, Desert Ratz, was now headlining some of the bigger venues in Vegas.

As he walked around the car to meet her, he decided to let her off the hook. He knew most people assumed he'd been snubbed by his family. That his not being part of the family business was not by choice. With all the growing fame and money that came with being one of the Santiagos of VDH, who in the world would *choose* not to be part of it? So asking him flat-out, he knew, was a bit awkward. "It's not that I'm not into classic cars or restoring them. Because I am. I grew up around all this, and I've done a lot of restoring cars myself. Including this one," he pointed at the Camaro they'd just gotten out of. "I just had a different calling than my father and Dimitri. This is what they love doing, and while I enjoy it, too, and still do it on my downtime, I'd always wanted to be a cop."

"And Diego a musician," she said. "I really like his music, and I have so much respect for the fact that he's stayed indie. I read somewhere that it was by choice, not from lack of any labels' wanting to sign him."

"He almost signed," Damian admitted. "But to Diego it's never been about the money. He's all about the music. They tried to take some of the band's control over the kind of music and songs they wrote, and he said forget it. He's perfectly content being a local band. But they still do *some* touring. He's just very particular about the gigs he accepts out of town."

"But even though he's got his own thing," Bethany eyed him, "*he* still makes the occasional appearance on the show."

Damian nodded with a smile. "He doesn't mind it. It's good exposure for his band. Which, let me tell you, I was one of the original members of Desert Ratz when they first put it together way back in high school."

"Really?" her eyes went all bright again, and this officially confirmed that no one could make Damian smile as easily and often as Bethany could. "You're a musician, too? What do you play?"

"Bass guitar, but I also play the acoustic, and it's what I usually grab these days when the mood strikes me. And I still get together with the guys every now and again and do some jamming."

Absentmindedly he reached his hand to her once again. Only this time, before he could pull it back, she took it. Feeling her soft, dainty hand in his felt nicer than he'd expected. Their eyes met for a moment as their fingers laced together. He had no idea what to make of her going along with his slip this time, but he wouldn't ruin the moment by addressing it. Instead he asked her what he had a feeling had made her nervous enough to *want* to hold his hand. "You ready to meet the stars of *Vintage Desert Heat*?"

She squeezed his hand. Her puckered lips and widening eyes instantly confirmed that somewhere between the security gate and where they stood now, she *had* lost a bit of her swagger and was now a little nervous. "You think they're both here?"

"I don't know about Dimitri, but I saw my old man's truck parked out front." They started toward the massive open doorway to the main shop, and he squeezed Bethany's hand, glancing back at her. "Don't worry. He's not nearly as crabby as he seems to always be on the show."

Bethany laughed nervously. "That's not what I'm worried about. I just can't believe I'm *here* in *the* VDH shop, and I'm about to meet Mace Santiago!" Swinging their intertwined hands as she turned to him, the unabashed excitement all over her face, she continued, "Up until I moved out here, because I don't have cable in my apartment and my Internet service is too weak for live-streaming video, I've followed this show from day one."

He smiled taking that last statement in. It only added to his already growing curiosity about her situation. She'd explained about *Desert Informer*, but it didn't make a whole lot of sense. Small-time presses like that were all over the place and likely short of interested interns. He was certain she could've found one nearer to home that was just as good, if not better. He'd lived here his entire life and not once had he heard anything *exemplary* about the *Desert Informer*. Now the *Vegas Sun-News* he might've understood her leaving her home behind to come all this way for and live in her crummy neighborhood. They were by far the biggest press in Vegas. But then she was also here for the opportunities in showbiz, so that kind of made sense.

The sound of a door opening loudly coming from the back of the shop as they walked in blasted him right out of his line of thinking. His old man smiled the moment he saw him.

"Hey, whatta ya know? Two of my desert rats come by this week to see me." He eyed him suspiciously. "You guys know something I don't? First Dominic come down all the way from New York unannounced just to say hi and now you?"

"Nic was in town?" Damian asked, wondering why he hadn't heard about it.

"Yep." His dad reached for a rag and wiped his hands. "Just two days ago."

"Is he still here?"

"Nope." His dad shook his head, glancing at Bethany. "Blew in and out like a desert gust. Stopped by, said hello, hung out for about half-hour, then said he had a flight to catch." He brought his attention to Bethany and smiled. "So who's this pretty little thing?"

His father's question interrupted his thoughts about how his brother Dominic hadn't bothered to so much as text him in weeks. Now he flew in and didn't even think to let him know he'd be in town? Damian hadn't seen him in months. "Oh, sorry," Damian said glancing at Bethany, who was already smiling nervously. "This is Bethany, Dad. A friend of mine and big fan of the show."

Damian didn't miss the way his dad glanced knowingly at their intertwined hands before looking up and smiling at Bethany. He was sure his dad was already curious about what kind of *friend* he'd be holding hands with and bringing to meet him out of the blue. "Bethany," Damian turned to her as he felt her squeeze his hand, "I think you know who this is."

"Yes. Wow." She nodded, letting go of Damian's hand to shake his dad's. "It's such an honor and pleasure, Mr. Santiago. I've been a fan even before you had a reality show."

"Call me Mace," he said, "everybody else does, and really?" Mace beamed as expected. "A young girl like you a fan? That's kind of surprising. Usually the only reason we get young girls watching is because of the boy."

Bethany explained briefly about her uncle and how much he'd told her about Mace and VDH way back when they were still touring all the classic-car shows. Damian stood back and watched as Bethany and his dad immediately hit it off. Her love for and knowledge of classic cars was obviously a big selling point for his dad.

Another thing his dad did that Damian had fully expected was offer Bethany a tour of the shop. Her excitement of course had Damian beaming just as much as his dad. The fact that she'd slipped her hand right back into his when she was done shaking Mace's hand was another thing that had Damian feeling strangely excited.

The tour was a longer one than usual. Damian suspected that was because aside from Lana, whom he actually lived with for nearly a year, Bethany was the only girl he'd ever brought here. No doubt Mace was already making more of this visit than his just dropping by with a *friend*.

They were nearly done when Mace got a call. He'd had a

few others during the tour that he'd ignored, but this one he said he had to take and walked off into his office. Damian decided to finish off the tour himself. "And this of course is where it all happens," he said raising his arm toward the open shop. "Not really. There's a lot viewers never get to see that happens in the other warehouses, but this is where most of the drama for the show unfolds."

She squeezed his hand, then surprised him by bringing it up to her chest. "Feel my heart," she said. "It's been pounding like this from the moment I realized what this place was."

Staring into her bright eyes, he couldn't hold back anymore. "My heart's been doing a lot of pounding today, too."

Her smile weakened a little as a reaction to his comment. He realized now it was probably too soon to be letting her in on what she did to him. But just as he had little to no control over the inexplicable smile that planted itself on his face whenever he was around her, he'd had no control over keeping this thought to himself.

She took a deep breath, and Damian braced himself for her response. "Maybe—"

The loud Dixie horn, like the one from the old *Dukes of Hazzard* show, and the even louder revving engine of his brother's car interrupted them. They both turned to see an impeccable replica of the General Lee coming toward them. It pulled right up to the warehouse door. His brother Dimitri was at the wheel, and Lazlo, their head upholstery guy, rode shotgun. Just like in the show, they both had to jump out of the windows, because the doors didn't open.

"Damian." Dimitri laughed. "What's with the surprise visits this week?"

"Yeah." Damian nodded. "Mace told me about Dominic. I had no idea he was even in town. At least he dropped by to see you guys."

Lazlo walked off, talking on his phone, waving at them to excuse himself, apparently needing some privacy.

Dimitri smirked as he walked up to them, holding a cardboard box of what looked like takeout. "Dominic's always been the beatnik of us desert rats. Never knows whether he's coming or going." He reached out his fist to Damian's, and they tapped fists, then he glanced at Bethany, who seemed once again to be speechless. "If I'd have known we were having company I would've brought more food. But as usual I bought way more than we're gonna eat, so there should be enough for everyone." He stopped long enough to take in Bethany from top to bottom. "You gonna introduce me to your little friend here or you want me to do that myself?"

Squeezing her hand gently, he lifted it toward his ever-flirting brother to make sure he understood Bethany was not someone he should be eyeing the way he was. "Bethany, I'm sure you know who this guy is. My kid brother Dimitri." Turning to his brother, who was already smirking at him deliberately as he lifted a brow, he said, "This is my friend Bethany."

"Friend, huh?" Dimitri leaned over to shake Bethany's hand. "Nice to meet you, Bethany," Dimitri practically murmured. "My brother here doesn't bring too many *friends* around."

Damian and Bethany exchanged glances, but she didn't seem fazed by Dimitri's insinuating comment. "It's very nice to meet you, Dimitri. I'm a big fan."

"Really?" He glanced at Damian as he walked over to the counter where he put down the box of food and turned back to them. "You watch the show?"

Damian knew what his brother must be thinking. Most girls who claimed to be fans of Dimitri's didn't know the first thing about cars. Diego and Dimitri both had lots of female "fans," and while Diego's fans seemed genuinely interested in his music, they all knew what these girls were really admiring. In Dimitri's case, it wasn't the cars he was famous for restoring.

"Not as often as I used to," Bethany responded, regaining a little of that swagger. "But I did when I had cable. Now I can only watch when I'm somewhere with a decent Wi-Fi connection."

Dimitri continued to eye her even as he began pulling some of the food out of the box. He turned to Damian for a second. "I got sandwiches from Earle's, but I also got some wraps if you're on one of your health kicks."

Damian shook his head quickly. As good as a wrap sounded, he was done sharing Bethany with his brother and his dad. She said she had an article she needed to work on, so the longer he hung around here the shorter his time would be once he got her alone again. "I'm good."

Holding up a sandwich at Bethany, Dimitri smiled a little too sweetly. "How 'bout you, beautiful . . . uh, I mean Bethany." He grinned sinfully. "You want something? Sandwich? Wrap? I got some pasta salad, too."

"No, thank you." Bethany smiled, and Damian let out a sigh of relief.

Beautiful had done it. He knew his smartass brother was doing it on purpose. His way of getting Damian to admit she was more than just a friend. If she was, he'd admit it, but at the moment he had no idea what was happening. All he knew was they hadn't stopped holding hands since they got there, and she was about to say "maybe" about something when his brother's crappy timing had interrupted them. Now he was dying to know what that "maybe" was about.

"We actually gotta get going," Damian said, already starting to walk.

"Dude!" Dimitri said, holding his hand out. "I haven't seen you in weeks."

"I know, I know," Damian said, feeling a little guilty. "I'll be back again soon, I promise."

Dimitri frowned as Bethany tugged at Damian's hand. He turned to her, still holding her hand, as she was walked over to the Charger Dimitri had driven in on. Leaning over to check out the grille, she turned to Dimitri. "Sixty-eight," she said, her lips curling into that lazy, smug smirk Damian remembered from the speed date. "Has the divider on the grille."

Dimitri's jaw dropped. Obviously she'd picked up on his suspicion about her being an actual fan of the show. Maybe this was her way of showing his a-little-too-full-of-himself kid brother that she wasn't watching the show just to watch him go off on one of the rampages he was so famous for, in his muscle shirts, showing off his tats and big arms, as most of his female *fans* were.

Lazlo walked over to Dimitri just then, handing him his cell phone. "He wants to talk to you now."

Taking advantage of his brother's distraction, Damian began walking back to his own car. "That was perfect," he said, squeezing her hand but not explaining why.

"I know," she said, laughing softly.

Damian turned to her, surprised that he'd hit it on the nose. She *had* done it on purpose. Able to hold back this time from saying what he really wanted to, that *she* was perfect, he addressed something else instead when they reached his car. "So maybe what?"

He was certain he was going to have to explain what he was asking, but before he could begin to she smiled. "Maybe my heart was pounding for other reasons as well." She dug her teeth into her bottom lip with a very sweet smile before adding, "Maybe my heart's been pounding from the moment I realized it was you knocking at my door today."

He stared at her now, wondering when she'd stop adding to the already incredible impression she'd made on him so far. She'd been thinking about her unfinished statement this whole time, too, otherwise there was no way she would've understood his question so quickly. But her response to it left him speechless, not to mention a bit breathless. And since he couldn't think of a more appropriate way to respond to that, he stopped fighting his need to do what he'd ached to do since he'd sat at her show, mystified by this beautiful woman who stood before him. He leaned in and kissed her.

CHAPTER 9

Even as her brain was screaming *No! What are you doing?* an even more convincing voice deep inside her was telling her to *just go with it. You deserve this.* God, but Bethany hadn't anticipated *this* being so good. His kisses were magical. His tongue moved flawlessly in rhythm with hers, almost as if they'd been kissing each other for ages. It was exhilarating. Every nerve ending in her body had come alive at the first touch of his lips to hers.

Halfway before they even got to the shop that far more convincing voice had pretty much convinced her to just go with it. Whatever *it* entailed. She couldn't be sure at the time, but one thing there was no denying was the incredible attraction they were feeling for each other. For her it was more than just that. Just like last week, that undeniable chemistry was still there and growing stronger with every moment they spent together. Even after her show, when they'd gone to eat and both of them played things down, not mentioning what had happened during her performance, the sparks were still there the whole time. She felt it as she spoke enthusiastically of Salvadoran food, saw the very thing she'd seen all through her show in his eyes still. Yet their unspoken agreement not to verbalize this secret thing they were both experiencing continued. Why say it when they could just feel it? And it felt *so* good she was willing to risk everything for it.

The only thing Bethany worried about now was that he might think his family was the reason for her sudden decision to go with it—to tell him her heart had been beating erratically from the moment she'd known it was him at her door. Because what she was feeling had nothing to do with his family. She'd thought about him *all* week—daydreamed about the possibility of something like this happening, and now it was.

His being a part of VDH was an incredibly exciting plus, but that's not why she'd given in. It hadn't been completely on impulse either. The question had actually been a constant source of distraction this entire week. If she ever got the chance to, would she? She thought she'd be scared. She thought she might fight it, but now all she could think of was, what was next?

His mouth continued to devour hers as urgently as she kissed him back. The thoughts going through her mind now were very different from what she'd thought they'd be all week if she actually gave in to this. She'd thought for sure she'd regret it the moment it happened. Instead, nothing had ever felt so right.

Just when she thought she could do this forever—when she'd even begun to scold herself for not showing him more interest last week, because she could've been doing this *all* week—he pulled away breathlessly, reminding her for the first time in the last few minutes of where they were. They were still standing in a parking lot. The very parking lot of *Vintage Desert Heat*. One of the few reality shows she'd ever followed closely.

Leaning his forehead against hers, both of them still breathing a bit heavily, he smiled. "Let's go somewhere else."

Her eyes went wide. "What? Why?" As perfect as this felt, she wasn't ready to take things further. Was he, after only one kiss, suggesting they go back to his place?

Then she heard the long, masterfully tuned whistle, so unlike Trinity's pathetic little whistle. With their foreheads still touching, they turned to the shop. Dimitri and Lazlo were standing there chuckling. "*That's* why," Damian explained.

"Bring your *friend* back soon," Dimitri's playful tone teased. "Delfi's gonna be pissed when she finds out about this."

Immediately hating Delfi without even knowing who she was, Bethany tried to stay calm but still pulled away. "Who's Delfi?"

Pulling her back, he smiled. "My incredibly meddlesome sister." Bethany stared at him, confused, remembering his sister's name was Fina. "Delfina or Delfi or Fina or whatever the hell you choose to call her is the oldest, therefore she likes playing mother hen to all her little brothers." He waved at Dimitri before opening the car door so Bethany could get in. "She'll be back all right."

"Oh, yeah, she will." Dimitri laughed again. "Delfi'll make sure of it."

Bethany watched Damian roll his eyes as she got into the car, feeling a little silly over the hasty but very real jealousy she already felt about having to share this man with someone else. Silly, maybe even alarming, but she was now enormously relieved.

"He just means," Damian said, leaning in, so close to her face she could almost taste his mouth again, and her heart started that familiar thumping, "that Delfi will be mad she missed this. That's all."

Having his mouth so close again, she couldn't resist placing her hand behind his neck and kissing him again softly. "Okay," she whispered.

"Okay." He smiled, pecking her one last time before pulling away and closing the door.

Letting her head fall back against the seat, Bethany took a very deep breath. Was she really letting this happen? Was she actually going to allow herself to be happy for once—do something *so* against her better judgment just to gratify her heart's sudden desires?

The driver's-side door opened, and Damian sat down next to her, smiling as he stared into her eyes in what was now becoming her favorite thing about him—those eyes and the unadulterated way they looked at her as if she were actually as incredible as he made her feel. He leaned in and kissed her once again, slowly, but profoundly. It was almost indescribable what his kisses did to her. They did the very thing she'd felt when she connected with him in such a way during her show. It was as if the very essence of him ran through every peak and valley of her soul, leaving his signature—his mark—etched deep down in places she never even knew existed. Hell yeah, she was allowing this to happen.

This was exactly why she was so excited about the idea of giving in to her heart instead of being afraid. After such an intense ending to her tour of his family's famous auto shop, the whole way back to the city their conversation was in no way strained or uncomfortable. Just as they'd engaged comfortably last week after putting on such a show for him, the entire time, she'd listened intently to him talk of Mace and Dimitri and how the idea of a reality show even came to be.

Not surprisingly, Mace had been against the whole thing in the beginning. The location of the shop had always been top secret, because once he'd gained enough popularity he was so overwhelmed with fans, classic-car enthusiasts, and reporters visiting the shop in the city that he wasn't getting any work done. All this was before the reality show ever aired. "The shop in the city is still open, but it's more of a showroom now, almost like a museum. They do some small jobs there still, but all the big clients and heavy hitters—celebrities that want their cars worked on by VDH—get taken out to the big shop."

It wasn't until he mentioned it on their way out of the place that she noticed how far out the land around the shop was fenced off. Her mind had been so busied all the way there with so many other things that she'd paid little attention to anything, other than to notice how isolated the roads they took were, and that they were driving deeper and deeper to the middle of nowhere. Of course now it all made sense.

She turned to him curiously. "You and all your siblings have D names. I've known other families that do that, but usually they follow the dads or in some cases both parents had the same first initial, but with you guys it should've been M, no?"

Damian shook his head. "Domacio is actually Mace's full name. They've just always shortened his name, and he always made all of us call him that, not Dad." He laughed. "Though little by little he's becoming the Old Man to all of us. I still think he prefers that to Dad."

Bethany was still thinking about that. *Domacio*. It made sense now. She'd always wondered if Mace was maybe a stage name.

"So." Damian rubbed his neck, turning to her. "I turned down my brother's food because you said you have that article you need to get written, and I was hoping for a little more alone time with you before I took you back." He said it so matter-of-factly and without reservations that it almost made her laugh, but it also made her insides tingle. He wanted *alone time* with her. "But I *am* hungry, are you?"

As if on cue, her stomach grumbled. Luckily, he didn't hear it. Her free hand, the one he wasn't holding because he'd held her other one the whole way back again, traveled down to her belly. "Yes, I haven't had anything since breakfast."

For the first time since his brother called her beautiful, she saw his expression go a bit hard. "That's why you get lightheaded, Bethany, and close to passing out. You shouldn't go so long without eating anything." As if he'd just scolded her and immediately felt bad about it, his frown softened and he smiled. "I haven't eaten anything since breakfast either. In fact all I had was some coffee and half a bagel. I should take my own advice. I'm starving."

"I am, too," she admitted. The tingly feeling in her belly was more than just hunger, and she knew it. Just the fact that he was actually worried about her added to her bubbling insides.

Coming to a red light, Damian brought her hand to his mouth, kissing her knuckles softly. Bethany didn't think her insides could go any mushier than they already were, but they did, and she could only imagine the lovesick expression on her face as she watched him kiss each of her knuckles one by one. "I know just the place to go, then," he said, staring at her after kissing the last of her knuckles, then smiling at her sweetly.

It wasn't until after she inhaled and exhaled that she realized how dreamily and cartoonishly she'd done so. It was so bad it made her blush. His sweet smile broke into a huge one. "Wow. That was awesome."

She laughed, now feeling as silly as her aunt when she whimsically watched the handsome hero on one of her *telenovelas*. Only this was real life, and the hero had watched Bethany do it! Feeling a bit mortified, she laughed, covering her face with her free hand. "That was ridiculous. Don't laugh at me."

"Who's laughing? I *loved* that. It was so genuine and spontaneous. I'll have to remember to kiss your knuckles more often."

This was another thing she'd noted since last week. How easily she could be this comfortable with him, even though she still didn't know him well at all. As dumb as she felt right then, she knew she didn't have to worry about his thinking her an idiot. "It's not *what* you did or said. It's *how* you did it. *You* were very genuine, too. Everything about you so far seems to be." She smirked, lifting an eyebrow. "Even that first time I met you. You had no qualms about admitting to a perfect stranger, who was there to make a connection, mind you, that you weren't into that kind of *shit*."

With a nod, she motioned to let him know the light had turned green. He laughed as he brought his attention back to the road.

"I mean really, Damian," she teased. "How rude was that?"

"Okay, maybe that was bad form." He continued to laugh, and she could hardly look away from him anymore. Everything about him fascinated her now. From his sexy smile to his strong chin, even the self-assured way he carried himself, something she had mistaken for cockiness but now knew was just well-deserved confidence. "You can't hold it against me, though. I was just being honest and straightforward. Something you obviously appreciate as much as I do, right?"

Feeling a twinge of guilt, because as comfortable as she felt with him already, there were a few things in her life she didn't feel ready to—couldn't—discuss with him just yet, she nodded in agreement and left it at that. The rest of the way to the all-you-can-eat seafood place he was taking her to, he told her about the food there. As she had been last week when she'd gone on and on about the *pupusería*, he seemed very jazzed about this place. The more he talked, the more her stomach growled.

Finally they were seated, and Bethany felt a little disappointed that it wasn't a buffet as she had expected. As far as she was concerned, all-you-can-eat meant buffet. Now they were going to have to order and wait. As much as Damian had talked up the place, she really was starving now.

A petite young waitress with her dark hair in a loose French braid approached their table with two glasses of ice water. "Detective Santiago," she said with a big grin as she placed the glasses down on the table. "Nice to see you dressed down for once and not all stuffy."

"Yep, the stuffy clothes take a hike on my day off," he said, returning the big grin. "And I told you, Olivia, it's Damian."

Bethany watched, a little perturbed at how easily Damian went on with the waitress. She liked thinking the rapport she and Damian had easily built was something special he'd only ever felt with her. Because she certainly had never felt as instantly comfortable with anyone as she had with him. Fortunately, their prattle didn't go on for too long before *Olivia* asked them if they were ready to order.

Since this was her first time here, Bethany sat back and let Damian order for them both. "Okay, for our first round we'll take the lobster tails, crab legs and steamed crabs, jumbo shrimp, clams, fried fish." He eyed the menu. "A tray of oysters sounds good." He paused for a moment, and Bethany didn't think he'd order any more, but he continued. "We'll have some hush puppies, and just to pretend we're being healthy, the sautéed vegetable medley."

Olivia smiled a few times, giggling as she jotted it all down, then took their menus. When she walked away, Bethany decided to let it go. She'd never been that kind of petty girl. Instead she leaned forward, smiling. "*Gawd*, that sounds so good!"

Damian took her hand and caressed her fingers. "It is, and they're very quick, so we won't have to wait long." That made her smile even bigger. "So," he said, staring into her eyes playfully, "you know about my siblings, my job, and all about my family's business. All I know about you is you're from Nogales, Arizona. You're a hopeful journalist out here on an internship, you're a helluva singer, and you haven't been out here too long living alone in downtown Vegas."

"You know a lot," she said, her eyes teasing right back, but already felt her insides tensing.

"Not enough," he countered. Playing with her fingers, his eyes searched hers. "First of all, were you seriously looking to make a connection at the speed date?"

Glad he'd chosen an easy topic, she smiled as his other hand reached for her other one now, too. It was crazy and a bit unnerving how just hours ago when he'd shown up at her place he was just Damian, the guy she'd shared such in-credible moments with last week. The cop she should not be letting herself get caught up with. Yet here they were holding hands across a table, and for anyone who walked by or took one glance at them, including *Olivia*, they were unequivo-cally a couple. At the moment, she felt like a girl staring into her boyfriend's teasing eyes. "No, I wasn't," she admitted. "And if you hadn't been so incredibly smug about it, I proba-bly would've told you I agreed. It *was* kind of dumb."

"So why were you there?" he asked, looking confused, then added, "and I wasn't trying to be smug. I just thought it was so stupid I wanted to make it perfectly clear I wasn't there by choice."

Bethany laughed. "I was there doing research. I had an article I was writing about dating in this day and age. I had to research five different ways single people go about try-ing to find a mate." She shrugged. "As silly as speed dating sounded, I thought it'd be something interesting to add to my article, besides the normal online dating and going to clubs."

For a moment she thought about sharing the very thought that had just popped in her head. She might use him as one of her examples in the follow-up article she now had to write. The most common way of meeting a mate, according to surveys, was being introduced by mutual friends. Jerry wasn't exactly a mutual friend, but ultimately he *was* the reason Damian had showed up at her show and why they were here now. But then she decided against mentioning it. She still had no idea where this was going, and as much as it felt like something was definitely happening between them, this still could be just an unexpected date with no follow-up. Though Damian *had* sounded pretty confident when he assured his brother that she'd be back.

Damian lifted a brow. "Have you met up with any of the guys you met that night?"

"No." She shook her head. "Like with Jerry, I responded to a few of their emails just to be nice, but never followed up to meet with them or even gave out my number."

"Speaking of," he pulled his phone out of his pocket. "I could've kicked myself in the ass last week for not getting your number." She watched him tap the screen on his phone and look up at her. "What is it?"

Without thought she gave it to him as her insides did a little dance. Everything was just *happening*. Yet neither of them had addressed what exactly *was* happening. She had to wonder now how this day would end and how much more she would allow to just happen. The other day she had been adamant that nothing could—should—ever happen. Not with Damian or anyone. Yet here she was anxious for him to put his phone down and reach his hand out to her again.

Just as he put his phone back in his pocket without so much as another word about it, the waitress arrived with some of their order. Bethany stared down at the plates, understanding why Damian had ordered so much. The place might be all-you-can-eat, but the portions were fairly small. The jumbo shrimp they ordered came in a serving of just four. And the lobster tails were on the small side. Still, everything looked and smelled heavenly.

Olivia giggled a little too much when Damian teased her about nearly fumbling the hush puppy basket. Bethany managed not to roll her eyes, but she didn't so much as crack a smile. Not even when Olivia grinned at her widely and told her to enjoy her meal.

They dug in, and after a few silent minutes of chowing down, Bethany laughed. "I *guess* we were hungry!"

Damian looked up just as he was about to smash into his crab with a wooden mallet. Olivia approached them once again, and Damian turned his attention to her. She took some of their empty plates away and dropped off a few more loaded ones. With one of the sexier smiles Bethany had seen on him, Damian winked at Olivia. "Keep 'em coming, sweetheart, we're gonna be here awhile."

Olivia grinned widely. The exchange wiped the smile off Bethany's face. She stuck a hush puppy into her mouth to keep her lips from puckering and chewed slowly. She wasn't sure what annoyed her more, the fact that Damian was so smooth or that their clueless little waitress would smile at him so eagerly right in front of her when she'd just seen them holding hands earlier. This was so unlike her. Just as she reminded herself she had swagger and that she'd never been catty or jealous in her life, Damian directed the sexy smile at her. He picked up an oyster and started squeezing lemon juice on it. "You believe what they say about oysters?"

Immediately, her annoying thoughts were dropped, and she sat up, smiling coyly. It was almost embarrassing how one smile from him could switch her mood so easily. "You mean about their being a natural aphrodisiac?"

"Yep," he said, nodding, his eyelids lowering a bit as he brought the oyster shell to his lips and sucked its contents dry. Watching him do that, especially the way he eyed her as he did it, made her breath catch, and she prayed he hadn't noticed.

"Funny," she cleared her throat, watching him squeeze lemon juice on the next one. "I mean it's funny you should ask. For a long time I thought I'd proven the myth to be true."

With the oyster shell at his lips again, he stopped and lifted a brow. "Is that so?" She nodded as he sucked the contents of the oyster dry, a little more slowly this time, then licked his lips as he continued to watch her. "How's that?"

She took a deep breath, trying to gather her thoughts again. "In high school me and my science partner read about it when we were researching and decided to put it to the test." Suddenly feeling silly, she bit her lip, trying not to laugh. "We kissed and—"

"Wait," he said, suddenly looking a little too excited. "Was your partner a girl or a guy?"

"Oh, you wish it was a girl." She laughed, throwing her napkin his way. "Of course it was a guy!"

Nearly frowning now, he sat back. "Go on."

"Neither of us was attracted to the other, so," she covered her mouth with a napkin because she could feel herself going into a giggle fest, "our very scientific hypothesis was that since neither saw the other in that way and our friendship was completely platonic, the kiss should not be at all arousing. And after our initial kiss, we agreed it wasn't." She shook her head. "So we decided to go to a restaurant and order a tray of oysters. Mind you," she brought one hand to her chest and covered her mouth with the other one, shaking her head again, "the idea of oysters back then was so gross to both of us. But it was all in the name of science, right? So we sacrificed our taste buds and forced down three oysters each. After brushing our teeth, we kissed again, and this time we ended up making out pretty heavy."

He rolled his eyes, the usual genuine smile a bit forced now. "How'd you figure out you hadn't proved anything, except that this guy managed to find a way to get you to make out with him."

"Exactly!" She wiped her mouth, smiling even more widely. "But it went both ways. It wasn't until later, when we'd been a couple for months, that we both admitted to secretly harboring crushes for each other from the very beginning of the semester when we were first partnered up. But for a long time I really did tell myself that the oysters were the reason I let him feel me up the very first time we made out."

"All right," he said, suddenly sitting up and reaching for a shrimp. "I don't think I wanna hear about this anymore." Bethany had heard his playful tone enough to know this wasn't it. "Tell me about your siblings. You have any?"

Out of nowhere a strange unease settled in her stomach. She knew it was for more than one reason, but for now she'd ignore the second reason and focus on the first—she had to share about her family. "I have a seventeen-year-old sister and a twelve-year-old brother."

"Wow. That's kind of a big age gap." He stopped before reaching for a crab leg. "How old *are* you?"

"I'm twenty-two," she said, pulling out a sliver of lobster

meat from the shell and dipping it into the butter. "After my parents married, my dad moved my mom down to the small town he was from in Oaxaca, but just a few months after I was born she left him. She said he was abusive, so she moved back to Nogales and divorced him. When I was two she remarried, but after initially not being able to conceive again, she thought maybe she wouldn't be able to, and when I turned five my sister was born. She and my stepdad agreed they were good with just the two of us. Then there was another unexpected surprise, and when my sister turned five they were blessed with my brother."

"Well, that's cool. It worked out." He chuckled. "Were they nervous when your brother turned four?"

"No," she pressed her lips together. "My mother passed away when he was only three."

Damian immediately reached his hand out and touched hers. "I'm sorry."

"It's okay," she lied, remembering that's when her life began to change and how it had ultimately led her to where she was now. But staring across at Damian's perfectly chiseled chin, and the eyes that made her melt *every* time now, she considered that maybe things really did happen for a reason. Smiling weakly, she decided this was something she could share with him. "It was very sudden and a huge blow, but I'm over it now. It's been ten years." He squeezed her hand and she continued. "She fell off a horse in Mexico. At first everyone naturally assumed that the blow to the head is what ultimately killed her, but later it was determined she had an aneurysm that burst in her brain. *That's* why she'd fallen off the horse. The doctors said she'd likely been born with an undetected aneurysm and over the years it got bigger and bigger until it just burst."

He stared at her seriously, shaking his head, taking in what she'd just told him. "I lost my mom very suddenly, too, so I can relate to it being a huge blow."

"Really? How?"

She noticed a strange shift in his expression. "The small charter plane she'd taken to San Diego went down in the middle of the desert. I was just a kid, too." Before she could offer any words of sympathy he shrugged. "But we're on you right now, so tell me more about yourself."

Hating to be such a downer and that the mood had taken such a turn when they'd been having such a good time, she decided she'd tell him about her stepdad another time. In an attempt to bring the mood back to where it had been before the talk of their mothers' deaths, she smiled, lifting her chin. "Another thing you don't know about me is I teach Zumba classes."

He sat back again in his seat, taking with him the warmth of his hand against hers, but Bethany could see the relief in his eyes that the mood had changed. She definitely wasn't telling him about her stepdad today.

"So let me get this straight," he said, lowering his head a bit. "You're an intern writing for the paper, you teach Zumba, *and* you have your own one-woman show?"

"*And* I do local theater," she beamed proudly. "I'm playing Iona in the theater version of *Pretty in Pink* at the Red Sea Theater." Remembering the speed date, she almost laughed. "That's why I was dressed so funky that day of the speed date. I'd just come from a performance, and I hadn't had a chance to change."

Both his brows lifted now. "No wonder! I meant to ask you about that. That was some bright-ass eye shadow." She nodded in agreement until his smile fell suddenly and his face went a bit hard again. "Of course you were passing out from exhaustion. When the hell do you sleep?"

"At night," she said reaching for one last hush puppy. She was done. Popping the hush puppy into her mouth she smirked. "And in the library sometimes."

That didn't seem to amuse him as she thought it might. "No wonder Amos was worried," he said, very seriously now. "As much as I loved your show, I'm glad you won't be doing it for a while."

Frowning, she sat back in her own seat now. "It was only one night of the week."

"Sweetheart, you were passing out from exhaustion. Your body can only take so much before it starts shutting down." Looking behind her, Damian's serious expression suddenly morphed into a sweet smile, immediately irritating Bethany, because she knew just who he was smiling at. His eyes met with Bethany's again. "Are we done here so I can ask for the check?"

She nodded, and he lifted his hand. Within seconds Olivia was there again, with a smile Bethany only remembered seeing this big at the speed date, from the hostess. Even then she had thought a smile that big was ridiculous. Now she found it annoying as hell.

Just when Bethany was getting over her annoyance about the amount of attention the waitress gave Damian each time she came to their table, she came back with the check and some hard candy. "I remembered which flavor you liked from the last time you were here." She actually twirled her stupid finger in her hair as he took it and thanked her.

Once Damian had paid, refusing to take any money from Bethany, they got up and left. Just like everything about being with Damian, his holding out his hand for her and her taking it, as soon as she stood up, seemed like something they'd been doing for years.

Still a little annoyed about his interaction with the waitress, Bethany snapped out of it when Damian pulled her to him as they reached the car and kissed her deeply. The watermelon flavor of the after-dinner candy that *whore* had given him immediately seeped into every crevice of Bethany's mouth. Once again he left her breathless as he pulled away with a smile and opened her door.

Their conversation on the way to the car had been mostly small talk about the food and how full they both were now. But when they got into the car, Bethany had to ask. She wasn't being petty, just curious. The fact that Damian had called the stupid waitress "sweetheart" again when he thanked her for her service had nothing to do with it. Well maybe a little. "Do you talk to all girls the way you did to that waitress?"

He turned to her as the corner of his lip tugged, and he adjusted his seat belt. "How's that?"

She shrugged, making light of it. "You called her sweetheart—twice."

Turning on the ignition, he seemed to ponder. "I've never really noticed. It's just something I do out of habit, I guess." Grinning as he pulled out of the parking spot, he turned to her again. "Did that bother you?"

Never really noticed, her *ass*. He smiled especially widely every time he said it. Not liking that he was enjoying this, and remembering how abruptly he changed the subject when she mentioned her ex-boyfriend way back in high school feeling her up, she considered doing something a little immature. This day was slowly coming to an end, and something had definitely changed between them from the time he picked her up until now. It wasn't like her, and considering the circumstances she knew she shouldn't, but she had a point to make before she even considered moving forward with this. Whatever *this* was. Because she'd met the type of guys she was beginning to suspect Damian might be, and she was not about to go against that nagging voice in her head and take a risk, giving in to a romance with a *cop*—something she had believed was out of the question—with someone who wasn't completely worth it. She'd get it straight now, before she made any rash decisions.

"No, I was just curious. But I suppose I know what you mean by doing things out of habit, like when I'm singing I get so lost in the songs sometimes I don't even notice how focused I can get on one particular person in the audience."

Smug smile obliterated—one point, Bethany.

He stopped just before pulling out of the parking lot and turned to her. "You do that with *everyone?*"

Making sure she made her point, she looked him straight in the eye. "No, Damian. I don't. You're the *only* one that's ever happened with. It's nice feeling special, isn't it?"

CHAPTER 10

Perfect. She had walked right into his plan. The whole time they'd been eating, he kept trying to think of a way to ask about her relationship with Simon but thought it too soon to be going there. Even when he picked up the instant blaze in her eyes at the mention of Delfi, he still didn't think it enough. Simon was obviously a friend of hers. One she most likely would argue was perfectly harmless. But there was no denying the guy wanted more.

Last week Simon had grated on his nerves, and Bethany was nothing more than the beautiful girl in the show who had blown him away. Not only were things different now, but what she did to him was unreal. Damian knew himself. Even with his ex-girlfriend he'd had very little patience for friends like Simon who were just a little too friendly for his liking. He could already sense everything with Bethany would be epically heightened. So when Damian thought he'd picked up on what might be construed as restrained irritation on Bethany's part at the extra attention Olivia was giving him, he took it up a notch in hopes that she might mention it.

Olivia's remembering what his favorite flavor candy was from the last time he'd been there couldn't have been better timed. That sexy little eyebrow of Bethany's shooting straight up, even though she'd looked away, had pretty much confirmed that he'd secured what he'd been going for. The only bad thing was, he was pretty sure that if things worked out as he was hoping they would, he and Bethany wouldn't be coming back here very often, if *ever*. Painless sacrifice. The food was good, but there were plenty of other all-you-can-eat places that were just as good. This was Vegas, after all.

Checking his rearview mirror to make sure there was no one waiting behind him, he delayed pulling out into the moving traffic a little longer. "Special doesn't even begin to describe what I felt during your show. And if you promise to never give anyone else that kind of performance, I promise I'll never call anyone but you sweetheart."

That didn't seem to satisfy her, because she still seemed unsure. "It wasn't just you calling her sweetheart, Damian." She sighed looking even more uneasy now. "I'm not sure what to make of today, but I think I should make it clear that kissing like we've been doing is not a casual thing for me. So seeing the way you behaved with that waitress just made me wonder if this is something you do often—so casually."

"No, it isn't," he said quickly, then put the car in reverse before someone came along and honked at him, blocking the driveway. *Shit!* Maybe he'd gone overboard trying to get her in jealous mode so she'd better understand why that picture of her and Simon in her front room—one of the few pictures she'd chosen to display—was beginning to really bug the hell out of him. "Listen," he said as he pulled into a parking space again. Turning the ignition off, he took her hand in his. "*This* is something I've never experienced, and I've had girlfriends, okay? I lived with one for almost a year. I know what it feels like to start falling for someone you think is different. I'm a grown-ass man, Bethany—a homicide detective. My heart is supposed to be hardened and unaffected, *impenetrable* by anything, because of the things I see day in and day out. I *should not* be feeling what I feel when I'm around you, especially this soon. But I am. And the craziest thing about it is I think you're feeling it, too." She nodded, the uneasiness in her eyes replaced by sudden excitement, and he had to smile and kiss her hand before he went on. "This is no way a casual thing for me," he assured her, then took it a step further. "I haven't been in a relationship in over a year, and since then I've had no desire to be in one. I was beginning to think I never would. And if I ever did, I thought for sure I'd play it ridiculously slow, maybe even blow it by taking things too slow. But all day today there've been these sirens going off in my head telling me I *need* to lock this down today—make it official. I haven't even taken you home, and already I know the only thing I'll be thinking about once I leave your place tonight is the next time I get to see you. It's *insane*."

She stared at him in silence, teeth buried in her bottom lip. Damian knew this *was not* the conventional way you went about declaring your feelings for someone. You were supposed to play it cool. Not lay it all out like that. Lock it down today? After just one unofficial date? That was crazy talk! But just as with everything else he'd felt up until now with Bethany, as utterly insane as this was, even this felt right.

Just like that first night at the speed date when she'd dismissed him so easily and her lip slowly lifted into a lazy smirk, it was happening again, and his heart nearly stopped.

"It is insane," she agreed, and he could barely breathe now. "But you're right, I am feeling the very same insanity."

His heart couldn't take it anymore. Either she was telling him they could somehow figure out how to deal with this beautiful *insanity* together, or she was saying this was too soon and too crazy to work. "So is that a yes?"

Her eyes widened a bit, but she still smiled. "What exactly does locking it down mean to you?"

That was close, but it still wasn't a yes, so he'd make this as simple as possible. "Means I'm the only guy you spend your free time with, and you're the only girl I spend mine with." He lifted an eyebrow, hoping she'd read between the lines here, in case she was still planning on doing things with Simon she might be taking more photos of. "No one else."

"You know my free time is very limited," she reminded him. "It wouldn't be fair to you that you might have more free time than me but will be restricted to spending it with only me, and I may often not be available."

"That's fine," he replied immediately. "Work keeps me pretty busy, too, and when I'm not working I have plenty of other stuff that keeps me busy that don't involve other women. I didn't say we can't spend our time with others, just no other men for you and no other women for me." He paused to make sure that last part had sunk in with no objections, but her expression was neutral, so he continued. "I still get together and jam with the Desert Ratz every now and again, and I've been meaning to get back in the shop and spend more time with Mace and Dimitri. I have a few projects I want to start on this year. So you don't have to worry about fair. Locking it down *does* mean a few other things to me, but I know you need to get back to your paper right now. This one thing is the one I'd like for us to agree on first. We can get to the rest later."

Her sudden smile relieved him. "I can agree to that, especially because I have few friends I spend time with at all and none of them are guys."

Smiling, too, Damian leaned in and kissed her softly. He could hardly believe this day had turned out as it had. When he'd left his place today, his expectations had been nothing more than to *try* to get her number. He certainly hadn't expected that he'd be in a relationship by the end of the day. He had made Jerry out to be a nut for getting so ahead of himself, and now here he was, ecstatic about the turn of events. He'd never live this one down, but at this point he didn't care.

Sucking her bottom lip before pulling away to look at her, he caressed her hair. There was just one more thing he needed to know. He knew he wasn't being paranoid either. He was trained to pick up on the smallest of clues, but he didn't even have to be for this one. Simon had made it blatantly obvious. The guy wasn't even trying to be subtle about the way he looked at Bethany. "What about Simon?"

Her brows pinched. "What about him?"

"What is he to you, if not a friend? I saw a photo of the two of you in your front room."

That seemed to catch her by surprise. He waited, making note of the fact that she broke eye contact almost immediately. Taking a deep breath, he reminded himself that just this last week he had made the argument at work that eye contact in itself was only one, if not the least reliable, of the signs of deception. While true, it was also a known fact that breaking eye contact was a good sign the subject was one that made the person you were interrogating uncomfortable.

"That photo is not so much about the people in it, but what it represents."

"And what's that?"

Again she looked away. This time not just with her eyes; she completely turned away and looked out the window. "That was taken just after I finished my very first gig here. Simon just happened to be in it, too. It was a skit show I got a very small part in, and it's where I met him." She turned back to him, lifting and dropping her shoulder. "It's just sort of a reminder of how far I've come since I first got here. And, yeah, I guess Simon is my friend, but I see him as more of a coworker who I'm pretty close to. Outside of the gigs we've done together and the times he's given me rides to and from them, we've never done anything social."

This was good to know, but it still didn't mean he'd drop his guard when it came to Simon. He could admit it now, because at the time he'd shrugged it off, not wanting to sound like Jerry, but Bethany had pretty much cast a spell on Damian almost from the moment their eyes first met. There was something a bit mysterious about those deep, soulful eyes. Then in his follow-up meeting with her, he was able to bask in that smile along with that so-easy-to-talk-to personality that had completely nailed him. He was certain he wasn't the exception either. Here he'd only been around her three times, and already he was putting it all out there. This guy had been around her for months now, and Damian had seen the way he looked at Bethany. There was no way Simon didn't see in Bethany what Damian did. And that "pretty close to" shit was a bit unsettling. Bethany might see it that way, but Simon, like most guys—and Jerry was a perfect example—might be reading way more into their "closeness."

He leaned in once again and kissed her softly, wishing he could hang out with her longer. But from what little he knew about Bethany, he was sure if he got her home late and she still had that article to write, she'd be up until she was done with it. No matter how late that was. "Let's get you home," he whispered as he pulled away.

The rest of the way to her place was a lot more pleasant than the sudden panic and angst he'd begun to feel in that parking lot. She told him a little more about her gig playing Iona in the *Pretty in Pink* show. "Maybe I'll take my sister to see it," Damian said, squeezing her hand. "She loves that movie."

"For a smaller theater group they actually have some really good talent. The guy that plays Ducky is just awesome," she said, running her hand up and down his thigh, distracting him no end. "It sucks, because this guy, who I think is an incredibly gifted actor—this isn't the first time I've seen him in action—will probably never make it in Hollywood. Sadly, not always, but too often, it's about who you know, and just like Justin there are a ton of incredible actors out there who won't make it past community theater before giving up."

Suddenly she had his full attention. "Who's Justin?"

"The guy that plays Ducky," she said, tilting her head. "He's had so many auditions and gotten callbacks, but nothing ever comes of them. And who can afford to continually fly out or even be driving out to California? He has a wife and kid he needs to support, so he can't just quit his job and move out there, you know?"

He started to relax again after hearing that last sentence, and then he remembered he'd been forced to watch that movie so damn much with his sister, it suddenly hit him. Ducky kisses Iona, and not just any kiss. He really plants one on her. He turned to Bethany for a moment as the unsettling realization set in.

"What?"

"Are the stage versions just like the movies, or are they cut down?"

She thought about that for a moment, then nodded. "There are a few scenes left out. The less entertaining ones like the ones of Andie's conversations with her dad. Some of those were just worked into the dialogue between her and Iona instead."

He squeezed the wheel, suddenly grasping the reality of what he was in for. Just like watching her onstage with Simon, the fact that more than likely this actor did get to kiss her, this was a part of Bethany's life. He was just going to have to somehow get used to it.

He glanced back at her, and she smiled, bringing his attention to her soft, pink lips. He swallowed hard and smiled back. There was no way he could be pissed at her for doing her job. He'd just have to deal with it, but one thing was for damn sure, forget taking Delfi to see Bethany's show. He'd avoid witnessing someone else's lips on *his* girl at all costs, even if it was just an act. He squeezed her hand, wondering why he hadn't thought of this shit sooner. Because saying he'd deal with it was one thing; actually doing so if he ever had to would be quite another.

This relationship thing with Bethany was going to be a bit trickier than he had anticipated. As her *boyfriend*, he'd be expected to show his support. Now he'd have to come up with excuses and reasons for why he wouldn't be able to make her shows. Maybe he should've thought this through a little more before *locking it down*.

———

Walking out of the Pump N Snack where Bethany wired more money back home, she let out an enormous breath as she pulled her phone out. She made her way to the bus stop, where she sat down and texted her sister.

> I sent the latest but there will be more as soon as I get paid again end of next week. A couple of things have happened that may change our plans a little. All good. I promise.

For a moment she almost chickened out before sending it but then remembered Wednesday and sent it. Since her agreement with Damian that past Sunday, she'd had a lot to think about. Once this nightmare that had started over a year ago was over, she could move on with that part of her life and do as she pleased. She was nearly there already, just a bit more to go, and she didn't see why she needed to deny herself what she was slowly beginning to believe was one of the best things that had happened to her *ever*.

The past Monday she'd begun to have second thoughts about having agreed to Damian's "locking it down" idea. As she had told him Sunday, she didn't think it fair to him. It made her feel a little guilty, though she knew there was more to that guilt than she cared to admit. The guilt was so bad that she'd even begun to put her speech together about why she'd been too hasty to agree and why she'd changed her mind. Then she got the texts from him right around the very time she'd been lost in thought about him. He said he missed her. Among a few other deep-sigh-evoking sweet things. Then Wednesday he'd shown up at her Zumba class. She didn't see him until it was over, but what she felt at the sight of him after not having seen him for just two days was utterly irrational. The only thing that kept her from running and jumping into his arms was the fact that she was drenched in sweat. Still, she hadn't been able to keep from kissing him back eagerly when he'd kissed her hello.

They'd gone back to her place, where she quickly showered, and then they spent the rest of one of her unusual afternoons off together. The night before, she'd explained to Damian how before Amos had given her a shot at her own show, she was waiting tables at his theater show. When he pulled the plug on her show so that she'd get some rest, he also pulled the plug on her waiting tables. So Wednesday, Friday, Saturday, and Sunday nights were wide open for her now and would be for a few weeks, or however long Amos would insist she take off.

It was perfect timing for her and Damian that she had some time off just when they were getting to know each other. But from a financial perspective, the timing couldn't have been worse.

Her third encounter with Damian, on Wednesday, had been no different from the second. They hadn't done anything special except grab something to eat, then walked through one of the more glamorous casinos Bethany had yet to visit. The whole time they'd laughed and talked like a longtime couple. It continued to amaze her how comfortable they both were with each other. The only way in which Wednesday was different from her first two times being with him was that now being in his arms and kissing were a common and sometimes frantic thing for them. She appreciated that Damian hadn't so much as mentioned doing anything beyond their kissing. The way she felt around him, she knew it wouldn't take much to give in to him completely, and she knew that in her circumstances, she *needed* to take this more slowly than normal.

She'd be seeing him again tonight after having spent an entire evening with the guy just the day before yesterday. She really shouldn't be this giddy and anxious about seeing him again so soon. But she was. *God*, was she ever. Trinity was the only person she'd told about her new *boyfriend*. It felt strange even calling him that, but as unusually quickly as things had gone down, it was already what he was calling himself. It's exactly how he'd introduced himself to Trinity when they ran into her on their way up the stairs Wednesday night. Trinity was also just getting home from one of her "dates." Of course, Trinity, being her bubbly self, hadn't given Bethany a chance to do the introductions, so when she took the initiative, offering her hand to him and introducing herself as Bethany's neighbor, good friend, and confidante, Damian had taken the liberty of adding his own title—Bethany's boyfriend.

Immediately, Trinity's face brightened, and no sooner had Bethany closed the door behind her, still breathless from Damian's amazing good-night kiss, when there was a soft knock and a pathetic little whistle at her door. Bethany had no choice but to spill it, and Trinity had been overjoyed, calling Damian an absolute daisy. Apparently in Trinityspeak that was a good thing.

It felt good to tell someone, and it sort of helped to practice for the conversation she'd be having with her sister this weekend. Though that conversation would be much more toned downed than the one she'd had with Trinity. There'd be a lot less gushing and giggling, because she was certain her sister wouldn't be quite as amused as Trinity was.

For now she needed to get through the interview she had with a local, small-potatoes comedian and try to concentrate on getting her questions together for him, even though it was almost impossible to do so. Her *boyfriend* had told her he had another surprise for her tonight. The very thought had her insides bubbling already. He'd mentioned being a good cook, and she wondered if he was planning on maybe making her dinner, which was something he sort of hinted he planned on doing eventually. Would that be tonight? This meant they'd be alone at his place. They'd hardly been able to keep their lips off each other as it was. It was craziness, but a kind of craziness she already felt herself becoming addicted to, because even as she stepped on the bus now she had the insane urge to get off and go shopping instead—shopping for the perfect set of lacy panties and bra.

The woman she sat next to on the bus must've thought Bethany was nuts. When she first sat down, she was sure she was frowning at having the thought of wearing sexy underwear for Damian. Her thoughts had immediately crossed over to what Trinity had said about Bethany's dilemma. She told Trinity she wanted to take things slow with Damian sexually. She said as fast as things had happened, she was still old-fashioned and thought hopping into bed with him this soon was just not smart. It was partly true, but she had bigger reasons that she left out. Then she told Tiffany how hard it was to stay in control around him and how certain she was that if Damian tried to seduce her, she'd be powerless to stop him, because his kisses alone drove her insane.

With the straightest face, Trinity sat up, squeezed Bethany's knee, and told her to make sure she wore the rattiest bra and panties anytime she went out with him until she was ready to take that next step. This would ensure that no matter how hot things got, Bethany would be too embarrassed to let him see her panties with the "bullet holes," as Trinity referred to the holes in her ratty panties.

Bethany went from frowning as she sat down on the bus bench to giggling into her hand, then frowning again as she scolded herself for even thinking about doing just the opposite of Trinity's brilliant advice. The lady next to her had actually scooted a little away.

Leaning her head against the window as the bus made its way slowly through the crowded morning commute, she listened to both arguments going on in her head. *You need to wait,* was the one niggling voice. *You owe this to yourself,* was the other. The latter had won out all week, and as usual, she decided a compromise was best. It'd been so easy to say no to Simon when he'd asked her out a few times, and to stick to her guns, but then he'd never made her feel anything close to what she felt with Damian. No way was she depriving herself of that incredible feeling, but she would hold off as long as possible on taking things to that next level—as long as she could manage to anyhow.

———

CHAPTER 11

The young girl who stepped out of Jerry's car was not what Damian had expected to see. Jerry said he'd be stopping by the shop Friday afternoon because his daughter Ashlynn had been asking him to take her there all week. Jerry had mentioned his baby girl was all grown up, but Damian could now see that had been an understatement of epic proportions.

"Hello, Damian," she practically purred as she reached him.

The dark hair he remembered was mostly blonde now. And though her curly locks still had flashes of dark in them, it was very dramatic, and Damian felt dirty thinking it, but very sexy—too sexy for a girl her age.

She wore very short denim shorts and a short tank that only came halfway down her midriff, exposing her belly button along with the pink piercing in it. Damian wasn't able to make out exactly what it was, because he felt weird even looking there too long. He knew it was hotter than hell and this was common apparel in the summer out here in the desert, but the girl was sixteen. Sure she could pass for eighteen, maybe even older, as tall and filled out as she was now, but the fact remained she was only *sixteen*. What the hell was Jerry thinking letting her out of the house wearing this? Not to mention she wore more makeup than some adult women. No wonder her mother couldn't handle her anymore. The way she was fluttering those long lashes at Damian didn't seem right either.

"Wow, Ashlynn," he said, trying not to make too much of the way she sized him up. "You really have grown up."

To his horror she lifted her arms in the air and spun around for him. Damian's eyes were immediately on Jerry, refusing to let them wander onto any part of his friend's daughter's teenage but very adult-looking body. Jerry shrugged, "She takes after her mom."

Her *mom*. The woman who got pregnant in the tenth grade after doing it in a parked car with Jerry, and he wasn't even her boyfriend. Damian had heard the story several times, since he and Jerry didn't actually become friends until after high school. But what Jerry did tell him was that they had to have a DNA test done on the baby, because even Shannon didn't know who the dad was. She'd jumped in cars with so many different guys she had no idea which of them could be the dad, except that Jerry had been the only one with whom she'd been lame enough to rely on the old pulling-out method. It was a wonder Jerry hadn't caught any diseases. Now he was letting his daughter dress and apparently behave like her mother?

Another thing Jerry had shared with him was that Shannon was very popular in school, just not so much with the girls. He had to wonder now exactly what Ashlynn was being bullied for in her school back home, and if she wasn't to be blamed for it. Jerry had also shared with him that Shannon hadn't discriminated against the guys with girlfriends. From the looks of Ashlynn that was probably the case as well. That explained why she might not be well liked by some pissed-off girlfriends and why she was getting bullied.

Damian hadn't seen her since she was about eight and

was a chubby little thing. She'd lost all the baby fat and then some. It all made sense now, and he prayed for his friend's sake she wouldn't make him a granddad prematurely, as Jerry had done to his own parents way back when.

Ashlynn hugged him, and he hugged her back, careful not to touch any exposed skin. It was kind of awkward, with him placing his hands carefully on the very small part of her top that covered her skin. "Umm, you smell good," she murmured as she pulled away and once again looked him over in a very inappropriate way.

"Jerry!" Dimitri called out as he walked back out from the office, getting everyone's attention at once. His eyes were immediately on Ashlynn, and they looked too pleased. *Well, shit.*

The only reason Damian had even stopped by was to see Jerry and Ashlynn for a few minutes and kill some time to give Bethany time to get ready. Now he had to find a way to get Dimitri alone and warn him to not even think about trying anything with Ashlynn. He could see that familiar spark he saw so often in his brother's eyes already.

"Well, well, well." Dimitri smiled, taking in Ashlynn from top to bottom, and if Damian had been close enough he'd have reached over and swatted his brother on the back of his head. "Is this little Ashlynn?"

She smiled back at him, the lashes already fluttering away, and she brought her hand to her mouth. "Oh, my God. I can't believe I'm meeting you in person. My friends are gonna freak when I tell them," she said, biting her lower lip, then added, "if they even believe me."

Dimitri laughed a little too much at that. It wasn't even funny. "We'll take pictures so you can have proof. The old man will be back in a few, too, and that guy's a ham when it comes to taking pictures." He turned to Jerry, reaching out his hand. "How's it going, man? It's been a while. And damn," he turned back to look at Ashlynn. "Damian told me you had a little girl, but I didn't know you got busy that early. What are you, my age, sweetheart?"

"No, she's not," Damian immediately said, shooting his brother a look. "She's only sixteen."

Dimitri's mouth fell open for a second, but he recovered quickly. "Actually I'll be seventeen in a few months." Ashlynn smiled, lowering her eyes in Dimitri's direction.

His brother's eyes were back on Ashlynn for an instant, then he glanced back at Damian, who shook his head just enough for Dimitri to catch it. He was going to have to get his brother alone one way or another before he left today and explain. Ashlynn might be his friend's daughter and just sixteen, but even Damian had to admit that a girl who looked like her could get even a young, semifamous stud like his kid brother wrapped around her finger easily. The only thing Damian had said to Dimitri before Jerry arrived was that Jerry was bringing in his daughter for a tour of the place. Dimitri might be years ahead of his time when it came to restoring cars—and not only helping his dad run this massive business but dealing with being one of the stars of his own show—but he'd only turned twenty just recently and was still very much inexperienced for his age when it came to matters of the heart or being ready for anything serious. Damian *could not* let his little brother get any ideas about Ashlynn.

If she was anything like what Damian was suspecting based on her appearance and behavior alone, she could talk his brother into something that might get messy if Jerry ever found out—not happening.

"Hard to believe, isn't it?" Jerry said, smiling proudly in Ashlynn's direction. "The years just flew. Before you know it, she'll be a young adult."

"Yep," Ashlynn agreed, smiling coyly in Dimitri's direction. "Very soon."

"And she's a big fan of the show. We were hoping she could get a quick tour," Jerry explained. "Hopefully that's not too much trouble. We could always come back another day if today isn't good for you. She's staying with me for good now."

"Are you really?" Dimitri's brows shot up. "So you're a Vegas girl now?"

"Sure am," Ashlynn said, smiling.

"Nice." Dimitri grinned at Ashlynn then turned to Jerry. "And not a problem at all, man. We're done filming for the day, and the old man went into town for some errands, but he'll be back in a while. Now's actually the perfect time for a tour. C'mon," he motioned to Ashlynn with a tilt of his head and a smile. "I can take you now."

Before Damian could do anything about it, Dimitri whisked away Ashlynn, who happily walked alongside him. Damian hadn't even thought to explain Jerry's situation to his brother. He hadn't thought there'd be any reason to get into the details until he saw her get out of the car today.

"She was really excited about meeting Dimitri and your dad," Jerry said, apparently very pleased to appease his *baby* girl. "Thanks for this."

"Not a problem," Damian said, turning to Dimitri and Ashlynn.

His brother was already laughing again as he had earlier, and Damian seriously doubted Ashlynn was *that* funny. He wasn't about to let Jerry in on what he was worried about. It felt too weird. Maybe it was because she was Jerry's little girl, but Jerry seemed to be oblivious to the fact that he had a hot daughter who looked way beyond her age and was probably experienced beyond her age as well.

Jerry told him all about how things were coming along

with Ashlynn getting situated and enrolled in school for the fall. Damian got the feeling that once again Jerry needed to vent. Because as much as he seemed optimistic about the idea of playing the father role full-time for once in his life, he still seemed a little worried. As he went on at length about the conversations he'd had with Ashlynn, about her behaving and being respectful and all the "rules," and how she really was a good kid, Damian grew a little more worried about his friend. The girl had murmured just loudly enough for only his ears that he smelled good. Not to mention he hadn't imagined her checking him out, because she'd done it twice. Now she was off with Dimitri fluttering her lashes at him. He didn't think Jerry had a clue what he was in for.

Dimitri and Ashlynn had been gone long enough. After hearing his brother and Ashlynn engaged in more laughter a few times too many, Damian decided he'd had enough. What worried him now more than ever was that the laughter was genuine, the kind he and Bethany got caught up in so often, and realizing now how easily and quickly he'd been awed into needing to make her his, the sirens went off. "I gotta get going, Jer. I have to pick up Bethany in a few. But I need to talk to Dimitri before I go."

He'd already filled Jerry in somewhat about Bethany, leaving out the part about his locking it down on what was only their very first unplanned date. He just told him he'd gotten together with her again during the week and that he was doing so again tonight. As smoothly and as naturally as things were moving along with him and Bethany, it still sounded too crazy to say it out loud to anyone else. He'd give it some time before telling anyone just how serious he was about her.

Jerry walked over to get a better look at one of his dad and Dimitri's latest projects, and Damian walked away in the direction where Dimitri was leaning into a convertible Ashlynn was now sitting in.

"Mitri," Damian said as he got closer. "I gotta get out of here, but can I see you for a minute in the office? I need to tell you something before I go."

His brother turned to him, then turned back to say something to Ashlynn that made her laugh again before walking toward Damian. Trying not to roll his eyes, he walked into the office and waited for Dimitri to walk in after him. He'd just leaned against Mace's big desk when Dimitri walked in. "What's up?"

"Close the door, will you?" With a pinch of his brows Dimitri did, but waited. "Listen," Damian began, not even sure where to start. "Don't get any ideas about his girl, okay? I know you're used to flirting and all that shit, and she's a big fan so I'm certain she'd be willing to go along with anything you suggest, but you don't know about this girl, and most important, she's Jerry's kid, so that makes her completely off-limits."

As expected, his brother's response was an unconcerned smirk. "Damian, I know she's seventeen, dude. I'm not trying to get arrested or anything."

"She's *sixteen*," Damian reminded him. "And besides," he glanced out the window to make sure Jerry wasn't anywhere around. "She could be trouble, too. That's why she moved in with Jerry. Her mom couldn't handle her anymore, and just look at the way she's dressed."

That wiped the smile off Dimitri's face faster than Damian had ever seen it wiped. "For your information, Gramps, that's the style. And she seems nice enough to me." He reached for the doorknob as if he was done listening to Damian. "What's wrong with you, man? She's your friend's daughter, and you're gonna bad-mouth her because of the way she's dressed?"

Damian shook his head, motioning for Dimitri to keep

the door shut. "Trust me on this one. He's had a lot of problems with her, and you don't know the history. I'd fill you in on it, but I don't have time right now. Just promise me no matter how much she flutters those pretty little lashes at you, you won't fall for any of her crap."

It almost amused Damian that his little brother was looking at him with that disgusted expression. Of course he had no way of knowing why Damian was so adamant about this. Maybe if he were on the other end, he might be thinking the very thing he knew his brother was thinking, that he was being a total asshole about this, but there was no way he was letting his brother get caught up with her. Normally Dimitri would've laughed, agreed, and not thought twice about it. His arguing and quick defense of Ashlynn's honor only made Damian more nervous, so he offered him a little more. "She whispered in my ear that I smelled good."

Dimitri scoffed, "Listen to you. You're so full of yourself!"

"And she checked me out twice. Very obviously, dude." When his brother still shook his head again in apparent disbelief, Damian added, "You *know* I wouldn't make this up, brother. But there's still more. Call me tomorrow, and I'll tell you if you want." Damian tapped his own chest. "Trust me."

The severity of Dimitri's disgusted expression had lessened with his comment about knowing Damian wouldn't be making something like that up. Dimitri knew Damian better than that. And even though he wasn't smiling or even smirking anymore, he still nodded. "All right" was his only comment about Ashlynn now. He turned the knob, looking back to him. Damian was glad to see the smirk back on his face. "You all dolled up to see Bethany, your *friend*, again?" Damian nodded but made no comment. "You know Delfi's been asking all week about her. You're lucky she's not here today, or she'd be grilling you."

"She already has," Damian informed him, following him out of the office. "You kidding me? She called me first thing the next day. I guess one of you busybodies made sure she found out ASAP."

Dimitri laughed heartily. Normally, Damian would've frowned at that, but he'd been right about Dimitri's possibly already falling for Ashlynn's obviously very skillful charm, so he was glad to hear him snap out of it so fast. "That was Mace. But, yeah, he beat me to it." He laughed again. "Hey, anything to get her off us for a while. She's always on Mace about his high blood pressure and all that bad shit he eats and on me about partying too much. Your turn for once."

Damian shook his head as he walked away. Although he felt grateful to have been able to snuff a spark before it turned into a flame, he still felt for Jerry. The guy was in for it with this girl. He'd have to consider warning him, but for now he'd hold off. This could be very touchy. She hadn't actually done anything but flirt—with both him and Dimitri—and while this wasn't the first time he and one of his brothers had the same girl flirt with them, this was his friend's teen daughter! He'd definitely have to think of a delicate way to let Jerry know he was going to have to keep a real close eye on his sweet little Ashlynn.

After saying his good-byes to Jerry, he was off, thoughts of Ashlynn and her fluttering lashes long behind him. The only thing he could think of now was that he'd be with Bethany again soon.

———

Pulling up at the sidewalk just outside Bethany's apartment, Damian had to smile at the puttering of his heart. The anticipation of being with her had mounted the entire way there.

They'd talked about her and her friend Trinity taking the precaution of having a signal when they came to each other's door. While he'd commended her for being so careful, he also suggested a simple text might be safer. It was just a matter of time before someone picked up on their signal and tried to trick them. She'd laughed, saying no one could imitate Trinity's whistle, then she cracked herself up for the next five minutes trying to do just that.

He chuckled as he walked up the stairs, texting her that he was on his way up. She hadn't responded by the time he got to her door, and he hesitated to knock, afraid to startle her. Aside from her landlord, coming up to collect the rent, and Trinity, she said no one else ever came over. Even the times Simon had given her a ride to some of their gigs, she said she always told him to just honk or text her that he was there, and she'd run down. It'd been a relief to know she'd never invited the guy up. But now he faced a conundrum. Deciding to spare her any alarm, he texted her again.

I'm right outside your door. Should I knock?

He gave it a couple of minutes and still nothing. Walking over to the rail that looked onto the sidewalk downstairs, he leaned on it. Maybe she was running late and wasn't out of the shower. They still had plenty of time to make the show he was taking her to, and he couldn't forget her admitting she'd knocked over the fan that first day he came to see her because his knock had spooked her. If she were still in the shower, it'd be just a matter of minutes before she'd see his text and come to the door.

Damian couldn't even imagine living in a place like this. He could hear snippets of conversations coming from each of the apartment's pathetically thin walls. That's when he picked up on Bethany's voice. She was talking to someone, but no one was responding, which meant one thing: She was on the phone. It made sense now why she hadn't responded to his texts. He'd wait until she was done and read the texts instead of knocking.

Trying not to eavesdrop, he focused on the homeless guy across the street. He was making a big show of rearranging his junk-filled shopping cart.

"I can't. No, not tonight. Tomorrow for sure."

As hard as he tried not to listen to Bethany's conversation, it was hard not to. She'd apparently moved closer to the window that faced the very street he was looking out onto, and her conversation was much clearer. She must've walked away from the window suddenly, because the conversation was no longer audible except for the last phrase he caught just before she moved out of his hearing range.

"I just can't tonight, okay?"

A few minutes passed as he stood there staring at the homeless guy but lost in a completely other thought. Why wouldn't she just tell whomever she'd been speaking to *why* she couldn't make it tonight?

A door opening behind him made him turn, and Bethany stood at her open door, looking amazing. He'd given her a clue earlier and told her they were going to a show but not whom they were seeing. The only clue he'd given her was to dress as if she were going to a bar for drinks, because it was a laid-back kind of show. Nothing too fancy. He'd even texted after he'd given her the clue to tell her she should wear comfortable shoes, remembering how much standing they'd be doing. He was glad that as her boyfriend now his eyes had the go-ahead to roam, because roam they did. The tight jeans she wore with her very high wedge shoes accentuated those curves he had once thought might be Photoshopped. Like

Ashlynn, she was also showing a little skin, but instead of her entire midriff being exposed, the loose-fitting, shimmery top she wore tied around her neck and was V-shaped, hanging low in the front so her sides were the only part of her midsection showing.

"You haven't been out here long, have you?" she asked, looking very sorry. "I just now noticed your texts."

Gulping but not even trying to hide the smile already on his face, he shook his head, walking toward her. "Just a few minutes."

"I was just—" she began, but Damian's lips were on hers before she could finish, and he wrapped his arms around her waist, only then noticing there was a lot more skin showing. Her entire back. The top she wore tied around her neck and her waist; everything in between was exposed. Running both his hands up and down her bare back had him moaning in her mouth, as he kissed her even more frenziedly.

"*Damn*," he whispered against her lips, before plunging his tongue back deep into her mouth.

Up until now he'd only touched her over her clothes. Even then he'd been careful not to be pushy in any way. The last thing he wanted was for her to think his urgency in locking things down was to get her into bed, because it had nothing to do with that. Sure, the anticipation of getting her under him was something that was mounting rapidly, but he had every intention of giving her all the time she wanted—needed. Because *he* needed her to know that while he sped the process of making her his exclusively, they'd take their time with everything else. Still, he was only a man, and touching her warm, bare skin nearly pushed him over the edge. Hearing her soft moans wasn't helping either.

"Maybe y'all should take that inside," he heard Trinity drawl as Damian forced himself to pull away from Bethany's body and glanced back at her friend, who was on her way toward the stairs.

"Have fun," Bethany said, covering her smile with her hand.

"Thanks, I will," her tall, all-done-up, blonde friend glanced back at them, with an extra-large smile. "I'd tell y'all to do the same, but I see you've already started."

Bethany giggled, pulling him into her apartment. "I'm almost done; I just need to throw a couple of things in a clutch, and I'll be ready to go."

Damian pulled her to him again before she could walk away and smiled, looking deep in her eyes. "You probably already know this, but I have to say it anyway. You look amazing."

She tilted her head with a smirk. "Thank you." She walked two fingers up the buttons of his shirt. "You don't look too shabby yourself. I love your shirt."

Damian glanced down at the shirt. It wasn't until she ran her hand over his chest slowly, then squeezed his upper arm with a smoldering gaze, that he remembered the saleswoman, who'd flirted with him when she sold it to him, said it accentuated his muscles very nicely. He was glad he had worn it now, because she looked sizzling hot, and he'd be standing next to her all night.

Kissing him softly before she walked away, she checked him out from top to bottom one last time. "I like the whole outfit," she said as she walked toward her bedroom door.

Damian glanced down again at his jeans and shoes. "Men don't have outfits," he said with a smirk. "We just throw on whatever isn't dirty."

He heard her laugh. "Well, you did good throwing it together, because you look fabulous."

"Men don't look *fabulous* either," he mumbled, this time

under his breath so she didn't hear him. "Hot maybe, but fabulous, no."

He glanced around, frowning when he saw her cell phone on the kitchen counter. She'd begun to tell him about why she'd missed his texts, but he hadn't let her finish. Now how was he supposed to bring up the conversation he'd overheard?

She walked back out of her bedroom fidgeting with her earring. "I'm ready."

"You sure you're going to be okay in those shoes?" he asked, looking down at her high wedge shoes. They were sexy as hell, but they didn't look very comfortable.

"Oh, yeah." She nodded. "Wedges I'm good in. I was going to wear my spikier heels until you texted me. *Those* I wouldn't have made it through an entire night of standing."

He let her know they wouldn't be standing *all* night, then reminded her not to forget her phone. "That's right," she said, doubling back to get it. "And I'll turn my ringer on while I'm at it. It's why I missed your texts."

Damian stared at her for a moment. "You weren't on your phone?"

"Huh?" she turned to him, her eyes widening for just a second, then she glanced away.

"I thought I heard you talking while I was waiting out there. I figured you were on the phone, and that's why you hadn't responded."

"Oh, yeah." She nodded quickly as if she'd just remembered. "You're right, my sister called earlier." That was it. She offered nothing more about it, and held out her hand as she reached him by the door. "I can hardly wait to see what this second surprise is going to be."

Feeling just a tiny bit uneasy about their little exchange, Damian decided to let it go. Again he had to be mindful that this relationship had come together. Maybe Bethany didn't want to tell her sister about her relationship with Damian yet. Hell, he'd even put off telling his family and Jerry that little but very significant detail of his life—that he was now in a committed relationship. The girl he'd "hit it off" with just two weeks ago when he hadn't even gone to her show with the intention of doing so, was now his *girlfriend*—one he was already falling for fast and hard. Yeah, that might be a little hard to explain.

He smiled, kissing her forehead and feeling that now familiar swarming excitement. This was just the beginning of the first weekend he planned on spending most of with his new *girlfriend*. "Not sure if this surprise is better than the first." He smiled, looking into those big, beautiful eyes that looked back at him with the very same intense excitement. "But it's up there."

CHAPTER 12

The surprise stayed under wraps until they pulled up to the Zodiac Casino Resort, because it was right there on the big flashing billboards:

Desert Ratz live this weekend only!

Bethany had to admit she had had a feeling she'd be treated to one of Diego's gigs sooner rather than later. The sparkle in Damian's eyes when he spoke of his brother's band was so proud that she knew that, like the surprise visit to the shop, it was something he'd enjoy *thrilling* her with, especially after she had told him she enjoyed their music.

Smiling, she brought her hands to her mouth and turned to Damian, who was smiling back and looking very pleased with himself. "It's standing room only, so no seats; that's why I told you to wear comfortable shoes. But we can go backstage at any time, so if you get tired during the show, we'll go to the back and relax. They have a bar back there and everything."

Now Bethany's mouth fell open again. "We get to go backstage during the show?"

"Not just during," he said smugly, then squeezed her

thigh. "We're going straight there before the show starts, so you can meet my brother and the rest of the band."

"Get out!" She straightened up in her seat, eyes wide, making him laugh.

Okay, maybe he *had* totally surprised her again. She shouldn't be this surprised that they could get in backstage to meet the band—this was his brother, after all—but that thought for some reason hadn't dawned on her.

After leaving Damian's car with the valet, they made their way through the fancy casino. Just like when she first laid eyes on Mace in person and then later when Dimitri had driven up and jumped out of the car, she could feel her starstruck heart thudding as they neared the back entrance to the theater where the Desert Ratz would be playing

Breathing in deeply, she readied herself for this, because one thing had already been established. The gene tree this family had pulled theirs from was planted firmly in the Land of Good Looks on the planet Just Not Fair. Even for a man his age, Mace had it going on. So if Diego was anywhere as good-looking as he was on television, on top of his incredible musical talent, she'd have to make sure not to go too gaga for her boyfriend's brother. Bracing herself for this, she could only imagine now what their sister and Dominic looked like.

The big guy with the yellow security shirt standing outside the back entrance smiled as they approached. He opened the door with one hand and held out his other to Damian. "It's been a while, my man," he said as Damian shook his hand. "Good to see you again."

"Good to see you, too, Doc." He motioned back at Bethany. "This is my girl, Bethany." Bethany smiled, still trying to let the idea of being Damian's *girl* sink in. "Bethany, this is Doc. He looks after my brother."

"I sure do," Doc agreed, shaking Bethany's hand very gently. "Nice to meet you, Bethany."

With the introductions done, Damian asked Doc a few more questions about the security for tonight's show. Once he was satisfied, they moved on and went in. Bethany could already hear guitars being tuned, some drum playing, and lots of voices and laughter.

They turned the corner, and there they were. The members of Desert Ratz in the flesh. Just as when she'd met Dimitri and Mace, seeing these guys, but especially Diego, in the flesh felt surreal. It's not like any of them were huge stars. Unless you were a fan of the reality show or a classic-car enthusiast, you'd probably never heard of Dimitri or Mace. And with Diego's band, unless you were a local or, again, followed the show, they were not very famous at all. As far as she knew, they had more of a cult following, though the line outside to see their show was an indication of just how big the cult following was getting. Still, at the moment, she felt like she was about to meet The Beatles.

Diego shot off the stool he was sitting on as soon as he saw them, put the guitar down, and walked over to greet them. "Damian! What's up, man?" Diego bear-hugged him for a second, then let go, standing back to look at him. "When you called to say you were coming, I almost didn't want to get my hopes up. You and Dominic have been such apparitions these past few months. Mostly Dominic, but at least he has an excuse; he lives out of state."

Damian nodded in agreement. "Yeah, I know. I've just been real busy with work, but I'm working on that now," he said, holding Bethany's hand a little more tightly.

Bethany was doing her damnedest not to stare too hard at Diego. Just like Dimitri, he was even better-looking in person. Even so, and she knew she was probably biased, she still thought Damian was by far the best-looking of the three. As much as her heart thudded away because she was standing just feet away from Diego Santiago, one glance at Damian and that same heart doubled over in delight. This beautifully sexy man was telling everyone *she* was *his* girl. And not just tonight or until he was bored with the idea. She was finding out now that in a matter of a week, he'd brought her to meet his family. A family that, apparently, he'd become fairly distant with lately. That had to mean something.

The thought scared her a little bit—made her feel guilty—but she pushed her apprehension aside. She'd decided earlier when she spoke with her sister that she was doing this because she deserved someone like Damian in her life, deserved to finally be happy after everything she'd been through. She didn't care what anyone said or thought about it anymore either. She'd made up her mind. If he wanted to be a part of her life like this, wanted her to be his girl, why should she fight it? Because the more she was around him, the surer she was that she wanted this, too.

Damian introduced her to Diego, only this time she wasn't just his girl, she was his *girlfriend*. Bethany wondered how long it would take for her to get used to hearing that, because each time she did she felt like doing a little dance.

Diego's bedroom eyes were immediately on her, and he smiled. It was funny how much the two brothers resembled each other, yet they were different in many ways. While the main things, their eyes, lips, the cleft, even the sexy way they grinned at her playfully with those suggestive eyes that made her insides crazy, were so much alike, Diego's hair was longer, mischievously messy, and his demeanor was more laid-back than Damian's. Something that went with his whole rock-star lifestyle, of course.

Damian's lifestyle was obviously much different. At first

she had thought him big, sexy, and full of himself. Now that she knew better, he looked every bit the clean-cut, no-nonsense, hard-nosed yet deliciously sexy detective.

"Nice to meet you, Bethany." Diego reached out his hand. "How come I'm just now meeting you?"

He was asking Bethany but glanced back at Damian for the answer. "It hasn't been very long" was Damian's only response, but she caught the humor in his eyes when he glanced at her.

"So you're the singer?" Diego's question surprised her. She'd assumed since Damian had been such an *apparition* to his family lately that he hadn't told them much about her. "Damian says your voice is amazing."

Feeling her cheeks warm, she turned to Damian. "I do sing." She smiled, trying not to appear as uncomfortable as she felt, because Damian was looking at her weirdly. "I don't know about amazing but—"

"We have guest singers all the time on our shows. It's something the fans get a kick out of, actually." Diego smiled at her, exchanging glances with Damian. "So would you mind coming up and doing a couple of songs with us? You know any of our songs? If not, we could play around with a cover of some classic, no biggie."

Of all the pounding her heart had done this past week alone, not to mention when she'd been singing to Damian last week, this was probably the hardest it'd pounded yet. "No," she said.

"Great." Diego started back toward the stool he had been sitting on, and Damian smiled.

Snapping out of her sudden excitement about the unexpected invitation, she remembered. "I meant no," she said shaking her head at Damian. "I couldn't."

"Sure you can," Damian said, tugging her hand. "And

you'll be great. Just remember what you promised," he said, his smile teasing.

She tugged back until he stopped and looked at her. Diego and the guys were already setting up for what she imagined was an impromptu practice with her before going onstage. She must've looked as panicked as she felt, because Damian suddenly looked concerned. "What's wrong?"

"Nothing," she tried toning down her alarm. "I've just never gone onstage this unprepared," she lied. "I'm not supposed to be . . ." She looked at his unwavering eyes and glanced away for a moment, cursing herself for letting that last part slip.

"You're not supposed to be what?"

Remembering her conversation with her sister earlier, she racked her brain to come up with something. She glanced back up at his concerned eyes. "If Simon finds out . . ." Seeing his brows shoot straight up and his expression go hard instantly, she shook her ahead. "I mean Amos."

"If they find out what?" he asked, his brows coming together now.

She gulped as she touched his arm, feeling how tense he'd gone. If it weren't for the topic they were on, she might be tempted to press up against him and kiss him, because even this intense side of him was sexy as hell. "I'm not supposed to be working on the days he made me take off. There are a lot of people out there, and your brother's shows get uploaded to YouTube a lot. Simon's a big fan of Desert Ratz, too. I mean from the looks of the line out there, I think everyone in Vegas is. I just don't wanna risk it getting back to them that I took time off my show only to get up onstage somewhere else."

Bethany stared at him as indifferently as possible, reminding herself to blink. She knew from the beginning, when she realized why Damian looked at her so intensely, as he was doing now, that he was studying her expressions—using his expertise to his advantage, which she didn't think fair, but at the moment she had to admit she wasn't being completely honest. It *was* partly true Amos would be mad if he found out she did a show somewhere else when she was supposed to be taking time off, even if her time onstage was just for pleasure. But he and Simon were not who she was really concerned about her performance getting back to. It's why she had never told her sister about taking over the lead in *Imagine* at the Crown that one weekend. She knew taking the lead in such a big show with that much exposure was a risk, but at least with that show she'd worn heavy makeup, and in the elaborate costumes she'd be hard to recognize. Tonight, while this was not one of the biggest venues in Vegas, it was pretty significant, and she'd be completely exposed. As much as she'd have loved to sing with them, she couldn't chance it.

Damian stared at her for another moment, his jaw clenching once before he turned to Diego and the other guys. "Diego, she's sort of playing hooky from her other show that she normally does Friday nights. If word gets out she got onstage somewhere else, her boss might have a problem with that. But," he turned back to Bethany with a strained smile, "she can do something with you back here if you want, so you can hear what I was talking about. "

"Sure." Diego nodded, patting his hand on the empty stool next to him. "Get over here, girl. If you sing half as good as you look, I may just have to beg you to come onstage with us another time when you're not being a *bad* girl playing hooky."

With her insides all in knots, she smiled at Damian nervously, letting go of his hand and walking over to the stool.

Diego did the introductions of the rest of the guys in the band. This was another thing she'd always liked about the Desert Ratz. They were less than a half-hour from performing in front of what looked like a packed house, and you'd think they were performing at a backyard party. Every single one of them looked completely laid-back, in jeans and T-shirts, except for Diego, who had opted for a white, snug-fitting tank that showed off his muscled, tatted-up arms and shoulders.

She informed them that while she did know most of their songs, she wasn't sure if she knew all the lyrics by heart. Diego shrugged, smiling at her with that heavy-lidded gaze, just another attribute his entire family seemed to have plucked off that tree on the planet Just Not Fair. She smiled, recognizing the song he'd begun to strum on his acoustic guitar as one of her favorites. "You know this one?"

"'Rivers of Babylon'?" she asked just to be sure.

He smiled in confirmation. "Does this key work for you?" She nodded, glancing at Damian, whose smile was full of encouragement. "Ready? On three." Diego mouthed the numbers one through three, giving her just enough time to clear her voice, and they began singing almost immediately in perfect harmony.

Just as when Damian's brows had shot up earlier at her mention of Simon, Diego's brows did the same after hearing her sing just the first verse. Only unlike Damian's darkened scowl, Diego was smiling as he sang with her. He turned to Damian with an approving nod and an even bigger smile. Damian returned the nod as if to say, I told you so. The whole band was smiling now, snapping their fingers along, adding a little more rhythm to the song. She hadn't sat in an open jam session in a long time. It felt so good she was almost tempted to just go onstage with them, but she knew the risk was too great.

After a few more songs, their short session was over. Diego reached over and placed his hand on her shoulder, the excitement all over his face. "You have *got* to go on with us one of these days. They'll go crazy for you. And now I'm gonna have to come see your show."

Feeling all warm and fuzzy, she took the compliments, not just from him but also from the rest of the band, with as much swagger as she could. But the whole time her insides were a skittish mess.

"You sticking around after the show?" Diego asked Damian. "We're gonna hang out here for a while after. They're bringing in a ton of food for us, so we're just gonna kick back, grub, have a few drinks, and chill." He turned to Bethany, "Maybe we can even do some more jamming." He smiled very sweetly, but like Damian's smile, there was also something very sexy about it. "I'd love to do a few more songs with you. You guys should stay. It'll be fun."

She was glad she knew the gaze and that smile were just something that came naturally to the men in this family, or she might have thought he was flirting with her.

Damian glanced at her, tilting his head, leaving it up to her. Since she couldn't think of anything more exciting than hanging out backstage with Damian and the Desert Ratz, she grinned, nodding, and the brothers exchanged pleased glances.

"Cool," Diego said, then punched Damian playfully. "Me and you can do some catching up."

Diego insisted they help themselves to something from the full bar they had backstage. At this point Bethany was ready for something to calm her insides; she felt completely ready to burst. She actually could think of something far more exciting than even this that she and Damian could do after the show, but she was glad they'd been given an alternative. She might have been good and not gone out and bought the sexy panties she'd been tempted to, but the panties she had worn were hardly ratty. Just thinking of Damian's kisses and his hard body pressed against hers while she got ready today, she'd made sure she chose one of her sexiest pairs. She wasn't sure she'd have the willpower to stop things from going further, and if she had done what Trinity had proposed, she was sure she'd be furious with herself if things got that hot tonight, and she *had* to stop.

Damian ordered a bourbon on the rocks from the bartender at the exclusive backstage bar, and Bethany asked for an Amaretto sour. She stood at the bar by choice, not wanting to get up awkwardly onto the stool, while he sat down on the edge of the stool next to her. They stirred their drinks gently, as they watched the band prepare to go onstage. She didn't know him well enough yet, but she picked up a negative vibe from Damian as he sat there quietly stirring his drink and staring at the band. She hoped he hadn't mistaken her excitement about hanging after with the band as excitement about hanging out with Diego. *That* did excite her, but she didn't want him thinking it was for the wrong reasons. His brother might be crazy sexy just like Damian, but there was something about Damian she'd never felt with anyone else. Not even with his semifamous brothers, who'd both been cordial to her. While meeting them excited her in a different way, for completely different reasons, it didn't even compare to what Damian did to her.

"Something wrong?"

His eyes were immediately off the band and on hers. "No, why?"

"I dunno. You seem quiet suddenly."

He squeezed her hand, pulling her to him between his legs. She'd felt his hard body against hers on more than one occasion now, but this was the first time she had felt his hard thighs wrap around her like this, and it made her heart pound like *only* he could make it. "Nothing wrong at all," he said, staring down at her lips, then kissing her long, deeply, and more passionately than she'd expected him to in front of all these people.

With a low groan, he pulled away, still rubbing his big, strong hands on her bare back as he had when he first arrived at her place. "God, what you do to me. It's insane."

She moved in closer to him, the naughty girl in her wanting to know *exactly* what she did to him. She didn't have to move much closer to feel it—his very male version of what she was feeling—and she was sure those panties she'd so carefully picked out would be soaked before the end of the night if they kept this up.

Bringing her hands to his face, she cradled his strong jaw in her hands. "I know exactly what you mean." Staring into his eyes, she wanted to make one thing very clear in case there was any doubt. "No one, and I mean *no one*, has ever made me feel this craziness I feel when I'm with you."

One brow lifted slightly, but it was enough. That one subtle gesture was pretty telling of what he'd clearly been doubting. *Gads*, had she been that pathetically starstruck by his brother? So bad it rattled Damian? She had to wonder if this was something that maybe had happened to him before. Having two brothers who were in the limelight like his had to be tough. She smiled, feeling a little guilty that perhaps she had gone overboard. "You believe me, right?"

Looking at her very seriously, he pulled her even closer, holding her firmly by the waist. She now stood between, and in the safety of, his hard thighs, her upper thigh very aware of what she was pressed against. Breathing in deeply, she concentrated on his eyes and tried not to think about how warm that made her entire body. The serious expression softened, and given where she was standing now and what she was feeling against her thigh, she thought she might see some of that smoldering desire she'd seen in his eyes before. Instead there was a sweetness—a tenderness she'd also seen in his eyes before, but at a moment like this it surprised her. "I do believe you." He smiled, his big, warm hands caressing her bare back gently. "This week should've been a bad one for me, given how bad the case I'm working on has been. Instead it's been one of the best of my life." He kissed the corner of her lips softly. "And that's because of you. So, yeah, if you're feeling anything like what I'm feeling then I absolutely believe you."

He kissed her again, softly this time, but still very deeply. His tongue did what it had so frantically done just earlier, only it moved much slower, very thoroughly tasting every inch of her mouth. Almost as if he were trying to demonstrate something to her with his kisses. *Show* her what he'd just told her. That he knew just what she meant because he was feeling it, too. A sigh escaped her as they continued to kiss. She couldn't help but smile as she wrapped her arms around his neck, pulling her body even closer against his.

How did this happen? How did this wonderful man pop into her life out of nowhere and sweep her off her feet? Because that's how she'd felt from the moment he first kissed her back at the shop. She'd felt it even before that, felt it the night of her show, but that kiss had confirmed it. Swept—he'd completely and utterly swept her off her feet, and she was loving every moment of it. She felt ready that very second to give herself to him—show him with every part of her body just what he made her feel. But she'd settle for just being in his arms like this, having his mouth devour hers blissfully . . . for now.

"Are you two gonna watch any of the show or just stay back here and do that all night?"

Breathlessly and with her heart still beating erratically, Bethany pulled her lips away from Damian, though he held her body firmly where it was—against his. She turned, feeling a bit embarrassed, to face a smirking Diego and Quirce, the bass player of Desert Ratz.

"We'll be out as soon as we finish these drinks," Damian informed him.

Diego laughed, walking away as he pulled the guitar strap over his head. "Your lips have to be available for chugging to do that, my brother."

If her entire body wasn't already on fire, Bethany's face might've warmed at the comment. She took a step back as Damian stood up, noticeably adjusting his crotch area. "I gotta give myself a moment or two to be able to walk without looking funny." He winked at her. "Maybe it's not such a good idea to get so worked up in public, huh?"

Taking a sip of her drink in hopes of cooling her insides, Bethany took a deep breath. If that ever happened in private, she already knew she'd be a goner. So much for taking things slower than usual. The way she felt already, just as everything with Damian, this might be happening sooner than usual. She wasn't sure if she should regret taking Diego up on his offer to hang out with them after the show or be grateful she'd done so. From the very first time Damian had kissed her, she hadn't held back at all—she couldn't. And now she was certain she wouldn't for much longer. Every single time she'd been powerless to so much as fake a little modesty. Instead she was eager, willing, and as anxious as he was. She really should be embarrassed, but strangely she wasn't.

That voice in her head warned again about taking this slow,

but her heart was screaming otherwise. She glanced at him just as he adjusted again, and she couldn't help smiling, sinking her teeth into her lip. He caught her smiling and flashed the most wickedly sexy grin at her, warming her insides all over again. Oh, yeah, fighting her heart for much longer was going to be a challenge.

CHAPTER 13

As usual Diego and the rest of the Ratz put on a hell of a show. Damian tried not to fixate on Bethany's refusal to get onstage and her initial reason for not wanting to get up being Simon's finding out. She'd backpedaled fast enough, and in the end her explanation had made sense, but he'd had a hard time pushing back the thought that maybe she hadn't wanted Simon to find out she was here with Damian for other reasons. There was no question that everything else she'd said to him since, about not ever having felt this way with anyone else, was without a doubt true. The honesty in her eyes practically spoke to him.

For that reason, and because he had no reason to think she'd lie to him about her relationship with Simon, he had to trust her on this. He reminded himself that what he was feeling was because of what he'd picked up from Simon, not Bethany. The guy obviously had a thing for her, and who could blame him? Damian would have to get a grip when it came to Simon and just trust her, especially because she worked with the dude, and there was no way around her spending time with him.

Taking a deep breath, and before he could get worked

up over that, he squeezed his eyes closed for a moment and remembered her very profound statement earlier.

No one, and I mean no one, has ever made me feel this craziness I feel when I'm with you.

He'd keep that in mind, because it was all that mattered. Glancing around, because she'd been in the ladies' room for a while now, he turned to the doorway she'd be coming back through, but nothing. They'd been catching up with Diego for almost an hour, until she walked away to the ladies' room, and Diego walked off to greet someone.

"So this must be serious," Diego said, plopping down on the empty bar stool next to Damian, holding a beer. "I heard you took Bethany to meet Mace and gave her a tour of the shop."

Damian shook his head, motioning to the bartender to get him and Bethany another round. "God, those two are like twelve-year-old girls. Which one called you?"

"Actually," Diego grinned before taking a sip of his beer, "it was Delfi who called, and boy was she hot. She wanted to know if you'd brought your girlfriend to meet me, too, before bringing Bethany to meet her."

Damian frowned just as the bartender set his and Bethany's fresh drinks down on the counter. "What is it with her anyway?" He reached for his drink, leaving the bartender a tip. "She called me the very next day asking how come she was the last to know, then grilled me for about twenty minutes. It's not like I've been with Bethany very long."

"But it *is* serious, obviously?" Diego eyed him for a real answer this time.

For once he decided to just admit it out loud. He could leave out the details about just how soon after he'd met her he'd decided to make things official. He shrugged to make less of it, but he wouldn't lie. "Yeah, well, when's the last time I've brought anyone to your show, or the shop, for that matter?"

"Not since Lana." Diego's eyes widened a little. "And before that *never*. Shit, you must be serious, because I've never seen you suck face in public like a teen before either. This girl must be something else."

His brother bounced his brows suggestively, then laughed. Damian ignored the last comment, taking a sip of his drink instead. He thought about how his brother had put it. Even when he'd decided to take Bethany to see the shop, it hadn't really been a whim. That very first night, when she'd mentioned being into classic-car restoration shows, and after having spent more time with her at the *pupusería*, he knew if he ever got the chance he'd be taking her, eventually. He just didn't realize it'd happen that fast. But the idea of bringing her around to meet his family had been a pleasant one from the very beginning. He knew she'd be an instant hit, just as she had been with him.

Glancing back at the door before addressing his brother's comments, he was instantly on his feet. Diego turned as if on instinct to see what had Damian glaring.

"Yo, Jake!" Diego said, holding up his hand at Damian. "I got this, man."

The guy holding his tatted arm against the doorway, preventing Bethany from getting by him and saying something way too close to her face, turned to Diego with a smirk.

Diego waved a flat hand just under his chin, letting him know he'd better cut the shit, and shook his head. "Not happening, man. Unless you want your ass kicked, let 'er by."

The guy pinched his brows but didn't move his arm, so Damian took a step forward. Diego placed his hand on Damian's chest, then turned to him with a very surprised expression. He jabbed Damian's hard and now very tense pec jokingly.

"Dude! You're like a brick wall." Turning back to Jake and Bethany again, he was even louder. "I'd move that arm right now, Jake, before my brother goes over there and rips it off."

Finally getting it, the idiot lifted his hand and let her by. Damian met her halfway. "You okay?"

"I'm fine," she said as she reached him and slipped her hand in his. They started back to the bar. "He said he was sorry."

Damian stopped and looked back at the guy. "For what?" he asked, trying not to get too worked up. "What did he do?"

"Nothing." She tugged at his hand. "He said he didn't know I was here with anyone. I hadn't had a chance to tell him when Diego called out to him. He was just flirting, that's all," she assured him.

Feeling the tension that had crept into his entire body ease up just a tiny bit, he gave in to her second tug and followed her back to the bar. Diego laughed as they reached him. "Damn, Damian." He glanced around. "No one's gonna even think about messing with her now."

Damian glanced around casually; he hadn't even noticed they'd gotten everyone's attention. "Good" was all he said before reaching for his drink.

Bethany reached for hers, smiling. "Last one, okay? I have a Zumba class first thing in the morning."

"Zumba, huh?" Diego checked her out slowly as she sipped her drink and wasn't looking his way. "No wonder." He glanced at Damian, who was glaring at him now, and nearly spat out his beer, holding his hand at his mouth. "Damian, you're too much!"

Bethany looked up at them, confused. "What?"

Damian shot his brother a look, and Diego laughed again, then hugged Bethany. "Nothing, hon. Your boyfriend's a little explosive tonight, that's all." He winked at Damian over her shoulder. "Or maybe that's just what you do to him."

Diego pulled away, but Bethany still looked confused. Damian shook his head at her with a smile. His way of letting her know she didn't need to worry about it. His brother was just being an ass. Diego pointed at two guys who had just walked in the door. "I gotta go talk some business, but if you're out after that drink, let me just say it was very nice to meet you, and you're gonna *have to* do a show with us, Bethany. I mean it. You're awesome."

"Thank you," Bethany said with a demure smile.

She turned to Damian and saw him watching her, then smiled very sweetly and leaned into him as Diego walked away. "So far your siblings are incredibly sweet. I can hardly wait to meet the other two."

Kissing the top of her head, he smiled. "You'll be meeting Fina real soon. She's gonna make sure of that."

Bethany turned to look up at him. "I get the feeling meeting Dominic will take a little longer."

"Yeah." Damian sipped his drink, trying not to frown. "He's complicated."

They finished their drinks, said good-bye to everyone, and headed back to her place. Damian gripped the wheel as she ran her hand up and down his thigh, reminding himself not to get too carried away when kissing her good night. It was his own fault for rushing this whole thing, and he wanted to make absolutely clear it wasn't for any other reason than him making her his. He was willing to take everything else as slow as she wanted. Though so far she hadn't given him any indication she wanted to slow things down.

Just as he parked the car outside her place, she got a text. Knowing they'd left the after party just after midnight, he had to wonder who'd be texting her so late, but he held back from asking. Watching her text something back quickly, he made note of how hastily she shoved the phone back into her purse without saying a word. They got out of the car, and he came around the front to meet her. Deciding he wouldn't be one of *those* types of boyfriends, he wouldn't question the late-night text.

She gave him a look as he reached out for her hand so he could walk her to her door, but she didn't say anything. They'd had this discussion already Wednesday night, when he dropped her off. She'd insisted he didn't have to walk her up, but he told her to get used to it. This entire neighborhood was dangerous. And that barely lit stairwell with the few shaky light bulbs that were hanging on for dear life was not something he wanted her to be walking up by herself. Not if he could help it anyway.

"So tomorrow you have dancing in the morning, then you're off for the rest of the day?"

She turned to him, eyeing him strangely. "Is that what you think Zumba is? Just dancing?"

"Well, no," he admitted, trying his damnedest not to smile. "I caught some of your class Wednesday. It's also a hell of a turn-on."

They reached her floor, and she turned to him, arching her brow. "Really? Did you enjoy watching a roomful of women shaking their thing, Damian?"

"I don't remember any other women in the room," he said as they reached her door, and leaned into her, his body already anxious with anticipation of what he was sure would be nothing more than the mind-blowing kisses he'd had with her so far. "Just like your show that first night, my eyes were glued to you from the moment I first spotted you." Lowering his eyes to her lips, he could hardly wait to taste her mouth again. "And just like in your stage show, your dancing was as jaw-dropping as your singing."

That was no exaggeration. Just thinking about it had

him heating up. Bringing his hands around her bare back, he pulled her against him, taking her sweet mouth in his once again. In an effort not to get too carried away, as he had earlier when he'd had to spend the next ten minutes trying to calm the aching in his pants, he paced himself, kissing her slowly, but it was already too late. Her body pressing against his only made it more torturous, but he was determined. Even if he had to drive all the way home again with another painful erection, because the lingering taste of her still in his mouth was enough to keep him hard the whole way home, he wouldn't push for more.

Hearing and feeling her soft moans against his lips as their kiss became more hungered had him throbbing again as he had at the concert. He sucked her tongue, mimicking the way he hoped someday he'd be sucking other parts of her body, as they fell against her door. She ran her hands through his hair, pulling away at times to gasp for air, but in no way was she slowing it down. In fact her moans were getting deeper, and she let her head fall sideways, giving him the go-ahead to kiss and suck her sweet neck.

As much as he wanted to say it, he wouldn't. He'd wait for her to say the magic words: *Let's go inside*. But he could hardly stand it anymore. He sucked her neck harder, biting down a little with his teeth. "Damian!" she gasped as her entire body trembled in reaction.

He left a trail of suckling kisses up her neck all the way to her mouth, and her body continued to tremble uncontrollably. He stopped kissing her for a moment, as they stared at each other breathing harshly.

"What, baby?"

If he could've he would've held his breath in anticipation of her answer, but he couldn't; he was breathing too heavily. She closed her eyes in an obvious attempt to regain her composure. The same composure Damian had nearly lost himself.

"I don't want you to think I don't," she said, still struggling with her breath and licking her lips. "Because, *my God*, do I ever. I just think maybe we should wait a little longer. Everything's happened so fast and—"

"Shh," he said, kissing her softly. "You don't have to explain, okay? I'll wait as long as you need me to. You'll just have to forgive my body's reaction to you. Everything about you drives me insane, but I promise you," he kissed her forehead gently, "you can take all the time you want." He looked into her apprehensive eyes, needing her to understand this much. "I won't push for anything *ever*. You'll make this call, all right?"

She nodded, and he smiled, eager to reassure her that he was in no way upset. Disappointed? Hell, yeah, but he could tell she'd be worth the wait. No matter how long that might be.

"When do I get to see you again?" he asked, kissing her softly, incapable of keeping his lips off her for very long.

"Is tomorrow too soon?" she asked tilting her head.

"Hell, no." He laughed. "I'll have to work in the day, but I can pick you up around sixish?"

She nodded eagerly, biting her lower lip. *Damn.* As hard as he tried, and as much as he wanted to respect her wishes to slow it down, he *could not* keep his lips off her. He dove in again, glad that she seemed to be having just as hard a time ending this night.

Even after things calmed, and he toned his final kisses way down, he still walked away with a massive hard-on. He knew what he had to look forward to tonight when he got home. The same thing he'd had to do Wednesday night when he got home. One *long*-ass cold shower.

Damian hadn't been lying when he'd told Bethany yesterday that if it hadn't been for her, this week would've been pure shit. The double homicide he'd been asked to assist with had become a convoluted mess. The couple found murdered in their hotel room last week were both married to other people. As if that weren't enough, it was now coming out that the male victim had a serious gambling problem and owed a lot of people money, including a few shady loan sharks. The list of suspects was longer than any Damian had ever had to deal with. This was why they were asking for his help even though it wasn't his case initially. Tracking down and interviewing each suspect would take weeks if it were left only to the two guys assigned to the case.

The worst part about it, and what had him slamming drawers in his office now, was that because Damian was the resident expert on body language, they'd requested, but it was clearly more of an order, that he stay and interview the biggest suspect so far. The female victim's husband. And it *had* to be done tonight, because all the previous interviews had gotten nothing out of him. They were certain the days were numbered before the guy's attorney pulled the plug and advised him to clam up completely. Then they'd be up shit creek, because so far all they had was circumstantial evidence. They hadn't even been able to get the guy to admit he was aware his wife was having an affair.

Knowing this could take hours, possibly all night, he'd had to cancel seeing Bethany tonight. She'd texted him earlier that this time it was her turn to surprise him. So hearing the disappointment in her voice when he called to cancel, he'd been flooded with memories of all the canceled dinners, dates, and family parties that ultimately ended his relationship with Lana last year, when he was trying so fucking hard to prove himself.

Damian would be damned if he would let that happen again. He didn't give a shit what these assholes thought of him anymore. He'd more than proven himself. It was one thing to be forced to stay late for something like tonight, but if given a choice, he wouldn't be bending over backward and going above and beyond as he had last year. After just one official week of being with Bethany, he already sensed his feelings for her could easily surpass anything he'd ever felt for Lana. No way would he risk having her get fed up and dump his ass because he constantly put his job before her.

Several hours into the grueling interrogation, Damian didn't have much, but one thing he knew for sure; the guy was hiding something. Throughout the questioning there'd been too many times when Damian was caught in a stare-down contest with the guy. Exactly the reason he'd argued eye contact or lack of it was unreliable. Some liars made it a point to look you straight in the eye when they were lying. This guy might have actually been coached, because some of this body language was so blatantly forced, to try to hide what he was really feeling. But there was one thing that wasn't easy to hide at all—raw emotions. Defensiveness was always a sure sign that someone was hiding something or lying.

"So you're telling me, Mr. Ridley," Damian leaned onto the table, looking the haggard and emotionally worn-down looking man straight in the eyes, "that in ten years of marriage, you never once felt the least amount of jealousy or even the slightest bit of insecurity?"

"I never said I didn't—"

"Because I gotta tell you," Damian sat back crossing his arms, "I've seen pictures, and with all due respect, she was a very attractive woman. I'm certain she turned heads and—"

"Look," Mr. Ridley laid his hand on the table loudly. "I know my wife was attractive. I know men looked at her a lot, and hell, yeah, it bothered me sometimes, but I never suspected she might be cheating."

"*Never?*" Damian lifted an eyebrow as he opened up a separate file. "Tell me about the night the cops were called out to your home last winter."

Just like that, Mr. Ridley's hand, the one he had so firmly dropped on the table just moments ago, began to tap that same table. Then he picked it up and ran it through his hair. "I can read you the statements taken from your wife that night," Damian said, flipping through the file, "but I'd prefer you just tell me yourself in your own words."

"I'd been drinking," Ridley admitted sitting back in his own chair. "Twice that week she'd acted strange about a few texts she got late in the evening. Each time she had some lame excuse for why a coworker or her cousin had a question so late at night. I'd noticed after the first two times she started turning off her phone after nine. I didn't question it, but that night I turned her phone on without telling her, and sure enough she got one just after eleven. When I asked her about it, and why she'd turned the phone off in the first place, she couldn't even respond, so I tried taking the phone from her. When she refused to let me see it, we started arguing." He shrugged. "Turned out it was her cousin. *She* was the one having marital problems and was texting my wife after her husband went to bed."

"All right, Ridley," Damian said trying to push aside his incredible annoyance that it was nearly midnight now and there was no way he was going to get to spend *any* time with Bethany tonight. "Let's just cut the bullshit already. Your wife's body was found naked in a bed in a hotel with another man. The very man you had an altercation with just a few months after this domestic dispute, where you blew up at your wife because she got a goddamned text late in the evening. You still gonna sit there and tell me you had no idea she was screwing around? That you didn't know this guy was the one texting her—"

"I suspected, okay!" Ridley sat up suddenly.

Damian sat up, too. "Then why the *fuck* are you wasting my time? I asked you this hours ago!"

"I loved my wife!" Ridley pounded his fist on the table. "Just because I thought maybe something was going on doesn't mean I'd kill her."

"Then why the hell have you denied it all this time?" Frustrated, Damian pounded his own fist on the table as well. "Two interrogations before this one and for hours tonight you've been saying you had no idea she was having an affair when all the while you knew she was?"

"I said I *suspected*," Ridley repeated, his teeth clenched now. "I stopped trying to get to the bottom of it, because I didn't wanna fucking know, okay? We had arguments sometimes, and she said I just didn't get her. Said there was a *disconnect*. I thought maybe it was just a texting or phone thing. She might just be having some kind of emotional affair with someone. Nothing physical, and I figured I could live with that," he continued, with conviction and even more loudly. "As long as she wasn't talking about leaving me or divorce I thought I could deal with her venting to some other guy about us."

"So why'd you lie?" Damian asked with just as much conviction. "Why didn't you just say that from the beginning instead of acting like you had no clue?"

"Because I didn't!" Ridley stood up suddenly, his chair falling back. Damian shot up just as quickly, but he held up a hand to the mirrors in the room, letting his counterparts watching and taping the whole thing know he didn't want them rushing in just yet. "I told my lawyer I suspected, and he thought that was enough for you guys to nail this on me if you couldn't find the real killer. So they advised me to not even mention my suspicions." He glared at Damian, undeniable pain in his tear-filled eyes. "I loved my wife so much I was willing to ignore my suspicions if it meant we'd stay together, no matter how much it hurt." He plopped back down suddenly in his chair, dropping his head into his hands, and began to sob. "But I would *never* hurt her."

Damian stood there staring at this broken man. For the first time in all these hours, he knew he'd been sitting in front of a man who had very tragically lost his wife just a week ago; his heart ached for him. Glancing back up at the mirrors, he shook his head. Their murderer was still out there. They weren't any closer to finding him yet. Ridley hadn't murdered his wife. Of this he was certain.

CHAPTER 14

———

I missed you, baby. I'm just now getting home. I didn't
want to call and wake you but I wanted to tell you I can
hardly wait to see you tonight.

Bethany stared at the text once again. He'd called her just
after six last night to tell her he was going to have to work
late and had to cancel. This text was sent just a few minutes
shy of one in the morning. Really? He'd worked *that* late on
a Saturday night? Ever since she'd closed her door behind her
Friday night, when she had to let that man and the enormous
erection she'd felt through his pants walk away, she'd wondered if she'd made a mistake. Would he really drive home
for the third time that week instead of somewhere he could
satisfy his needs? A man like Damian would certainly have
go-to girls who'd be more than willing to help him out with
that. *She* was his girlfriend now. She should be the one not
only helping with but also enjoying his *needs*.

The entire night she'd hardly slept, thinking of how incredibly aroused he'd been, and though she had also been left
breathless, she knew it was much worse for men. She'd let
that incredible man leave her, hot, bothered, and unsatisfied

once again, when there were tons of women out there, like Olivia, the seafood whore, who'd be more than willing to accommodate him.

Her life had always been about timing, and once again this was proving to be the case. Her cut-short conversation with her sister, Stella, Friday night had been another reason for her sleepless night. Since she'd told her she would explain about Damian the next day, Stella had texted her just after midnight to say it was tomorrow already, but Bethany had informed her she needed to sleep. Truthfully, she needed more time to come up with a better explanation for why her seeing Damian was not as bad an idea as her sister seemed to think.

As much as she'd like to say that the reason for her holding back with Damian was what he was probably thinking—her morals, and that she simply wasn't the kind of girl who would jump in bed with a guy this soon—it was and it wasn't. Normally, and with any other guy, that would certainly be the case. She'd wait until she was sure about taking things to that next level, because it *was* a big deal to her, but as absurd as it sounded, and she knew she'd never get Stella to understand, with Damian she was already certain. There was something so inexplicable about everything she felt for him from day one. All she knew was that she was absolutely convinced Damian was the real deal. She felt it in every one of his kisses. Even if she couldn't explain it—didn't fully understand it. She just knew she didn't have to worry that he'd disappear on her after going there. But under the circumstances, she knew none of that would matter to Stella.

After her Zumba class yesterday morning she'd dreaded calling her sister, and then when she did she got the best news ever. Stella had gotten word that things were definitely moving forward as planned without any snags. Her sister didn't even care anymore that she was seeing someone. All she wanted to know now was why and how their plans had been changed and how soon they'd all get to be together again.

Bethany had spent the rest of the day running around collecting more faxes and sending some of her own. She'd been over the moon and immediately started planning her surprise for Damian that night. Then she got his call canceling their plans.

Now, sitting here staring at Damian's 1:00 a.m. text, she wondered if going any further Friday night would have even mattered. She was already very openly *his* girl. Anyone who'd witnessed their behavior in public would certainly come to their own conclusions about what was going on behind closed doors. The unease that crept up her spine now, wondering if this had been about timing, too, turned her stomach. Maybe she'd screwed this up.

Bethany shook her head, pushing aside thoughts that perhaps he'd decided at the last minute to spend a more fulfilling evening with someone else, and he'd done so until almost one in the morning. Rushing off the bus, she hurried home, reminding herself this whole exclusivity thing was *his* idea to begin with, and he'd been incredibly sweet when he assured her he was willing to wait as long as she needed him to. He really did sound disappointed about having to cancel—almost angry about it even.

Enough. She wouldn't give it another thought. Damian was by far the most genuine person she'd ever met. And she knew firsthand all about being lied to and deceived. She had no reason to believe that Damian's text and his phone call yesterday evening were anything but sincere. The surprise she had for him yesterday was half squashed, since part of it could only happen Friday or Saturday night. The other half, however, could happen whenever. And today's plans were perfect for it. He told her he wanted to show off his barbecuing skills.

They'd be alone at his place, and she couldn't think of a better place for it.

He'd be there to pick her up soon. Determined not to ruin today by giving in to her insecurity about where he might've been and with whom until one o'clock on a Saturday night, she decided he deserved the benefit of the doubt. If he said he had to work late, then she had no reason to doubt him. Besides, she had other things to worry about now. Real things, not just something her insecure imagination invented. Her sister had left a message earlier saying there was a problem. She'd already tried calling her back twice, and it'd gone to voicemail. She texted her also to tell her she was making her nervous and to call her back the second she had a chance.

Rushing into her apartment, she tried again, and once again the call went to voicemail. Surprised and beginning to really worry that Stella wasn't answering or calling back, she jumped into the shower. Once out, she tried not to freak out because there was still no call or text from her.

She tried to take her mind off it, because it was probably just a fluke. Stella had likely gone somewhere and forgotten her extra phone at home as she'd done in the past and would call her as soon as she got back. Instead of freaking out, Bethany continued to get ready, concentrating on putting her hair up in a loose French braid. She always wore her hair like this for her Zumba classes. When Damian had showed up at her Wednesday class, even though her hair was a sweaty mess, he commented on how adorable she looked with her hair up that way. Just thinking about how he'd looked at her when he said it, in that same way he so often did, as if he was in awe of her, made her feel *so* special it had her smiling already. Figuring today they'd be spending a casual day barbecuing and knowing how hot it was supposed to get, it was as good a time as any to look *adorable* for him again.

Since she finished getting ready ahead of time, Bethany went and stood in front of the fan so she wouldn't be a sticky mess by the time Damian got there. Her phone rang, and she grabbed it, rushing back to stand in front of the fan again. It was her sister. With everything being a done deal, she couldn't imagine what kind of problem there could be. She held her breath as she answered the call and prayed it wasn't too bad.

"Stella."

"Bethany, I'm sorry I couldn't answer or even respond; Max was here."

Nearly gasping, Bethany brought her hand to her mouth. "He went to the house? Why? What did he want?"

"I told you each time I went to make the exchange, I've gotten the runaround. And he's never there," her sister huffed, sounding very irritated. "The bitch assistant of his told me this morning that Max had instructed her to tell me to just leave the money, and he'd deliver the goods himself."

"You didn't, did you?"

"Of course not. Am I really supposed to believe anything that bastard says?"

Bethany let out a sigh of relief, thanking God that although she was very young, her sister was eons beyond her age in wisdom. Stella told her about how she'd refused, and the woman's saying Max would be very disappointed. "So what did he want?"

"He says he wants to deliver it to you himself."

"No!"

"That's what I told him. But he says he deserves at least that much, since he's been so patient."

Clenching the phone, Bethany paced her small kitchen. "I don't care what he says, Stella. Whatever you do, *do not* tell him where I am."

"You know I wouldn't," Stella assured her, lowering her voice, but there was no masking the familiar, growing alarm in her sister's voice that Bethany knew could very quickly turn into so much more. "Here's the thing. He said we were naïve to think he couldn't find you if he really wanted to. Claims all this time he's been biding his time, but he'd hoped that we would give him this one thing after everything he did for you—for us. He's acting like there was never anything in it for him. Like he didn't have his own ulterior motives from the very beginning!"

Feeling the perspiration begin to trickle down her back, Bethany went and stood in front of the fan again and attempted to sound as calm as possible. "Did he say why?"

"Yes! He says he wants to talk to you. That he wants the opportunity to *make amends*. And that he has a proposition he's certain you'll be pleased with."

"I don't buy it." Bethany chewed her bottom lip.

"Neither do I!" Her sister was sounding more and more panicked by the minute. Bethany needed to calm her before she had one of her anxiety attacks.

"Okay, what if you give him my number?"

"What? No!"

"Hear me out, okay?" Bethany said quickly. "That's why I got us both prepaid phones, Stella. I didn't have to register them under my name or give an address. I made sure they don't have GPS. As far as I know, they're not traceable. He can talk to me and tell me what he wants to say." She rolled her eyes. "*Make amends*, and I'll pretend to consider whatever crazy proposition he has, then we'll be done with it."

"You really think it's gonna be that easy? He's just making excuses, Bethany!"

"Listen to me!" Her sister was near the blowing point, her voice high-pitched and alarm-stricken. She spoke again very calmly, trying to sound as sure of herself as she could, pacing in her front room. The technique usually worked with Stella. She was too close to having this all behind her, and she wasn't about to blow it by panicking now. "First of all, breathe, Stella. I need you to remain calm, okay?" She heard her sister take in a deep breath, then spoke in the calmest voice she could muster. "Tell him I want to talk to him, too."

Stella groaned loudly, *"Why?"*

"Because I do," Bethany said, in the most credible tone she could manage. She and Max *did* go back a ways, and she'd spent enough time with him to know just what he needed to hear, but at the moment she needed to convince her sister that she really meant this. The last thing she wanted was for Stella to think that she was getting desperate. Because she wasn't—not yet. "I wanna thank him for everything he's done." Hearing Stella's exasperated gasp, she spoke faster. "He really did do a lot to help buy me time. Even if . . ."

"You *can't* be serious—"

"I am," Bethany said, this time with even more conviction. "Give him my number and tell him I'm looking forward to his call."

For a moment her sister was silent, then Bethany heard her take another, even deeper breath. "Okay. He said he'd be back tomorrow. I'll give it to him and tell him then. I really hope you know what you're doing."

Though she still sounded uncertain, Stella's high-pitched responses had calmed significantly. Bethany's attitude had done just what she was hoping. "I do." Bethany assured her. "Now I gotta go. Damian should be here soon."

"About that," Stella said, sounding a little nervous again. "You're not gonna tell Max about him, are you?"

"Of course not! My social life is none of his business,"

Bethany said, holding her arms up in front of the fan, deciding for now it was best if she made less of her relationship with Damian. Stella was already worried enough as it was. "Besides, I told you already. I've only gone out with Damian a few times. It's not a big deal *at all*. He's just someone to pass the time with."

Hearing her sister exhale in relief, Bethany smiled, knowing she'd successfully managed to talk her off the ledge—for now. Tomorrow she really had to turn up her acting abilities and hope that all that she'd worked for, and everything she'd sacrificed, had not all been for naught.

Once off the phone, Bethany wasn't sure how to feel. This could be just a bump in her very carefully laid plans—one last obstacle before she could get at least this part of her life back—or it could be *bad*. Things weren't going as smoothly as she'd hoped. One thing after another seemed to be slowly unraveling. But she wouldn't start thinking negatively now. She couldn't. And she certainly wasn't changing her mind about what she'd decided yesterday.

That suddenly reminded her of something, and she glanced down at her phone. Her stomach tightening at the sight of the text indictor flashing, she clicked on the texts from Damian.

> I practically ran up the stairs . . . Okay I did. I'm right
> outside. =)

Even though his text made her heart start to dance a little, she glanced at the time he'd sent it to see how long he'd been waiting, but most important, to see how much of her conversation he might've heard. Her dancing heart puttered as she realized it'd been sent over five minutes ago. The second one was sent just a minute ago.

> This is torture. I guess you're on the phone again. I
> don't want to knock so just come out when you're
> done.

Already rushing to the door before she'd finished reading the second text, she replayed her conversation with Stella in her head, cursing her thin walls and herself for letting this happen again. With very little time to think about it as she swung the door open, nothing too compromising came to mind that Damian might have heard.

Standing there in a black tank that once again displayed his hard-muscled arms and shoulders, Damian stared at her, his blank expression impossible to read.

"Sorry," she said with a nervous smile.

"You were on the phone?"

He took a step forward, and the smile tugging at the corner of his lips gave her hope he hadn't heard much or any of her conversation. Her mind was suddenly completely muddled. Every time she saw him was even more exciting than the last, and just feeling his big hand in hers now and knowing his lips would be on hers any minute had her heart going like crazy. For a fleeting moment, she couldn't remember a thing she and her sister had talked about.

Damian leaned in, kissing her softly, his arm already around her waist, pulling her body against his. "Jesus," he whispered against her lips. "It's only been a day, and I could hardly wait to be near you again."

Sighing in response to that, she smiled. "I know exactly what you mean."

He kissed her a bit more deeply before pulling away with an almost pained grin. "These shorts are too thin for me to be getting too worked up."

She looked down and realized she hadn't even noticed he

was wearing swimming trunks—the long kind that tied in the front—and they hung just slightly off his hips. From the way the snug tank clung to his abs, she could tell she was in for a treat once that shirt came off. "You didn't forget to pack a bathing suit, right?" he asked her as he smoothed a hand over the front of his shorts. "It's supposed to get close to one-ten today. Plan on being in the pool a lot."

"Yes, I packed one," she said, gulping back the extreme visuals she was having, of his wet and shirtless body pressed against hers in his pool, as she walked back into her kitchen.

She didn't mention she'd also packed a light overnight bag just in case. Her mind was made up. Nothing, not even the revelations her sister had made today, would change it. This incredible guy was her boyfriend now. Although things had happened so fast between them, that didn't take away from her very real feelings for him. The fact that he'd been the one to suggest exclusivity so quickly said so much about his feelings for her as well. Everything else, his taking her to meet his family so quickly and what she felt when he said the amazing things he said to her, like the fact that he'd been dying to be near her again, only further confirmed why this felt so right.

Taking the small grocery bag out of the fridge, she turned to Damian again. "Just let me grab my stuff in the room, and I'll be good to go."

"What's that?" he asked, pointing at the grocery bag in her hands.

She glanced down, then lifted it with a smile. "Stuff for a salad."

"I got all that stuff, babe. You don't need to bring anything. Just leave that here."

Ignoring his suggestion, she walked into her bedroom. "You gotta let me bring something," she said as she picked up the small duffel, hoping he didn't notice there was obviously more than just her swimsuit and sunscreen in it.

"Why?" he asked as she walked back out into the front room, taking him in and once again feeling her fluttering insides go wild. "It's *my* barbecue. I picked up a boatload of stuff at Costco today. You know they sell everything there in bulk, but also," he added, his expression falling for a moment, "we gotta talk."

Stopping suddenly, she stared at him nervously. "About what?"

"My sister called this morning. When I mentioned you were coming over today, she insisted on dropping by." Feeling massively relieved, Bethany refrained from letting the breath she'd been holding pour out. Instead she exhaled very casually and waited for him to go on. "She said she'd just come by for a little while, but then later I got a call from Dimitri. He *heard* about the barbecue at my place and wanted to know what he should bring besides his trunks and his appetite." He walked over to her, taking the small grocery bag from her hand, then slipped his hand into hers. "I'm sorry, sweetheart, but this may not be as romantic as I'd hoped." He tilted his head, kissing her on the forehead and looking even more rueful. "We Santiagos are die-hard Rockies fans. They play today against the Dodgers, who they need to beat to take the lead in the West, and he assumed that's why I was having it. He invited all the guys from the shop, including Diego and the Ratz. That's why I made that trip to Costco this morning. Looks like instead of just you and me today, I'm having a houseful now." The second she stuck her bottom lip out in a playful pout, he kissed it. "I'll have them out of there as soon as the game's over. I promise." He grinned now. "It's an early game, too."

Laughing softly, she shrugged. "It'll still be fun. I'm not

really into baseball, but I can't even remember the last time I went swimming. With this heat I'm *really* looking forward to taking a dip."

She didn't argue with him when he walked her small grocery bag back to the fridge. The stuff she'd gotten would barely be enough for two salads, maybe three. But no way would it cut it for a houseful of people.

They made their way out down the stairs. It wasn't even noon yet, and it was already scorching hot. Deciding she wouldn't worry about anything else for the rest of the day and just enjoy her time with Damian, she glanced up at her smiling, sinfully sexy boyfriend. Today was going to be great, and she hoped it would end even better.

They reached his car and as usual he opened the door for her, leaned in, and kissed her sweetly once she was in, then closed the door. While he walked around the front to get to his side, Bethany sat there enjoying the view and savoring the delicious taste of him still on her lips, her insides warming already. Maybe they'd get a little alone time before anyone arrived.

He got in, put his sunglasses on, and turned on the ignition. If she hadn't been staring at him like a lovesick puppy, she might've missed it. His eyebrow lifted and his lips opened, but he quickly pressed them together as if he were about say something, then changed his mind. She was about to question it, when he glanced at her, the eyebrow lifted even higher now. "So who were you on the phone with when I got to your place?"

———

CHAPTER 15

After a few moments of tense silence, Bethany smiled, placing her hand on his thigh. "Stella," she said, very relaxed.

She turned away and looked out the window just as he glanced at her again. It made total sense that Bethany would say things between the two of them were not a big deal yet. Technically it'd officially been just over a week now. But *at all*? *Just someone to pass the time with?* That's not how Damian saw things between them, and he'd been certain she was right there with him on that. He wasn't sure if he should quote exactly what he'd overheard. In fact he'd almost not brought up the call at all, but this time he couldn't just let it go. His curiosity had reached another level.

"I imagine you and your only sister must be pretty close." He ran his hand over her hand, which now lay flat on his thigh, lacing his fingers through hers over it. "Do you tell her everything, Bethany?"

She straightened out and actually cleared her throat. A sure sign of anxiety or uneasiness that only made him more anxious. Turning to him with that same relaxed smile, or one she was attempting to make appear relaxed, she traced a finger over his hand slowly with her other hand. "You mean have I told her about you and me?" With his eyes back on the road now, he simply nodded. "Yes, I have, actually. But to be honest, she tends to worry about everything, so I've toned it down a lot. I'm not sure I could explain what's happening so quickly." She shrugged when he glanced back at her. "I don't think she'd understand, Damian. Most people wouldn't. Don't you agree?"

He thought about that for a moment and how incredibly relieved her explanation made him feel. Lifting her hand up, he nodded, then kissed it. She was right. Most people wouldn't understand it. It was the very reason he was still playing it down to his own family. Even when his sister had grilled him again that morning, saying that this was clearly getting serious if half the family had already met Bethany. Apparently, she'd made Diego promise to tell her about it if he met Beth. Diego had actually waited a day, but Fina called Damian first after getting the call from his brother that morning.

Bethany obviously had figured out he'd overheard her "not a big deal at all" comment. And while he agreed that toning it down made sense for now, he wasn't so sure about adding the "just passing the time" comment. But maybe her sister did worry too much and maybe she had good reason. Again he had to keep in mind he still knew very little about Bethany and her family. Maybe she'd had her heart broken badly or something, and she was reassuring her sister she was taking it slow this time. Who knew?

Feeling satisfied he'd calmed his anxious curiosity, he decided he'd let go of the part about her asking her sister to give "him" her number. He didn't want Bethany thinking he'd been purposely trying to listen in to every word she'd said, because he hadn't been. For all he knew it could be a relative she was talking about. An uncle or her dad even. He still had no idea of her family's dynamics. Maybe that's why she was out here so alone. There could be lots of reasonable explanations, so he wasn't going to go there. Asking if she'd told her sister about them was one thing, but this would sound accusatory, and that's not how he wanted this relationship to start.

Determined not to let something so petty ruin what had the potential to be another excellent day with Bethany, he kissed her hand again. "Yeah, I sort of did the same with my sister this morning, too." He shook his head. "But Fina's not so easy to convince. She's on to me. Without having even met you, she seems acutely aware of just how serious I am about this."

He left her with that thought. Making absolutely sure she, too, was aware of just how seriously he *was* taking this. In case there was any doubt, *he* wasn't just passing the time. He wanted this point perfectly clear.

Not wanting to harp on it, he changed the subject to the barbecue. "I hope you like pork tenderloin."

She turned to him, squinting in that cute way she did so often. "I'm not sure I've ever tried it. But anything with pork is always tasty."

"It's one of the few things more complicated than mac and cheese that I'm actually pretty good at making."

"Well, that's one place where you have me. I've never been really good at cooking. My sister," she said, looking out the window again, "she's always liked being in the kitchen with my aunt, but me? No, thanks." She turned back to him with a smile. "I can barely warm a *tortilla* without burning it. So whatever it is you make, I'm sure I'll be thoroughly impressed."

He smiled at her, then brought his eyes back to the road, where they should be. It was damn hard keeping them there with her sitting next to him. But he liked the idea of thoroughly impressing Bethany.

They reached his place just as his sister pulled up with his niece, Carey. They weren't even out of the car when Carey was already waving at them feverishly. Damian waved back, chuckling. "That's my sister, and the little one in the backseat is my niece, Carey," he said to Bethany just as she opened the door and began to get out. "Word of warning. I'm not sure if all four-year-olds are like that, but she says it like it is and is always full of questions, so be prepared for the inquisition."

Bethany nodded at him, looking a little nervous, before stepping out of the car. Fina opened the back door of her car and helped Carey out. Damian met Bethany around his car, taking her duffel in one hand, then slipped his other hand in hers as they walked toward Fina.

As soon as Carey's little feet hit the ground she rushed toward them. "Are you Uncle Damian's new girlfriend?"

Bethany and Damian exchanged glances, before she looked back at Carey. "Yes, I am. Are you his niece, Carey?"

"I am!" Carey said, eyes gleefully open. "I know *your* name, too. It's Bethany."

Bethany bent over and extended her arm. "That's right, it is. So very nice to meet you, Carey."

They shook hands just as Fina began to walk toward them. She'd been busy taking something out of her trunk. "Potato salad?" Damian asked.

His sister nodded. "My specialty," she said, grinning. "Mitri put in his request."

She glanced at Bethany, but before Damian could begin the introductions, Carey took the initiative. "Bethany, this is my mommy. She says you might be the one."

Bethany and Fina looked at each other, eyes wide. "Carey, honey, I never told you that," Fina said, her face flushing.

"Not me. You told Uncle Diego this morning. You said she—"

"That's enough, Carey." Fina patted her daughter on the bed, eyeing Damian, who took the cue. No telling what else Fina had said to Diego that Carey might let out of the bag. Letting go of Bethany's hand, he picked up Carey and whirled her around in the air as she giggled uncontrollably. "Nice to meet you, Bethany." Fina extended her hand to Bethany. "I'm Delfina."

After the awkward introductions, they all started toward the front door of Damian's place. Damian did his best to keep Carey distracted as his sister and Bethany chatted. If he knew Fina, she would probably know more about Bethany before the day was over than he did.

"Bethany's pretty," Carey said as he put her down in the front room.

"Yeah, I think so, too." Damian said, turning back to Bethany, who was heading into the kitchen with Fina.

"Are you gonna marry her?"

Damian laughed. "Did your mom tell you I was?"

Carey stared at him very seriously, apparently failing to see the humor. "She said if you do, Bethany would be my auntie."

"I think your mom is jumping the gun a little." He could see in his niece's eyes that she didn't understand, so he nodded, giving up. "Maybe. We'll see. But don't tell Bethany. If I do ask her to marry me," he winked, lowering his voice, "I want it to be a surprise."

Carey's eyes opened wide, but she nodded. If he knew one thing about his niece it was that she loved secrets and surprises, though she wasn't very subtle with either. "Okay," she whispered loudly.

Needing to change the subject and distract his niece so he

could go steal Bethany from his inquisitive sister, he pointed at the box near the corner of his front room. "Go see what I got you. I'll be right back."

In a sprint, Carey was off toward the box, and he took off just as quickly in the opposite direction, toward the kitchen. Fina was already making herself at home, pulling pots and Tupperware out of his cabinets as she complained about there being no rhyme or reason to the way Damian put his dishware away.

Reaching out his hand to Bethany, who was leaning against the center island, he smiled, because it felt so good just to touch her. "I'll be back and help you find whatever you need, Fina." He tugged Bethany along with him toward the back door. "Carey's in the front room checking out a couple of things I bought her. We'll be back. Just let me give Bethany a quick tour of my place."

Fina turned suddenly in Bethany's direction, lifting a brow. "This is your first time here?"

Bethany nodded, but before Fina could ask anything more, Damian tugged at Bethany's hand again. "We'll be back."

Sneaking through the back door of the kitchen, which led outside, so they could bypass Carey at least for a few minutes, they walked out into the patio that wrapped around the back and led to the pool area. "I wasn't expecting your house to be all this." Bethany glanced around his big yard. This wasn't even half of it.

Damian stopped as soon as he knew he was completely out of his sister's and his niece's sight and pulled Bethany to him. "I bought it mostly for the garage space." He kissed her softly and smiled. "You'll probably notice, my whole family is kind of big on cars."

She smiled just as he went in for a longer, much deeper

kiss. He'd never get enough of kissing her, touching her, feeling her body against his. He'd wait as long as he needed to for more. It sucked that things had worked out the way they had today. He'd been looking forward to having her all to himself, and they would've been in the complete privacy of his own home this time. Unlike all the other times he'd hung out with her this past week, where the most privacy they'd had was the few hungered kisses they'd shared in his car and the equally feverish kisses they'd shared outside her apartment door. But in a weird way, he liked how easily they were getting past the formalities of introducing her to his family and friends. None of this had gone nearly as smoothly with Lana. Fina had never liked Lana either. The verdict was still out about Bethany, but Damian couldn't imagine even one thing his sister wouldn't like about her. He knew he was completely biased now, but so far everything about Bethany was fucking perfect.

Forcing himself, he pulled away from her, and he had to smile. He loved the way she often kept her eyes closed, like now, even after he'd pulled his lips away from hers, as if the experience was still lingering for her, and she didn't want it to end. "C'mon," he whispered, unable to resist pecking her one last time. "I'll show you the rest of my yard, then we can go see the inside. But something tells me we'll have a mini tour guide with us along for the ride in there, and I can guarantee you she'll be doing most of the talking. I wanted to take advantage of her distraction with some of the pool toys I got her today, to be alone with you for at least a few more minutes."

Bethany laughed. "You weren't kidding about her saying what's on her mind. My sister was just like that even before she was Carey's age." She laughed even more now. "I remember being in the backseat with her, when she was still in a car seat. She'd be talking everyone's ear off, and my stepdad would make snoring noises; she never even noticed."

Damian smiled, nodding. Having been on quite a few long rides with his niece, he knew the feeling. "Well there you go. At least you know what you're in for, because that's Carey."

They came around the side of the house still talking about his niece, and Bethany stopped walking and talking. Damian turned to see her staring out into his luxurious yard. "Wow," she said, shaking her head slowly. "I knew when we drove up and saw the house that it would be fancy, but . . ." She turned to him. "I had no idea being a cop could be this lucrative."

Squeezing her hand, Damian gave it another tug and they began walking again. "It isn't. I mean, the pay is better than most jobs, but you're right, it wouldn't get you a place like this." They walked down the long arched concrete stairway that opened up to the pool. "I never became a cop for the money, Bethany," he explained. "And it was never a goal of mine to live in a place like this. I don't need all this, but Mace has always made it a point to say the family business is the *family's* business, regardless if some of us are not as involved as Dimitri is. He insists on everyone getting their share. Even me and Dominic, who have the least to do with the reality show or even just the shop. I tried protesting for years. Telling him I didn't think it was fair, since Mitri was the one doing all the work, but he says he started this business before any of us were born, and he always said every penny would go to his kids no matter the circumstances. If it weren't for the nature of my job, I'd make appearances on the show myself. Because of my age, it was a real challenge to prove that I was ready to make detective. They have nothing they can use against me. I've followed the rules to the letter from day one, but even going on the show could give them something to hold against me."

"Why?" Bethany asked, staring at him very seriously. "What's so bad about going on the show? They do a lot for charity, right?"

"Yeah, but you've seen it, right?" He laughed, though he didn't feel all that much humor. "They go at it pretty bad sometimes. A lot of bleeping this and bleeping that and even throwing stuff around. That temper of Dimitri's is no act. It's stupid, but even something that small could be held against me. I just don't want to give those assholes *any* ammunition. Most of my coworkers don't even know I'm related to Desert Heat," he said, shrugging and hoping she got the most important point. He didn't want her thinking him a mooch, which was what he had felt like for a long time. "I do take care of all the security for both the show and the Ratz. A lot of retired cops or even current deputies do security on the side. I set my family up with only the most trustworthy applicants, and the ones who don't come straight from the force, I take care of running all the backgrounds." Looking out into his big backyard, he couldn't help but frown, because he still didn't think he did enough to deserve his lifestyle. "None of my siblings or myself have a greedy or selfish bone in our bodies. So we all get our share every month and that's that. As you can see, our shares are pretty significant, and I needed to start investing it. Uncle Sam was killing me. And I've invested pretty well."

They reached the bottom and started toward the poolside bar. Even though he didn't think Bethany was anything like Fina said most girls were, he refrained from telling her about those investments—his many other properties. Including an entire development of townhomes he had recently closed escrow on.

He wasn't refraining from telling her because his sister had warned him and his brothers again and again about letting women know how much they were worth; he did it because she already seemed a bit overwhelmed. Judging by her tiny apartment in that horrid part of town, she was obviously not used to any of this. He'd have to wean her into his lifestyle slowly. It was also why he cut the explanation of his mother's death short, too. Saying she'd been on a charter plane was one thing. But telling her it was their family's private jet was another.

He flipped a switch when they got to the bar, and the water mists turned on immediately, cooling them down. "Oh, that feels so good," Bethany said, not moving away from the perfect spot where the mist showered her.

He clicked another button, and the electric awning started out from the top of the bar area and slowly began shading half the pool. "That's the only way we'll be able to be out here today or we'll fry under this sun."

She nodded, staring at the moving awning, and he wondered if already he'd overwhelmed her. "You okay?"

Turning to him, a bit surprised, she smiled. "Yeah."

He pulled her to him, hoping to get a few last moments alone with her; he kissed her again then stared at her for a moment. "You're so damn beautiful."

"Thank you," she responded, then smiled timidly, bringing his hand to her chest, moistened by the mist. "I'm still trying to get used to how a few words from you can make my heart beat so frantically."

Just the touch of her wet skin had him feeling frantic, too. He was about to tell her so when the splash of someone jumping into the water interrupted him. He turned to make sure someone hadn't fallen in, but saw Dimitri pop up from the water, then looked up at the stairs to see the rest of the gang from the shop, including the Ratz and some of their girls, coming down the steps, all of them in swim gear and most holding boxes of beer or some kind of alcohol.

To his surprise, because his friend had never responded to the text telling him about his sudden Rockies barbecue party, he saw Jerry with a woman he didn't recognize and his bikini-clad daughter on their way down as well. Suddenly a bit unnerved, Damian still couldn't get over how oblivious Jerry was to his daughter's being extreme jailbait. This was already starting to look like an adult pool drinking party, with far more guys than girls, and he'd brought his overly developed sixteen-year-old daughter to it wearing *that*. But that wasn't the only reason he felt unnerved.

"You gonna get that barbecue going or what?" Dimitri asked, swimming up to the side of the pool nearest Damian and Bethany. "Hi, beautiful." Dimitri shook his head with a smirk, like the ass that he was, pretending it had slipped again. "I mean Bethany."

"I didn't know everyone was getting here so early," Damian said, slipping his hand into Bethany's after she said hello, making sure she didn't feel obligated to acknowledge his obnoxious brother's comment. "The game doesn't start until one."

"Yeah, but we wanted to get our swim in first," Dimitri said, dipping his head back into the water. "I brought some stuff you can throw on the barbie, too. Everyone did, actually."

Walking away and toward Jerry, because his brother had already disappeared back underwater, Damian turned to Bethany, feeling the tiniest bit weird. "You remember Jerry from the speed date?"

Nodding and smiling, she focused on Jerry, still too far away to hear them. "Yes, yes, Jerry. I'm *very* fond of Jerry, actually."

Damian stopped walking and stared at her. "What?"

"Well, if it wasn't for him I wouldn't be here with you, right?" Her smile teased him. "I owe him big time."

Sliding his hand around her waist firmly, he kissed her. "No. You don't owe him shit. But let's go say hi and do the reintroductions. I wasn't even sure he was gonna be here today."

They walked over to where Jerry stood by a couple of the lounging chairs with both girls. "Hey, Jer. I see you got my text."

"Yeah, and it was perfect timing, because I was just trying to figure out what we were gonna do today."

He turned to the unassuming brunette standing next to him and introduced her as Janis. Glad Jerry didn't give her a label of any kind, he left out the "my girlfriend" part when asking him if he remembered Bethany. He could tell Jerry was very surprised about how different she looked now, compared to the way she'd looked at that speed date. "Wow, I would've never recognized you."

He watched, maybe a bit too closely, as Bethany explained how she'd been in costume that night. It wasn't that he expected to see any sparks, but he still wanted to be sure. Satisfied that he saw absolutely none, he turned to Ashlynn. He began to introduce her to Bethany as the girl removed her sarong revealing her very tiny bikini bottom, which matched the equally revealing top. "Damian," she said, smiling coyly, the lashes already doing their thing. "I didn't mean to keep you up so late last night."

That got Bethany's attention instantly, and she turned to Ashlynn, then back to Damian. "This is Jerry's daughter, Bethany," he said quickly. "Ashlynn, this is Bethany. And don't worry about last night. You did the right thing calling me."

Not even sure if Ashlynn and Bethany had acknowl-
edged each other, Damian had the sudden urge to walk
away. "Make yourselves at home," he said, patting Jerry on
the shoulder. "I'm gonna go grab the stuff to get the grub
going."

"Let me know if you need any help," Jerry offered as Damian walked away with Bethany.

"She kept you up last night?" Bethany asked immediately.

"Not really, I was already up anyway." He turned to her,
wondering if he should tell her everything or just the need-
to-know stuff. Damian was all for complete honesty, but this
was the kind of thing Bethany *did not* need to know. "She
went out last night and I guess Jer had a date, too. Her date
got drunk. Jerry's made her promise to call him if that ever
happened instead of getting into a car with a drunk driver,
but she couldn't get hold of him, so she called me." Bethany's
sexy but suspicious little eyebrow had been up the entire time
he explained. "I was on my way home from the station, so
of course I picked her up and took her home. She's only sixteen," he added the last part hoping it would soften Bethany's
still-apprehensive stare.

Clearly it didn't, because she didn't seem at all satisfied
with that explanation. "She said she kept you up," she reminded him.

"Yeah, well, she's a little like Carey and your sister," he
said with a short chuckle, eager to lighten the mood as they
reached the top of the stairs. "Even after I got her home, she
went on and on talking for a while."

"Really?" Bethany didn't look or sound at all amused. "So
what did she have so much to talk to you about?"

Damian followed Bethany's eyes as she glanced back at
Ashlynn, the sixteen- going on twenty-five-year-old vixen
lying on the lounge chair rubbing suntan lotion on her long

legs. Most of the guys around her seemed to be trying but failing miserably not to gawk. "She's a long story, babe," Damian said as their eyes met again. "I'll have to tell you about her another time. All I know is Jerry's got his hands full with that one."

Bethany still didn't seem at all satisfied with that, but she didn't press further. Maybe he would just tell her the whole truth. It might actually be better. He thought about Ashlynn's being bullied, and judging by the way she'd fluttered her lashes at him even while he stood there holding Bethany's hand, she was probably a lot more like her mom than Jerry would ever admit. He knew what Bethany must be thinking. She was partly right. Ashlynn had laid it on thick, very possibly in the hope of causing some friction, but not for the reasons he was sure Bethany was thinking.

Carey was already in her bathing suit when they got into the house. Fina was spraying sunscreen on her. "Get that on good," Damian said as they walked into the room. "It's blazing out there. Mitri's already in the pool. Have him make sure she stays under the shade."

Immediately, Carey started up. "I can swim all the way to the deep side now without my floaties," she informed them all. "And I can float for a long time." She turned to Fina. "Huh, Mommy? You can time me, Uncle Damian. My longest is almost a minute."

His niece was off and running, but that seemed to change Bethany's mood. Bethany smiled at Carey's excited babble, seemingly forgetting, at least for the moment, Ashlynn's fluttering lashes. She even stayed in the family room chatting with Carey as Damian went into the kitchen.

Gathering all the stuff he needed to take outside, he cursed under his breath about this unexpected twist to what should've been a pleasant day with Bethany, even with the entire gang there. Ashlynn had an agenda, and he might just have to let Bethany in on it before she misinterpreted her actions. Damian was *not* planning on dealing with this shit today. He'd wondered about it after he left Ashlynn last night, but now he was sure of it. He'd fucked up, and this could be *bad*.

CHAPTER 16

The giant inflatable turtle finally made its way into the pool, and Carey happily hopped onto it. Bethany had helped her inflate it. The entire time she'd heard *all* about Carey's own five mini musk turtles, not to be mistaken for the slider-type turtles, because those were not really minis, just baby turtles that actually grow big and usually die very quickly—they found out the hard way. After her rather long tutorial on turtles and how to tell the difference between musk and baby slider types, Bethany had been able to get away for a moment to change into her own two-piece bathing suit.

His sister was everything Bethany had expected, tall, thin, and *very* pretty. Her medium-length wavy hair was highlighted and complemented her perfectly tanned skin. Bethany didn't even have to wonder. She was certain it was a natural tan. Yep. Another native of the planet Just Not Fair. But to her relief, she'd been just as easy to talk to as Damian and his brothers. Bethany had expected his older "mother hen" sister to be a bit snooty. That couldn't have been further from the truth.

And Damian definitely hadn't exaggerated about Carey's being a chatterbox. Fina had actually told her to take a breath a few times, which she did very dramatically, then she'd start right back up again. Fina had also more than once shaken her head at Bethany apologetically. Bethany didn't mind. She thought Carey was adorable, but that mouth of hers was a bit of a loose cannon. To her mother's dismay, she'd let Bethany in on a few things. One: She'd be an excellent flower girl *if Bethany ever needed one*. Two: Her mommy said all her uncles were *comittyfolic*, which, after explaining it meant they could never have just one girlfriend for very long before getting a new one, Bethany realized meant *commitment phobic*. Bethany thought that was interesting, considering how quickly Damian had brought up the whole subject of committing and exclusivity.

Last, but most disturbing, and this came so out of nowhere that Bethany had been left speechless: Uncle Dominic's mom was not her grandma, and she was so sad she took a lot of sleeping pills so she'd never have to wake up again, and that's why she was in heaven now.

That's when Fina had finally pulled the plug. She'd changed the subject quickly, and they'd all headed out to the pool. Carey's unexpected announcement about Dominic's mom explained a little about why, in what appeared to be such a tight-knit family, he chose to live so far away, but Bethany dared not ask further details about something so personal.

Bethany joined Fina and Carey in the pool. The water felt heavenly, and Damian told her he'd join her just as soon as he got the meat on the grill. He and his brothers would take turns watching the grill, so he could relax, too. She'd only been in the water for a few minutes when she noticed Ashlynn walk over to the grill and talk to Damian. He'd looked up in her direction, and their eyes had met a few times.

The fact that someone as young as Ashlynn could be attracted to Damian didn't surprise her. What *had* surprised her was how nervous Damian had become when explaining Ashlynn's comment about keeping him up late last night. Even now, as Ashlynn leaned on the island around the grill, flashing Damian her overly developed sixteen-year-old cleavage, he appeared a bit unnerved. Bethany had a feeling she knew what Damian had meant when he'd said Jerry had his hands full with Ashlynn.

Bethany was no stranger to premature overdevelopment. She and her sister had both been cursed with developing far too early. But unlike Ashlynn, who clearly enjoyed flaunting it, Bethany remembered trying to hide hers. She'd been tormented in middle school by the immaturity of the thirteen-year-old boys who'd dubbed her "Turbo Tits" very early on. Stella was worse, constantly cursing her overly developed curves.

She watched as Damian closed the grill, said something to Diego, who stood nearby, then something to Ashlynn, before walking away toward the pool. There was no hiding the disappointment on Ashlynn's face, as she kept her eyes on Damian even as he removed his shirt. Bethany's focus was immediately on Damian's chiseled abs and amazing chest. He jumped into the pool, and Bethany took the moment he was underwater to snap out of her stupor and glance back up at Ashlynn, who smiled at her strangely before lifting her brow and looking away. The fact that she was a sixteen-year-old minor didn't lessen her irritation with girl. Bethany knew her type already. She'd been around plenty of girls like her back in school, the girls who had no qualms about flirting with the young but adult school narks and even teachers if they were attractive enough.

Damian's head popped up from the water, and he swam up to Bethany, immediately kissing her. It wasn't any different from how he had been all day, but Bethany sensed his unease.

Feeling his hands glide all over her underwater took a little from the tension that had begun to develop inside her. She glanced back and noticed sweet little Ashlynn was watching them, so she wrapped her legs around him, cupping his face in her hands, and kissed him very thoroughly. As juvenile as she felt for even thinking it, she hoped to squash any ideas or fantasies running through that girl's head about Damian—her boyfriend. She came up for air sooner than she wanted, because she had to be mindful that they weren't alone in that pool, but she did smile sinfully, licking her lips.

"Wow," Damian said, staring at her. "I would've jumped in sooner if I knew this was how I'd be greeted."

Without letting her respond, he devoured her mouth again, this time pulling them both lower into the water, where his big hands roamed her entire body, even squeezed her behind gently over her bikini bottom. With her mind now completely off Ashlynn, her heart pumped, and all she could think of as he sucked her tongue was how she wished to God they were alone.

Carey's squealing made them finally pull apart for a moment. They both turned to see Dimitri on the other side of the pool spinning the giant turtle around while Carey held on for dear life, giggling loudly. "Keep her in the shade," Damian said loudly, pulling Bethany to him and wrapping his arms around her middle.

They were both facing Dimitri and the others now but were far enough away that Bethany gave in to the urge to press up against the very solid confirmation that Damian had been just as quickly aroused as she'd been. It made her heart beat even faster, and her burning insides begged for time alone now. She should be ashamed of the utter temptation she had to lower her hand and stroke him even if it was just over his shorts. Instead she rubbed her ass up against it; the sensation alone was enough to make her tremble.

"Stop that," he whispered in her ear, but moved his hand down, his fingers just under the top front of her bikini bottom. "I'm already gonna be stuck in here for a while."

Running her hands down over his big hard arms until they reached the tip of his fingers, she fought the urge to push his hand lower. *God*, she wanted him so bad. If they'd been alone, she would've already pulled her bottoms off and straddled him right there in the pool. She'd known since yesterday just the feel of his hard, near-naked body against hers would be enough to get her going, but his hand this close to her pulsating need for him had her squeezing her eyes shut and gulping hard.

"Hey, Damian," Diego called out from the grill. "Do I just flip these over?"

"Yeah." Damian pulled his hand away from her bikini. "Lower the fire, too. Mitri can take the next shift."

"Nah," Dimitri countered. "I'm on Carey duty."

"*Shit*," Damian muttered, pulling away from Bethany.

"I got it," Fina said, headed toward the stairs of the pool already.

Carey called out for Bethany and Damian to come hang on her giant turtle. They started toward her, though Damian took a quick swim to the other end of the pool before coming back and meeting them. Bethany bit into her bottom lip, visualizing him adjusting himself again as he'd done Friday night.

After relieving Dimitri from *the duty*, Bethany proceeded to get the inquisition Damian had promised she would get from Carey. About fifteen minutes later, and as Damian very noticeably kept his hands to himself, mostly playing and spinning Carey around, it was apparently safe to step out. Damian said he wanted to check his pork tenderloin. When

Carey protested that she wanted Bethany to stay with her, Damian insisted Bethany needed a break from the water, and a drink. This was true, but Bethany couldn't shake the feeling he didn't want to be caught alone with Ashlynn again. More than gladly, she stepped out with him firmly attached at her hand. Carey stayed back, with Diego now taking on the duty.

On their walk toward the bar area and the barbecue, they heard someone yell out, asking Dimitri where he was going. Bethany and Damian turned at the same time to see Dimitri and Ashlynn headed up the stairs. Bethany turned back just as the unmistakable irritation swept over Damian's face. His jaw even worked as he waited for Dimitri's answer, which was that he'd be right back down.

"Something wrong?" she asked, determined not to jump to conclusions.

Damian turned back to her with a strained smile, shaking his head, but otherwise didn't address her question. As they reached the bar, he walked around it, and Bethany pulled out a stool on the other side.

"What do you feel like drinking?" he asked. "We have everything. Mixed drinks, wine, beer. What's your poison?"

Ignoring how her insides had gone tense over his reaction to seeing Dimitri walk away with Ashlynn, Bethany decided a drink was exactly what she needed. "Hmm." She thought about it as she sat down across the bar from him.

He reached over and opened the full-sized, stainless-steel fridge. "Well, shit. Someone brought readymade drinks." He pulled out a pitcher with a pink drink in it and read the label. "Pink Panty Droppers." With an evil smirk, he glanced back at her. "Maybe you should try some of this."

Matching his evil smirk, she nodded. "Sounds good, but if the drink is supposed to serve a purpose, I'll tell you right now, I don't need it."

His eyes widened for a moment, and he glanced up at one of the screens mounted on the walls of the bar. "Fourth inning," he said, pulling a glass out for her, pouring her the drink, and setting it in front of her. "As soon as this game is over, I'm kicking everybody out."

Bethany laughed, picking up the glass. She had a nagging feeling about the whole Ashlynn thing; her gut told her it wasn't anything she needed to worry about, but still she didn't like how uncomfortable it made her.

Jerry and Janis, a girl he'd apparently met at the speed date, joined them at the bar. Bethany made small take with Janis, as Damian and Jerry discussed the game. Ashlynn came over to ask Jerry for the keys to the car at one point, so she could get something from it. Bethany kept a close eye but noticed how little flaunting she did in front of her dad. Damian had seemed unnerved again, and he all but ignored her, keeping his eyes on the TV monitor the entire few minutes she stood there. It was all a little too weird for her to disregard.

As the day went on Damian and Bethany had gone back into the pool a few times. Each time they'd been "stuck" in there for a while because their touching and rubbing underwater had gotten a bit out of hand again.

Fina and Carey were the first to leave, and though Bethany could see just where Carey had picked up her interrogation skills, Fina wasn't nearly as bad as Damian had warned her she'd be. Bethany had managed to dodge some of the questions that might've had her embellishing or even lying a little.

When Dimitri left, he announced to Damian's obvious annoyance that he was giving Ashlynn a ride home, since Jerry and Janis were hanging out for a while longer. Finally, about an hour after that, Jerry and Janis, the last to leave, drove away.

Bethany had planned on just letting the whole Ashlynn thing go, because she didn't want anything ruining the time she'd finally get alone with Damian. But after a few more uncomfortable Ashlynn moments, she decided she needed to get one thing straight first.

"So what's the deal with you and Ashlynn?" she asked straight out, as she took a seat on the big comfy sectional in Damian's family room.

Damian walked up to the armless sectional, pushing the pieces together, and she saw that the pieces that served as footrests actually could come together and turn the sectional into a huge bed. "Lift your legs," he said as he moved another flat piece toward her.

She lifted her legs onto the flat piece, and he pushed it against the sofa she'd been sitting on, so she was now sitting on what had come together as a bedlike sofa.

"There is no deal with me and Ashlynn," Damian informed her as he slid in next to her, sideways, lifting himself up on an elbow. "She's Jerry's sixteen-year-old daughter who thinks she's found the answer to all her problems."

Bethany stared at him, waiting, but when he didn't go on, she gave him a look, tilting her head. "Well, you can't just leave me with that, Damian." She paused for a moment as she watched his fingers caress her leg in a circular motion, moving slowly up to her knee. Feeling the excitement with just that simple touch, she knew she couldn't beat around the bush. She looked straight into those sexy bedroom eyes, which were already looking at her in a way that made her breathe a little deeper, and decided to be completely honest. "Something about her makes me uncomfortable. I know she's young, and you would never—"

"It's not what you're thinking, Bethany," he said, his fingers moving further up her leg. "I thought the same thing."

"That she wants you?" Bethany asked, making sure he knew *exactly* what she was thinking.

He nodded, moving his hand off her leg for a moment to reach for the pillow behind Bethany. Placing it behind her, he whispered, "Lie down."

Staring at him, she realized she was beginning to feel the very thing she'd felt the night he'd shown up at her show—utterly captivated. She needed to snap out of it, because she needed answers first. Still, she did as he asked and lay back, unable to break the eye contact she was now locked into. "So what is it?" Finally, the feel of his fingers back on her legs, only higher up now, made her close her eyes. "I need to know, Damian. I didn't like the vibe I got from her today when she was around you."

"She's not interested in me, babe," he assured her as his fingers moved slowly up her thigh. "She's interested in Dimitri."

The slight change in his tone made her open her eyes. "And that bothers you?"

"It does," he admitted, to her surprise, and it almost made her sit up, but she didn't. She continued to stare at him, trying to concentrate on his words, but his fingers moving in small slow circles further up her leg made it nearly impossible. "I think she's bad news, and I don't want my brother getting into any trouble. She's also a minor, remember?"

"But the way she looks at you—"

"She doesn't want me, Bethany. I'm certain of that, but she *did* make me a proposition last night."

Now Bethany began to try to sit up, but Damian held her down, pulling his body half over her, pinning one of her arms under him and lacing his hand through her other hand, holding it down next to her head. "I knew it—"

"Shh!" he said, kissing her softly. "It's not at all what you're thinking, and it's such a nonissue, if it hadn't been for the way she behaved today, making it obvious to you that something was up, I hadn't planned on telling you at all."

"Telling me what?" she demanded.

Again she tried moving, but she was no match for his strong body pressed against her. It really should've made her mad, furious even, yet shamefully, feeling certain hard parts of his body pressed against her was turning her on.

He stared deep into her eyes with those heavy-lidded bedroom eyes she was certain he knew drove her crazy. "Last night Ashlynn asked me if I was lonely."

Bethany squirmed under him, not just because of the jealousy that suddenly consumed her at knowing that baby whore had been alone with *her* man and obviously she *did* want him, but because he just admitted he had had no intention of telling her. "And you weren't going to tell me this?"

"No," he said, moving over her even more now and holding her hand down as he licked her bottom lip. "She wanted to know if I was tired of my single bachelor lifestyle."

Bethany turned her face so his lips wouldn't touch hers anymore, because she was officially pissed now. "Get off me, Damian. I don't even wanna know what the hell her proposition was. From the way she behaved around you today clearly you didn't turn her down flat."

Damian moved, and for a second she thought he might be moving off her. Instead he brought his big body entirely over hers now, pressing the massive hard-on this conversation had apparently given him against her. He took her other hand and held it down, too, rendering her immobile. As much as she knew that this should piss her off even more, his pressing himself between her legs made her breath catch. "She's trying to set me up with her mom, sweetheart." He leaned down and kissed her hard, then sucked her bottom lip before pulling away. "The whole reason she ran away and is living with Jerry now is that she hates her mom's boyfriend. I guess her mom told her once upon a time she found me attractive, and her mom and Jerry have never even gotten along. So she thought maybe if she could convince *me* to hook up with her mom that would get rid of her mom's boyfriend."

She stared at him, not sure how she felt about this, but she tried desperately to concentrate on everything he'd just said, because the way he'd begun to sway his hips, rubbing his erection—that felt bigger now against her—was a huge distraction.

"Her line of questioning last night caught me off-guard, okay?"

The emphasis on that last word had her attention. He sounded nervous—guilty. Any growing anticipation about what might happen between them in the next few minutes was squashed. *"And?"*

"I thought the very same thing you were thinking before she brought up her mom. That she was coming on to me. I panicked. So I may've gone a little overboard telling her just how much I enjoyed my single bachelor life. How much I wanted it to stay that way." He stopped and searched her eyes for a moment, all the passion replaced with what almost looked like fear. "I didn't even mention you or that I had a girlfriend. I'm sorry."

This is what had him feeling guilty? That at a moment like that he hadn't thought of telling this underage girl, who was in no way entitled to an explanation of his personal life, about his brand-new girlfriend?

Unable to touch his face, because he was still holding her hands down, she smiled. "Kiss me."

A very relieved smile replaced the fear in his eyes, and he kissed her deeply. Continuing to make love to her mouth, he took some of the pressure off, though she hadn't minded it at all, by going back to his original position, lying next to her rather than on her. He let go of her hand as well and brought his hand down to her thigh again, making her tremble.

His fingers glided up and down the inside of her thigh, and that alone had her breathing harder. She moved away from his lips to catch her breath for a moment, and his mouth slipped down her jaw, kissing and sucking as she let her head fall back to give him full access to her neck. He moaned with each suck of her very tender neck. As he began sucking harder it made her tingle in the very part of her body that yearned for his fingers to move a little higher, and she began to squirm.

"Did you mean what you said today?" he whispered breathlessly against her neck, "or were you just—"

"No," she said sharply, knowing exactly what he was talking about. Swallowing hard, she moved his hand up between her legs, gasping when he immediately moved her bikini strap aside and slipped a finger in her. "I meant it," she said, instinctively lifting her hips as he slipped in a second finger.

She was so wet she should have been embarrassed, but it was all she could do to stop herself from moaning loudly as his fingers slipped in and out of her now, and he continued kissing and sucking her neck. She squeezed her eyes shut, her entire body trembling wildly. His thumb worked that magical place that might have her screaming soon if he didn't slow down. Gasping again suddenly, but this time from the disappointment as his fingers pulled out and his mouth moved away from her neck, she opened her eyes and watched him bring his fingers to his mouth.

He licked one clean then sucked it for a moment. "Delicious," he said with a sinful grin, and the burning desire in those sexy eyes of his had her nearly exploding. He brought his other finger to her lips, spreading all of her own juices on them, then kissed her, licking and sucking on her lips so hard it hurt, but in such a good way it made her moan with pleasure. She'd never been so close to coming from just a kiss, but then she'd never tasted herself on someone else's tongue before. It felt very erotic, and if he continued to suck her mouth as intensely as he did now she just might.

Once again she gasped as he pulled away from her mouth and began to pull off the short mesh cover-up she'd thrown over her bikini. Feeling almost frantic with anticipation, she sat up a bit, helping him pull it off, then pulled his T-shirt off, too. Just as she had in the pool all day, she ran her fingers over his hard chest and muscles, then kissed his shoulder. But, unable to stand it anymore, she wrapped her arms around his neck and pulled him back down with her.

Kissing her roughly again, he sucked her lips and tongue harder than before. The shameful noises she made now surprised even her, but it seemed to turn him on, because his kiss became even more frenzied. His hand moved down, and he slipped his fingers in her again, pushing in deep this time. Gasping for air, she arched her back, and she felt the sudden emptiness as he pulled his fingers out of her again. In the next second she had both his tongue and his fingers in her mouth, the taste of her own juices turning her on so much, she grabbed his hand, sucking and licking his fingers clean as he watched her in awe.

Groaning, he lifted himself over her, his entire body pressing against her again as he pulled her bikini top up, exposing her breasts. He sucked one hard as he massaged the other and pinched her nipple, making her yelp with pleasure. "Beautiful," he said as he pulled away to stare down at them, then into her eyes.

Just like everything she'd felt from the beginning with him, this kind of arousal was something completely new to her. She'd been with her first boyfriend enough to know what horny felt like. But she'd never had the urge to beg someone to just fuck her already, and it dawned on her that this, too, could be something new Damian brought out in her, because she felt a desperate need to have him in her *now*.

He sucked her breasts softly, then so sharply she felt it all the way down to the very part of her body that ached for his touch. Bethany finally gave in to the pleasure, and she cried out loudly, making him suck harder. The sensation was unbelievable. The only other times she'd felt even close to the frantic need she felt now were the few times their kisses had gotten really heavy.

She ran her fingers through his hair, moaning each time he sucked her nipples a bit harder, at times fisting chunks of his hair in her hands. He moved slowly, raining soft kisses down her belly, until she felt him tug on her bikini. Kissing the area just above her bikini bottom, he began pulling it down slowly. His kisses moved down as her bottom did, and her already wild heart sped up. If he kept moving this slowly, she was going to scream; she could hardly stand it anymore.

Once her bikini bottom was down to her knees, mercifully he pulled it the rest of the way off with a yank, leaving her trembling with eagerness. With another fast move, he startled her as he pulled both her legs, sliding her almost to the edge of the sofa. Surprising her again, he didn't just spread her legs as she'd anticipated; he pulled one leg over each of his shoulders, her ass completely in the air, and his face right there. His hands caressed her behind as he leaned in, and his lips kissed her softly, making her lift her behind even higher, shamelessly, *needing* more of his mouth on her.

Taking that cue, he sank his tongue into her, his hands squeezing her ass and lifting her even higher; then he ran them up and down the sides of her quivering thighs.

"Oh, my *Gawd*!" Bethany's eyes watered from the pleasure. She had never known a body could react to pleasure like this.

As he continued to fuck her with his tongue, he slid his hands up the outside of her thighs, past her waist, until they reached her breasts, and he squeezed gently.

She squeezed her hands over his, showing him how hard she wanted him to squeeze them, and he did. Seeing her arch her back in reaction and gasp in ecstasy, he lifted his hands away from her breasts and laced them with her hands instead, just as he began to suck, making her moan and squeeze his hands in reaction. Each time he swirled his tongue and sucked, making her feel like she was that close to bursting, he'd pull back, unlatching those perfect lips from her throbbing, aching *need*.

As slowly as he'd done everything else, and as much as she could tell he was trying to take his time, she now sensed the urgency had picked up for him as well. Latching on again to that perfect spot, he sucked more intensely now, his tongue moving in a perfect rhythm as the quivering buildup to her climax increased.

Unable to keep from swaying her ass along with the movement of his tongue, she began to moan louder and louder as everything she'd been thinking of all week, all day, finally peaked, and now she cried out his name, squeezing his hands as current after current of pleasure shot through her body.

Even though he was sucking her more softly now, she still couldn't stand another second, and she squirmed, trying to turn to the side. He finally pulled away, letting her bring her thighs off his shoulders, and she sat up and hugged him. She wrapped her arms around his neck tightly, her body still feeling the sensations pulsating through her. Then he kissed her, his lips very warm and wet, that now-familiar taste of herself in her mouth again. Never in a million years had she thought that would turn her on so much. But at the same time, she got the distinct feeling it wasn't so much what he did to her or the eroticism of it all, but, like everything else she'd experienced since she met Damian, it was what she was feeling *because* of him. *Indescribable* was all she could think. From the very beginning. She felt as excited about being a dirty girl for him now as she had when she'd watched him sweetly kiss her knuckles one by one.

Getting up on her knees quickly, she sucked his lips, his tongue, and all around his mouth, wanting to lick every bit of it off him. He groaned, squeezing her ass with both hands, molding and spreading as he continued to kiss her frantically. It amazed her that even though her body had felt spent just a moment ago, kissing him like this got her going again that quickly. They were both on their knees now as they kissed wildly, his hand running up and down one side of her naked body. His other hand worked on pulling his wallet out of his trunks' side pocket. Right then she realized he wasn't naked yet, and she wasn't having that.

Her hands were instantly on the rope tied at the front of his trunks, and she began easily undoing the knot. Her heartbeat nearly doubled at the sight of his huge erection. The thin material of his shorts did nothing to hide what nearly burst out. She'd felt it and rubbed it all day in the pool, but seeing the bulge now made her nearly gasp.

Seeing him toss his wallet on the floor and rip open the condom packet, she knew what he'd been digging so desperately in his pocket for. "You sure about this?" he asked, bringing his hand behind her neck.

"Yes!" was her quick and only response as she began sucking his lips again.

He squeezed her ass hard, groaning in her mouth. "You

have the sweetest ass I've ever seen," he said against her lips. "And, damn, I can't wait to flip you over and take you from behind, but this first time I wanna look in your eyes when it happens."

Bethany was convinced now. It was Damian that made all the difference. She and her horny teenage boyfriend had tried just about every position, but never once had she felt what she did just hearing Damian say what he wanted to do to her. "I can't wait for you to take me every way you want to."

With another loud groan, Damian pulled her down with him and then rolled on top of her, spreading her legs. "Ready to be mine in every way?" he asked as he rolled on the condom faster and easier than she'd ever seen it done.

She nodded eagerly, feeling even more excited now, and a bit nervous at the same time. Since her only experience had been with her equally inexperienced, first and only boyfriend ever, they'd fumbled through all of it. Damian was by far superior to her only other experience in every way. Though she suspected he was superior to most, not just her fumbling first boyfriend. But one other thing had her heart beating nearly through her chest. Damian was also *much* bigger than her teenage boyfriend.

Slipping a finger in her, he smiled. "Yeah, you're ready." He glanced up at her with an evil grin, rubbing himself against her wet, eager opening. "You want this?"

"Yes, *please*," she said with an urgency she'd never felt before.

He squeezed his eyes shut with a groan. "Please what, baby?"

Their eyes locked for a moment. She should be mad he was doing this, but as usual she felt more aroused than she ever had in her life. "Please fuck me," she whispered.

"What was that?" he asked, rubbing her right on the perfect spot with his erection, and as good as that felt she wanted him—needed him in her *now*. "Fuck me, Damian, please!" she begged.

Groaning even louder, he lowered his body onto her, and she felt him begin to enter her as his lips reached hers. He kissed her softly as he pushed in farther. Feeling the stretch and even slight burn as he went even deeper, he suddenly stopped and pulled away from her lips. "This isn't your first time, is it?"

"No." She shook her head, spreading a little more for him. "But it's been a while," she gulped. "Like since high school. Don't stop . . ." And since he obviously liked hearing her beg, she added, "*please*."

His eyes went a little wide, then he kissed her again and slid farther in, but more slowly now. She could feel he'd gone a little tense, so she ran her hands over his big arms and shoulders, reassuring him he wasn't hurting her, especially since he'd gone past the burning part, and having him inside her nearly all the way felt amazing.

She lifted her hips, wanting him even deeper, and he complied, burying himself deep inside her. "God, that feels so good," she gasped as he began to speed up.

Lifting her hips, needing him to speed up even more, she panted loudly, mouth wide open, then bit his big hard shoulder in an effort not to scream out, it felt *that* good.

"You're so tight, baby," he said, lowering his face to her ear. "*You* feel so damn good, I can hardly stand it."

He sounded a bit panicked. "Do it, Damian," she said, running her fingers through his hair. "I wanna feel you come inside me."

"Stop," he urged, but slammed in and out faster and harder now.

"Do it!" she cried out, unbelievably feeling that she, too,

was close to exploding again with every stroke. "Make me yours in every way, baby. Please!"

"Damn it, Bethany," he grunted pumping into her a few more hard times until he lifted himself up away from her face with a harsh groan, drove in one last time *deep* into her, and held it there as he collapsed on her, his heart beating wildly against hers.

Make me yours . . . gulping back the slightest lingering of guilt, because she shouldn't feel guilty. Not the least bit. She wrapped her arms around his hard back, stroking his beautiful muscles. *Her* muscles. *Her* man now, because she'd just given herself to him in every way, and she had every right to enjoy this bliss.

CHAPTER 17

One pesky ray of bright sunlight directly in Damian's face was enough to force him to finally open his eyes. He'd been fighting it for a while, not wanting to move and possibly ruin the most perfect sleeping position he'd ever been in—sideways next to his beautifully naked girlfriend. Able to caress her warm body slowly from her bare back to her delicately soft yet very firm ass as she lay there on her stomach, her hair so close to his face every breath he inhaled was all her. That fragrance of her shampoo mixed with the lingering of her sunscreen and all the femininity that was the soft sweet scent of Bethany.

With one eye open now, squinting because of the sun, he scanned her body from top to bottom, bringing his hand over her naked behind. She looked peaceful and content; the expression she wore was a very satisfied, soft smile. He'd almost felt bad touching her because he might wake her—almost. Unable to take his hand away, he squeezed a perfect ass cheek gently. Immediately he felt his insides begin to heat. He'd already woken up hard, but realizing who was lying next to him, the intensity of it had doubled.

She shifted a tiny bit, and he stopped his squeezing until

he was sure she was still deep in her sleep. Moving carefully so as not to interrupt what appeared to be a very happy slumber, he inched his way downward until his face was just beside her behind, and he kissed one beautiful ass cheek while squeezing the other softly. Glancing up to see if she'd noticed or moved at all, he smiled when he saw she was still very deep in sleep.

Bringing his attention back to her beautiful ass, he kissed it again, this time sucking a little as his hand traveled down slowly between her legs. Just as his hand made it down to the warm opening between her legs, there was movement. He glanced up to see her sleepy eyes looking at him. With her teeth biting into her lower lip, she blinked in that slow-motion way she'd done so often during that first show that had floored him. Moving again, she spread her legs a little, lifting her behind just so, instantly jump-starting his breathing.

Taking a very deep breath, he turned back and bit her flesh just hard enough to make her squirm and moan; he released a carnal groan. Instantly he was on his knees, with one hand under her belly. He lifted her behind, his full-blown and ready erection already feeling the moisture between her legs. She was on her knees now, too, fisting the sheets in front of her and rubbing her ass against his throbbing hard-on.

"Jesus, Damian, no more torturing me. You did that enough last night. Just do it."

Bending quickly over the side of the bed, he grabbed one of the condom packs on the floor. After their initial first time yesterday, Damian had made sure that, each time after that, he took it real slow, making it last good and long, at times tormenting Bethany in the process. He ripped the pack open, feeling like a teenager as he fumbled to get a condom on as fast as possible, but Bethany's ass in the air was a hell of a distraction.

As soon as it was on, he grabbed hold of her hips and slammed in hard. Bethany's crying out in pleasure as she did only heightened his crazed arousal. He had had a feeling that being with her would be like this, but he had never anticipated feeling this kind of madness. Just hours ago they'd collapsed, completely drained, and he'd been certain they'd sleep late into the day, but from the moment his brain had awakened enough to remember who was lying beside him and all that they'd done last night and into the early morning hours, it was all he could do to keep his eyes closed and keep his hands to himself.

He'd also managed to draw out their lovemaking a few times last night. So much so that Bethany had accused him of teasing her for his pleasure. Partly true. Her panting and begging him not to stop or even slow down had been such a fucking turn-on that he'd actually enjoyed her agonized pleas, so much so that he'd been able to hold off a bit just to hear them longer. But this, this was his absolute weakness. Rocking into Bethany as he stared at her gorgeous ass would have him bursting in no time.

Yesterday hearing her beg him to make her his in every way had done him in the first time. Now, looking down as he spread her to watch himself slide in her sweet wetness had him grunting already. Her panting and crying out, then feeling her own throbbing was all it took. He slammed into her one last time, pulling her by the waist to him as he clenched his teeth and squeezed his eyes shut, releasing what felt like something he'd been holding in for years.

He drained into her, trying desperately to catch his breath, his profoundly satisfied body also drained of any strength. Once again just like last night, he felt completely spent and utterly satisfied.

Certain they could sleep for a few more hours after that,

he cleaned up and climbed back into bed next to Bethany's warm body. Last night he'd upped the air conditioner so high that cuddling now felt perfect. Damian spooned her, and she felt perfect in his arms, as if their bodies were made for each other.

He kissed the side of her face tenderly and then nuzzled his nose into her neck, where he knew he'd be able to sleep like a baby. "Mmm," she said, then sighed in complete contentment.

In the next second the words nearly escaped him, but he caught himself before saying them. Words that had his eyes wide open now. *I love you.*

So stunned at how close he'd been to saying them and how natural the thought had been, he hadn't even noticed he'd gone completely tense until she turned her head slightly. "Something wrong?"

Easing up a little, he tightened his hold of her. "No, not at all."

He felt her body ease up, too, and heard her sigh. "This feels so perfect," she said in a very sleepy voice.

"Yeah, it does," he whispered back, kissing the side of her face again.

For the next few minutes, as Bethany quickly fell back asleep, Damian lay there thinking about Bethany and what exactly his feelings for her were. He couldn't be in love already. Sure, he felt for her something he'd never felt for anyone before. He was certain of that now. But even though he'd begun to believe he might go his whole life happy being alone, he hadn't totally ruled out the possibility that he might meet someone who'd make him change his mind. Even if he'd never imagined that if and when that happened, things would move this fast, or that he'd fall this alarmingly hard, he'd never said never.

But love? He caught himself shaking his head and stopped

before he woke Bethany again. Love was an entirely different ballgame. He wouldn't overthink this. Bottom line was he'd begun to think that he was feeling for Bethany the way he was because it'd been a very long time since he'd felt *this* attracted to someone and even longer since he'd had to wait to seal the deal all the way. He'd reasoned that as soon as he did it with Bethany, it would alleviate the intensity of what he felt for her. Now that he knew that wasn't the case—now that it felt as if it'd only stepped it up more—he was confused.

So everything up until now had come together a lot faster than the norm. His being in love this soon was out of the question. He'd already risked scaring her off by demanding exclusivity so quickly. Even if she had repeated his words last night. The ones he *had* let slip: *ready to be mine in every way?* Hell, she'd begged him to do it. It could've all been in the heat of passion. Damian wasn't about to risk really scaring her away by jumping the gun on this, too.

He closed his eyes, holding Bethany even tighter, never wanting to let go now. With his heart already beginning to argue that love wasn't out of the question, his father's cheesy catchphrase suddenly came to mind. *You better slow your roll.*

Half asleep, Damian let his hand roam around with his eyes still closed and came up with nothing but an empty mattress next to him. That was what ultimately woke him. He glanced around the now bright but empty bedroom, wondering if maybe Bethany had left. She couldn't have. He'd driven her here. Pulling his legs off the side of the bed, he bent over for his trunks. Just as he'd begun to pull them on, he was relieved to hear her voice. It was distant, so after pulling up his trunks, he stood completely quiet and confirmed hers was the only voice speaking, so obviously she was on the phone, but what she was saying, he could barely make out.

". . . I'm working," her voice either lowered or she walked away farther, because the rest of what she said was a mumble. Damian started toward the door. Sleeping with her had definitely heightened what he felt for Bethany, or maybe his feeling of entitlement, because the unease he'd felt yesterday when he'd heard her tone down her relationship with him was a slow-boiling annoyance now. Had she really just told someone she was working instead of admitting where and with whom she was?

". . . not now I can't, but tonight for sure."

Instead of standing there eavesdropping as he was tempted to, Damian decided to walk out into the front room, where her voice seemed to be coming from. As soon as he opened the door, he was surprised to see she wasn't even inside. She'd stepped out onto the patio.

Even though Bethany smiled as soon as she saw him, Damian hadn't missed how her head had jerked in his direction when he opened the door. He managed to smile back, but just barely, as he walked toward her. As much as he had every intention of not jumping to conclusions and giving her the benefit of the doubt, it was already pissing him off that she turned away and lowered her voice.

He opened the patio door, and she turned, lifting her hand for him to give her a second, then turned her back on him again. "I gotta go now, okay. Yes, tonight."

He'd give her a second or longer if she needed it, but he wasn't leaving, if that's what she thought. Wrapping his arms around her waist from behind, he noticed how she stiffened. As much as that, too, made him wonder what the hell her sister was asking about now that she couldn't talk about until tonight, he still tried to shake the unease and leaned in to kiss her neck. This time he was asking her straight out the second she was off the phone. No more dicking around.

This close, he heard the other person on the phone, and it wasn't her sister. It was a *guy*. "Okay, tonight then. I'm really looking forward to it, Bethany."

Damian yanked his head back.

"I am, too. Bye." She turned to him as soon as she was off the phone.

"Who was that?"

This was another first for Damian. He'd never felt anything like what he was feeling at that moment, as he stared at her, his heart pounding as it always did when he was around her, but for an altogether different reason now. It had actually been a chore to refrain from cussing and asking her who the *fuck* was that on the phone.

"That was Simon," she said, as if it were nothing.

That only spiked the annoyance that had already boiled over and was reaching a new height. He wouldn't even attempt to hide what he was feeling now. "What's he looking forward to tonight?"

"Seeing me." She said it so calmly, it gave him hope this was a complete misunderstanding.

Still, he fisted his hands tightly, trying to remain as calm as she was. "Seeing you?" He lifted both brows, unable to hide the anger now. "You're gonna see him tonight?"

She nodded, touching his face softly. "What's wrong with you?"

While her touch did calm him a little, it wasn't nearly enough. "What do you mean what's wrong with me? You're gonna go see this guy tonight, and he's looking forward to it? And so are you?" Then it hit him. "You told him you were working. Why?"

Pinching her brows together to think about it, she tilted

her head. Damian took a few steps back—away from her. As cute as he normally thought it when she did that, right now he was too damn pissed to appreciate it.

"No." She cleared her throat. "He asked why I said it'd be better if we talked tonight instead of now, and I told him I was working tonight."

"You're lying," he snapped.

Never had he been so sure about anything in his life. Every word she'd just said to him had been insincere.

"*What?*"

Damian stared at her, taking a step forward now. He had to calm down. He was getting too fired up to read her. She looked stunned, but was it because he'd called her on her lying or was it because she was pissed he'd just called her a liar?

Her eyes pinched together again, but it wasn't in that cute way anymore. This he could read loud and clear. She *was* mad. Glancing down at his fisting hands, she looked back up at him, shaking her head slowly. "What *is* wrong with you? And why are you calling me a liar?"

Feeling a little panicked now that maybe he *had* jumped the gun—let the seething jealousy cloud his judgment—he took a deep breath to compose himself and spoke more calmly. "You told me you were off today. Said you had the whole day off. Remember?"

Swallowing hard, it was frustrating that his anxiousness wouldn't let him concentrate as he normally would on even the smallest details of how she responded to his questioning. Her eyes had opened slightly at that last question, but she held her chin up, looking straight at him. "Amos's call woke me. He needs me to come in tonight. They've had a few waitresses call in. Then he told me to call Simon because he wanted to talk to me."

Instantly wound up again, he couldn't wait when she paused. "About *what*?"

"About my show," she said, crossing her arms.

As irritated as she appeared to be getting, Damian couldn't put his finger on it. For someone who'd just been accused of lying, her irritation was understated. "Your show?"

"Yes. My show," she said with a little more conviction. "He has some ideas he wanted to go over with me, but I told him it'd be better if we talked tonight when I go in."

They stared at each other for a moment silently. He was beginning to feel a little stupid, but something still didn't sit well with him. "I'm sorry," he said, bringing his arm around her neck and kissing her head. "I'll just be honest with you, sweetheart, I don't like him. I don't like the way he looks at you."

She pulled away from him a bit roughly. "Or trust me, obviously." She glared at him now, but he almost welcomed it. Finally a real show of someone whose boyfriend had just accused her of something *way off*. "You really think I'd leave your bed to go do something inappropriate with another guy? Regardless of what you think of Simon, after everything that just happened between us, you're worried about me doing something with him?"

Okay, it took her a minute. Maybe she'd been too stunned at first, but this was genuine disgust she was spewing—disgust at him. She started to walk away, but he reached out and caught her hand, pulling her back to him. "Baby, I'm sorry. I really am." He shook his head. "I don't know." He kissed her forehead, then her nose, anxiously staring into her eyes. "It's just that everything I feel for you is so different from anything I've ever felt. Every reaction to you feels different—untamed."

He held her hand to his bare chest, needing for her to feel

just what she did to him. A moment ago his heart had nearly pelted out of his chest because he'd been ready to spit bullets. Now it pounded because he feared he'd pissed her off so bad she'd leave here tonight and never come back.

Bringing that same hand up to his mouth, he kissed it several times. "I'm sorry. I'm sorry. I'm sorry." He kissed her lips this time. "I'm an idiot. A jealous fucking idiot, and I've never been like this, *ever*. I swear to you. I'll work on it. I will. And I *do* trust you. No matter what I feel about Simon, I'll trust that I don't have to worry about you doing anything *inappropriate* with him ever."

Finally she smiled, and he leaned his forehead against her, the relief enormous. "You're not an idiot," she assured him.

"Yes, I am."

"No, you're not," she insisted, pulling her forehead away from his and looking him in the eyes a bit seriously now, "And you're right about Simon. He has asked me out."

Damian had just admitted that he was a jealous idiot, but he'd also promised he'd work on it, so he clenched his teeth and said nothing. Taking long, deep breaths he stared at her, waiting for her to finish.

"He did so way back when we first met, but I declined." This time *she* kissed *Damian's* knuckles, and he took another long breath, gulping hard and continuing to listen to her calmly. "When he asked a few times more, I let him know that while I liked being his friend I wasn't interested in anything else. I told him his continuing to ask me out made me uncomfortable and maybe we wouldn't be able to be friends if he was gonna keep asking. He promised me he would respect my wishes and not ask anymore. He wanted us to stay friends, and ever since he hasn't brought up the subject of anything between me and him again."

"How long ago was the last time he asked?"

She shrugged. "It's been a while. Maybe six months ago?"

Damian wrapped his arms around her waist. "And you're gonna tell him about us now? Tonight?"

"If it comes up, sure." Without even thinking, Damian lifted a brow. "My private life is none of his business, Damian. I don't want him thinking that I feel I need to report anything to him. So I won't. But if it comes up, of course I'll confirm it." She brought her hands to his rough chin and rubbed it. The corner of her lips lifted in that sexy way he loved seeing. "The fact that I have a big, tough, sexy-as-hell boyfriend now won't be a secret, if that's what you're asking."

Damian lifted her suddenly, making her yelp, then squeal, but her legs were wrapped around him instantly. "You forgot horny," he said, diving into her neck as he pushed what was so ready for her again against her crotch. "And crazy about you." He started toward the patio door. "I think you need a little reminder," he said, biting her lower lip.

Just like that she did one of the things he'd loved so much about her from the first time he kissed her. She cradled his face in her hands and kissed him, just as frenzied as he was.

———

"You told Stella you agreed with everything." Bethany got off her bed, no longer able to sit still. "She said it was a done deal."

"I did agree to everything, Bethany. There were just some minor details I needed to look into further, and I take full responsibility for the delay," Max said, sounding every bit as remorseful as he claimed to be. "But you have my word that it'll all be taken care of. This is why I wanted to talk to you. You know how your sister gets. I didn't want to be responsible for one of her little . . . *episodes*."

Play nice. You have no choice. She'd already done her part by acting genuinely happy to hear from him after all this time. She'd cheerfully told him all about the fake job she'd made up and how excited she was about getting back home when this was all over. She even assured him that once back she'd take her old theater job back, and things could go back to the way they were so long ago when she first met him. They'd start over again. She was anxious to let bygones be bygones and get back to the dream life she had once upon a time.

For most of the call she'd watched herself in the mirror, practicing all the fake expressions that went along with all the bullshit she had to feed him.

With an exaggerated deep breath, she looked in the mirror again and smiled. "I suppose waiting a little longer won't kill me. I'll explain it to Stella. But you won't get the money, Max," she said this very firmly. "Not a cent until I have what I need in my hands." She knew that wasn't the part he was worried about. The whole needing-the-money thing had just been an excuse. She knew what he really wanted. "And I won't set foot back in California again until you give me what's rightfully mine."

"Understood," he said without hesitation. "But I'd like the opportunity to deliver it to you."

This was what made her nervous. The only reason he'd want to deliver it himself would be to ensure that once it was done she'd either have to reinvent herself elsewhere or follow through with coming back to California and pretending none of this had ever happened. Something she had been fairly certain she couldn't do even before Damian, but now she was absolutely sure she wouldn't. She'd already explained to Stella that once this was over, they were all moving to Vegas permanently.

But they had to hold on to that house in California. It was all they had. Without it, and Bethany being the only one working, she just didn't see how they could make the move. There was no way she could fit them all in her little apartment, and she could barely afford the rent there now. She'd figure out how to catch up on the mortgage payments one way or another.

After just one week, but especially after the night she'd spent with him, and then almost the entire day today, until she was forced to leave to make this call, she was certain of one thing: She couldn't leave Vegas now. Everything she lived for could easily be transplanted here. Stella had even been excited about it. But as insane as it sounded, she could already feel it: Leaving Damian was not an idea her heart would entertain.

"It'll give us a chance to speak in-person about this proposition I mentioned to your sister. I'm quite certain you'll agree; it's a very reasonable offer and a win-win for both of us."

Bethany refrained from groaning. She wasn't remotely interested in hearing his proposition, but again she humored him. "When the time comes, we'll talk," she said simply. "For now just work on getting this taken care of."

Without her having to ask, Max assured her he wouldn't "blow up her phone" with texts or calls. Considering how badly things could've gone today with Damian, Bethany couldn't have been more grateful for that. An entire hour after getting off the phone with Max, Bethany still lay there staring at the ceiling. On top of the usual feeling of the weight of the world, heavier than ever because her siblings and aunt were counting on her, she was now also wrestling with her conscience. There was no way she could tell Damian about this. Not yet. He'd insist on getting involved, and there was no way she could allow that. Especially not after what he'd told her about his image at work being so important and his not wanting to give them any kind of ammunition. His being involved with this could ruin him.

She squeezed her eyes shut, shaking her head, remembering the look in Damian's eyes today when he'd hit it on the nose, calling her a liar. No way had she anticipated his getting close enough to hear Max, so it was no wonder he'd picked up on the lie she pulled out of her ass when she couldn't say it was her sister.

Fortunately, she'd been able to come up with something believable. And after the initial shock of nearly being caught, she was able to sound a bit more convincing. It helped to use the anger at realizing he actually thought that after the night and morning she'd spent with him, giving herself to him in every way imaginable, she was actually going out with another man and blatantly standing there informing him of it. Before that, she'd been drowning in the guilt that she had so boldly lied in his face that she couldn't conjure up the least bit of resentment at him for calling her on it.

She brought her hands to her face, nearly groaning. But did he have to be *such* a sweetheart again about apologizing to *her*? First he was so remorseful about not telling Ashlynn he had a girlfriend and now this. As if she didn't already feel crappy about having to keep something so big from him. The one thing that gave her conscience the tiniest bit of relief was that evidently he, too, was of the opinion that some things were better left unsaid. He had made it very clear that if Ashlynn hadn't shown up being so obvious, he'd had no intention of mentioning she'd "kept him up," and especially not of mentioning her proposition to him. Knowing this, and based on his reaction to what he *thought* she was lying about, she was more convinced than ever that she was right to hold off until everything was done.

She vowed that until she could tell him everything, she

wouldn't be so careless about letting him overhear things that might have her fumbling again. Because staying away from him or slowing things down until this was really a done deal was out of the question now. She could hardly stand knowing that because of her internship, work, and his job, it'd be at least a few days before she could be with him again.

CHAPTER 18

For almost two weeks Max kept his promise about not blowing up Bethany's phone. Clearly, not blowing up her phone did not mean he'd cease contacting her, because he hadn't gone too long without texting or calling now and again. Each time was supposedly to update her, but the updates were no more than to tell her there wasn't anything new. He claimed he wanted to keep her in the loop because he knew she was anxious.

Tonight was the first time since Damian had all-out called her on her lying that Max's texts had ignited his suspicions again. Since she'd gone back to doing her show, she'd been really busy, though Amos had insisted on cutting her waitressing hours a bit, so she wasn't as busy, but her social life and time with Damian *had* taken a hit. Several times in the past couple of weeks Damian had had to cancel their plans because of work, too. So she was finally getting to surprise him like she'd wanted to weeks ago.

They'd been at his house while she helped him get ready, because he didn't know where they were headed, and she didn't want to tell him, so she was going to dress him. Determined not to screw up again, she'd resorted to keeping her phone on vibrate when she was around Damian. He'd asked her about her phone always being on vibrate several days ago, and she explained she had so little downtime that when she finally did get some, she didn't want to be bothered, but in case her sister called, she didn't want to turn it completely off.

With that he let the subject go. But earlier tonight when she'd glanced at a text from Max, then shoved her phone back in her bag the moment Damian walked into the room, he called her on it.

"Why do you do that?"

She looked up at him, her heart already thumping. "Do what?"

"That's not the first time I noticed you hide your phone suddenly when you see me coming."

She shrugged. "I didn't realize I did that."

"You do."

"I'm always in a hurry, Damian. I think I just have a habit of shoving everything in my bag without thinking."

The mood had gotten a little tense, since she hadn't had much else to add. But after a while they were back to cuddling and laughing playfully as she tried in vain to get him fully dressed in the appropriate attire for tonight's surprise, and they'd end up entangled in each other's arms for too long.

"We're gonna be late," she reminded him as his hands were already making their way down inside her skirt and squeezing her bare ass.

"Mmm," he groaned. "It'll be worth it."

Giggling, she pulled away. "No, I've waited weeks for this. I don't want the surprise to be ruined."

He was already in black slacks. She'd almost pulled out a black tank from one of his drawers. The kind she loved seeing him in so much. But then she saw the black sleeveless shirt and pulled that instead. "Try this on."

"With slacks?" he asked, lifting the shirt in the air.

"Yeah, I think it might be just the perfect thing."

He pulled off the shirt he was wearing, allowing for a very pleasurable view of his beautiful chest and shoulders, then threw the sleeveless shirt on. It was so perfectly snug, it accentuated his big chest and abs. His hard shoulders looked even bigger in it somehow, too.

"Perfect," she said, unable to help herself and reaching out to caress his big arms.

"Are you sure about this?" he said, looking into the mirror.

"Yes. Just tuck in the shirt."

He began to just as her phone buzzed. She'd pulled it out from her purse earlier and it was now on the table in front of the mirror Damian was looking into. Their eyes met in the mirror as he continued to tuck his shirt in, then she saw his eyes travel down to her phone again. "You gonna check that?" She shook her head, but again he didn't let it go. "Why? 'Cause *I'm* here?"

"*No!*" she said, reaching for it and praying it wasn't from Max. "I just . . ." It wasn't Max, but she still got caught up reading it.

We're heading out now. Send me the address or name of the place. See you in a few.

"You just what, Bethany?"

He wasn't looking into the mirror anymore, and the expression on his face was the same as the day he'd accused her of lying. The same as earlier when he asked her about her *habit* of shoving her phone away whenever she saw him coming. She really had to work on her poker face, but this time she could actually use it to her advantage. She texted the name of the place where they were meeting to Jerry. With a smirk she put the phone down and ran her hands over his now very tense abs and chest and brought her arms all the way around his neck. "I just have some things going on tonight, and I don't want any texts or calls ruining the surprise." He eased up a little, staring at her, but didn't say anything. "You'll see what I mean when we get there. Trust me."

Those last two words nearly twisted her mouth into a pretzel as she said them, considering how much she was keeping from him. She could only pray she'd be able to tell him everything soon. She just needed at least one thing done first.

Giving in to her embrace, he hugged her back, squeezing her tight before kissing her very sweetly. "I'm sorry," he whispered. "Work has me wound real tight lately. We're not any closer to closing that case, and having to cancel on you so much has been making me a little crazy. I don't mean to sound so paranoid."

"It's okay," she said, running her finger over his bottom lip. "Maybe after tonight, no more surprises. At least until you close that case. This way I don't have to be so sneaky. I didn't realize being sneaky around a homicide detective trained to pick up on deception would require such skill." She laughed nervously at the hidden irony. "A skill I'm obviously lacking."

His sudden huge smile made her feel better about his once again doing the apologizing when she knew damn well he had every reason to be suspicious. She did stink at this sneaking-around thing, and obviously Damian was very well trained at picking up the stench of dishonesty.

"It's probably the one thing you're not very good at," he said, smacking her behind lightly. "But I'm glad. I don't want you to be good at lying to me."

"Never," she said, choking back any glimmer of unease. At least she could say, with all honesty, "I'd have to try *really* hard to get anything by you." Before he could read too much into that, because it was something her subconscious was screaming at her, she added, "So it's settled, after tonight, no more surprises for you."

He smiled, kissing her once again, then pulling away to look in the mirror again. "You sure about this? I'm assuming you're taking me to some kind of club. I'm just trying to figure out what kind dresses like this."

She frowned but nodded. "Yes, this is perfect, and I'm not saying another word about where we're going. Now let's go."

Feeling a little disappointed, she grabbed her small clutch and put her phone in it. Damian was right. She did suck at this. He'd figured out part of the surprise. Now if she could just get him there before he figured out the rest.

———

They arrived at Mi Vida Hermosa, and she was glad she knew the doorman, because the line to get in was outrageous. Way back when she first got her gig as a Zumba girl, the other instructors had brought her here once a week to practice and put together new routines, but they didn't want it to feel like work. Once she picked up her second and third job, there was no more time for this, and she hadn't been back in months.

She'd arranged this days ago, giving them Jerry's and Janis's names, and had texted Jerry to just walk up to the front of the line and let them know he was on the list. Just as she and Damian would, they'd bypass the line and walk right in.

She'd purposely steered clear of wearing a shorter skirt with ruffles, like those so many of the girls in line wore, so that Damian wouldn't immediately figure out where she was taking him. Her longer, hip-hugging skirt with slits up both sides didn't scream salsa quite as loudly, but it was still sexy as heck. Proof of this was how quickly it'd come off her as soon as Damian set foot in her apartment when he'd picked her up. He attacked her with a growl the moment he saw her.

They left Damian's car with the valet attendant and walked along the enormous line of people waiting to get in. Damian's head fell back now as they neared the front of the line, and he could hear the music, not to mention seeing how the people in line were dressed—a sure giveaway. "Salsa, babe?" He squeezed her hand with a smile. "I don't know how to salsa."

"It's easy, Damian," she said, squeezing his hand back. "And I promise you won't be the only one here new to it. There are a lot of beginners that come here to learn or just have fun."

They reached the door where Rigo, the handsome door guy and a friend she hadn't seen in months, stood checking a few girls in. He looked up and did a double-take when he saw her, then smiled. "Hey, chica! How *are* you?" He held his arms open. "C'mere!"

Bethany let go of Damian's hand to hug Rigo. *"Ay, mami,"* he said hugging her tight and rubbing her back. "You look so *good.*" He pulled away and checked her out from top to bottom, still holding both her hands, then let go of one and twirled her around. "Look at you. *Dayum!*"

She'd forgotten how touchy-feely and over-the-top Rigo could be. But it was good to see him again. She kept saying she had to come back and visit with him, but her schedule just never gave her a chance.

With one of her hands free now, Damian quickly slipped his hand back into it and squeezed a bit harder than when he was being playful. That was her cue. "Rigo, this is my boyfriend, Damian." She glanced back at Damian, his rigid expression so telling of what he must be thinking.

Rigo lifted a brow, checking Damian out from top to bottom, but she knew it wasn't for the reasons Damian would probably think. "Nice to meet you, Damian." Rigo held out his hand.

Damian shook it, at the same time pulling Bethany closer to him. "Likewise," he said without so much as a smile.

Rigo smirked, looking back at Bethany, and she lifted a menacing brow, warning him to behave, since he'd obviously picked up on Damian's chilly reception.

Unhooking the rope that blocked the entrance to the club, Rigo motioned for them to go right in. "*Cuidado* in there," Rigo said as she walked past him ahead of Damian, then leaned into her, lowering his voice. "*Es un poco celoso, no?*"

Bethany shook her head. "No," she said with a smile, but kept walking.

She felt Damian's face near her ear as they walked into the club. "*Sí,*" he said, surprising her that he'd heard.

She turned to him with a smirk. "Well, you have no reason to be jealous."

"Are you kidding me? With his fucking hands all over you like that? He didn't get that—"

"Damian," she said, leaning against him as they walked through the crowd.

"No, I'm serious," Damian continued, sounding more irritated as the scene outside seemed to be getting to him the more he thought about it. "Douchebags like that guy act like—"

She touched his face to calm him. "Baby, he's gay." Damian stared at her, a bit stunned.

He looked as if he was about to comment on that, but

something behind her caught Damian's attention. "Whaaaa?" he asked, with a big smile, then shook his head.

She turned to see Jerry dancing toward them with a beer in his hand. "Ready to get down?"

Bethany laughed, surprised to see how well Jerry moved his hips. Janis came up from behind. Jerry's hand held one of hers and he held a drink in the other. "This is cool," Jerry said, taking a sip of his beer. "I haven't been salsa dancing in a while, but I have a few times."

With a teasing smile, Bethany made sure Damian knew. "This is who texted me earlier, and I was trying to keep you from seeing who it was from."

Damian's smile waned a little; he looked a bit remorseful now. Pulling her against him with one strong arm around her waist, he kissed her temple. "Again, I'm sorry about what an ass I've been lately."

She smiled, trying not to let on how much she hated that he felt so guilty about not trusting her. She also hated to think that because of her, he might start questioning his natural instincts. It was just a matter of time before she'd be able to come clean, but the more time passed and the more he apologized for his valid suspicions, the harder it was to sleep at night.

No matter how tempted she was at times to tell him, she knew she couldn't. No way was she getting him involved and telling was all it would take. She'd tell him everything. But not until it was all over, because if she was losing sleep now over her guilty conscience, she knew it would be a million times worse if she told him and somehow his name was smeared with her mess. It would just have to wait.

Shaking it off, she took his hand from her waist. "Let's go dance."

"Whoa," he said, tugging at her hand. "I think I need a drink before I get out there."

"The bar in that corner is not as crowded as this one," Jerry informed them, still dancing in place. "We'll be right here when you get back."

Taking his advice, Damian and Bethany headed toward the less-crowded bar in the darker corner of the club. The rhythm of the song blaring loudly made her want to move her own hips. It was one of her favorites, and one she often used in her Zumba class.

While the bar wasn't nearly as crowded as the main one, it was still too crowded for both of them to step all the way to the front. "I'll wait here," she said, letting go of his hand just outside the crowd that surrounded the bar.

"Amaretto sour?" he asked, and she winked, with a smile.

Swaying her hips to the song, she stood there enjoying the music until she noticed out of the corner of her eye a guy in white watching her. She stopped swaying her hips so much, not wanting to give the guy the idea she was hoping to be asked to dance. Rigo was right. She did need to be careful with Damian. He'd already made it very clear how he felt about this kind of stuff.

Even with the distraction of the blinking light in her clutch, she could still feel the guy staring at her as she pulled her phone out, refusing to look in that direction. She had a couple of texts. She read the first one, from her sister.

We got a letter from the bank. They returned the check we sent them and it says we have ten days to send them the entire amount past due to bring the account current or they'll start the foreclosure process.

Bethany's heart sank. "They can't do that," she whispered under her breath.

She turned to see where Damian was, because the other

text was from Max. Damian was still at the bar paying the bartender, so she clicked on Max's text quickly.

I always knew you were a resourceful one.

Bethany reread it, not understanding what it meant. *Resourceful?* The last text she had from him, the one she'd shoved back into her bag before being able to read it in its entirety, hadn't made sense either. She scrolled back up, feeling a little irritated about the constant texts from Max that had nothing to do with what she really wanted to know. It was always some blithering nonsense like this that she was sure he sent with the hope of drawing her into a chat. Maybe together both texts would make sense. She reread Max's previous text.

It crossed my mind but I can't believe I never seriously considered you might do this.

Rereading the most recent text, she still wasn't sure what he could be talking about. Just as she was about to glance back at the bar to see where Damian was, her phone buzzed in her hand, making her flinch suddenly. She clicked on it and read.

Did you tell your new sugar daddy EVERYTHING?

Instantly her heart jumped. He knew about Damian. But how? Then she thought of the guy staring at her earlier. She jerked her head up, certain she knew who the guy who had been staring at her so hard was, but he was gone. Her eyes scanned the area frantically. With her heart beating nearly out of her chest, she took a deep breath, trying to gather herself. Was she just being paranoid?

She glanced back down at her phone to reread the text. "Hey."

Nearly jumping out of her skin, she gasped, bringing her hand to her chest. Damian stared at her, concerned, then glanced down at her phone, and she quickly turned the screen away from him. As concerned as his expression remained, a brow slowly lifted as he brought his attention back to her face. "Something wrong?"

CHAPTER 19

Talking himself down, because he'd already almost blown it twice tonight, Damian took long breaths as he patiently waited for Bethany's response. But there was no fucking way he was letting this go. She'd been on her phone again, and once again she was jumpy as shit. This time she hadn't shoved her phone back in her purse, but clearly she hadn't wanted him to see whatever it was she'd been reading.

She waved the phone at him for a second before dropping it back into her small purse, and Damian studied her closely as she tried to shrug it off. "My sister," she said, then took a deep breath. "She just texted me some not-so-good news." She took the drink he held out for her. Downing nearly half the glass, she smacked her lips and smiled. "I needed that."

"Why, what's going on? What kind of bad news? Is everyone okay?"

"Yeah, yeah." She nodded. "Everyone's fine. It's just some financial stuff I've been dealing with." She waved her hand in front of her and shook her head, slipping her purse under her arm. "It's nothing I want to discuss tonight. Trust me, Damian," she added as her hand slid into his. "You don't wanna hear about it. It's all this boring stuff. Just a few bills we're behind on is all. I'll deal with it tomorrow."

He started walking alongside her but slowed, tugging at her hand. "Well, wait. Maybe it's something I can help you with."

Immediately she shook her head adamantly. "No, no way."

"Why not?" he asked, feeling frustrated. He already hated that she was stuck living in that crappy apartment, but now she was also dealing with bills from back home, and he had more than enough to move her out of that shithole and possibly pay off whatever bills had her looking so worried just moments ago. "You said it was bad news. Let me help you."

"No!" she said, making no attempt to hide the agitation anymore. "Can we please just forget about it and go dance?"

This entire night had gotten off to a shaky start. Clearly this was going to be a challenge, but if these bills her family was behind on had Bethany so agitated she seemed almost ready to snap, Damian was going to help her with them. He'd talk her into it one way or another. Bethany had been looking forward to this for weeks. He'd drop this for now. Smiling, he kissed her softly. "Okay. Let's go find Jerry and finish up our drinks. Then I get to see that sweet ass of yours move for me like it did in your Zumba class."

It took a few moments, but slowly she came back from that dark place she'd begun to sink into. With another long swig of what was left of her drink, an evil smile spread across her face, and she sank her teeth into her bottom lip. "We'll see if you can keep up."

They found Jerry and Janis and stood off to the side of the dance floor watching the dancers. Some of those guys moved their hips faster than the women, and there was an awful lot of dirty dancing going on. "I don't know about this."

"You don't have to dance as fast as they do," Bethany

assured him, "And look." She motioned casually at one guy doing the two-step in the middle of all the spinning going on around him. "They're not all good at it."

Damian laughed. "I don't think I'll be *that* bad."

"Good," she said, smiling, then looking down at his bottle. "You almost done with that?"

He took the final swig and braced himself. They waited for the next song, since Bethany said the current one was nearly over, and then all four of them made their way onto the dance floor as the next song mixed in. Immediately Bethany's hips and arms were moving just as skillfully as those of the other women on the dance floor, who seemed to be pros at this. It didn't surprise him. He'd seen her in her Zumba class. She was a natural, and damn, she looked sexy doing it.

It was happening again, as it did so often with Bethany. Damian didn't even try to fight it anymore. Watching her, especially doing something like this, moving her beautiful body so perfectly to the rhythm, could quickly put him in a trance. Although he was certain now how he felt about her, even if her body weren't as beautifully shaped as it was, he'd still fall into her spell. Most of the time it was her eyes and smile that had him feeling this way anyway. He wasn't even paying attention to his own moves; he was too busy smiling stupidly as he watched her dance.

Dancing up to him, she swayed against him, as he'd seen so many of the other couples do earlier. After several minutes of her swaying her body against his, Damian had to wonder how the fuck these guys did this without going rock hard in the process. Just watching her had begun to get a rise out of him. Now having her soft but very firm body pressed up against him and looking into her sensual eyes, he felt ready to throw her over his shoulder and take her home that minute.

He pressed his hips up against her now in an effort to

conceal what was undeniably out there now. Her eyes opened wide, but sparkled at the feel of him up against her. "You can't move away from me now," he whispered in her ear.

"I don't want to," she whispered back, grinding into him even harder.

Glad the music was so damn loud, he groaned in reaction to her grinding him like that, not to mention feeling her breasts against his chest. He leaned into her ear again and said, "We gotta move into a dark corner so I can take care of this."

Her shocked eyes looked up at him. "Here?"

She started to grin wickedly, so he hugged her, laughing. "No, that's not what I meant. I mean I need to get somewhere dark so I could at least adjust. I move away from you now, it'll be like something out of a dirty cartoon." Unbelievably, she giggled. "It's not funny," he said, but laughed, too.

Only Bethany could get him in this predicament. By the time they made it to the darkest corner of the dance floor, pretending to dirty dance all the way there, they were both laughing so much they were turning heads.

"Stop!" he whispered. "People are starting to notice."

Chewing her lip with a smile that said she was up to no good, she reached down and wrapped her hand around him over his pants. "Bethany," he said through his teeth, leaning his forehead against hers, "you're being bad."

"You said you liked it when I was bad," she whispered, squeezing him softly before letting go.

"Yes, but not in public. Not here."

Pulling her off the dance floor and into a dark corner, he adjusted himself while Bethany attempted to help, giggling out of control the whole time, as he swatted her hands away. He knew even remembering something this silly would have him missing her like crazy the next time they had to go days without seeing each other. Their damn jobs kept them both so busy.

He finished adjusting, knowing it had been pointless, because he needed her in his arms again, and he'd be adjusting all over again in a few minutes. Pulling her to him, he leaned against the wall as she fell against him, and he kissed her long and deep. When he came up for air, he heard her sigh the way she did so often after he kissed her like that. It reminded him of the way she'd sighed that very first time he kissed her knuckles in the car. "God, I love you."

They both froze suddenly. He'd thought of telling her so many times in the past few weeks, and each time decided he'd wait for a better time. Each time he didn't think the moment special enough, romantic enough, and now it'd just slipped out. *Here* in a darkened corner of a noisy nightclub where they'd laughed all the way there so he could adjust his *boner*. Could he be a bigger idiot? Before he could get too angry with himself, she leaned in and kissed him softly, then whispered against his lips. "I love you, too, Damian." She sighed again softly, something he loved hearing her do now. It was always so real—so pure and spontaneous—when she did so. Sort of like his telling her he loved her. It just poured out. "So much," she added making his heart swell even further.

Feeling suddenly panicked that his grown-ass detective self could feel choked up, he kissed her. The emotion of hearing her say she loved him had taken him completely by surprise. He knew it'd be special the day he finally told her, but he hadn't prepared for hearing her say it to him. Her adding *so much* to it only intensified the happiness of knowing that once again they were on the same page, because now he knew he wasn't crazy for feeling this way about her this fast.

Hugging her tighter, he kissed her even more deeply, finally admitting to himself he'd been nervous that she wasn't feeling nearly as captivated as he was. He could now attribute his insecurities, his paranoia, and his gut feeling that something wasn't right to this. He'd always been a sensible guy. The way things had happened between him and Bethany, the two of them so perfectly in tune, felt unrealistic—so improbable. He'd been sure he was being delusional to think this was really happening. And he kept waiting for something to happen, looking for something to justify that notion.

Now he knew this was all he needed. Confirmation that sometimes things just happen because they were meant to be. They didn't have to make sense or follow every rule in the book of love. This was possible, and now he had proof he wasn't nuts for thinking so.

Lifting her off the floor, he spun her around slowly. "I love you," he whispered against her mouth over and over again, until she kissed him, forcing him to shut up.

"I almost wish I hadn't invited Jerry here tonight," she said as he put her down. "It feels rude to leave, but all I wanna do now is go back to your place and make love until I have to leave."

The thought of her having to leave almost ruined the moment. "Move in with me, Bethany."

Her eyes opened wide, the smile flatlining. "What?"

"So you'll never have to leave," he said quickly. "I hate knowing that after tonight, it'll be days before I get to see you again."

She shook her head slowly, eyes still open wide. "I . . . I can't."

"Why not?"

She blinked twice before she responded, and he saw the tiny flicker in her eyes. "I signed a lease."

"Fuck the lease. I'll pay it off." The more he thought about it, the better this idea sounded. "You'd be there every night when I get home." Now there was a glimmer of excitement in her eyes. "You could use one of my cars to drive to and from work."

He'd stop short of saying she could quit her job if she wanted to. She didn't need to work, but he knew that was crossing the line. Her jobs weren't just jobs to her. They were part of her dream. He wouldn't ask her to give that up.

Just as fast as the glimmer of excitement had begun to appear, it was gone. "No, I can't. Not yet."

"Why?" he said, a little calmer; he didn't want to be pushy. He'd just sprung this on her.

"Because I have things I have to take care of back home." She chewed the corner of her lip, something he'd noticed in the past weeks as her nervous quirk. "My sister and brother—we've been talking about moving them here instead of me moving back home."

"Move back home?" he asked sounding more alarmed than he'd intended. "You *can't*."

She smiled now, touching his face softly. "I know. You're the reason why I've been talking about getting them out here instead of me going back. But I have to get that taken care of first." She smiled even more sweetly now. "Trust me, Damian. I can't think of anything," she closed her eyes, sighing deeply, then opened them with a blissful smile, "more heavenly than going to bed *and* waking up in your arms every day. There are just a few things I need to work on first."

Damian thought he had a solution for this, too, but he'd already sprung enough on her for one night. He'd wait for another time to tell her about it. Right now he needed to figure out how to get her back to his place without her feeling bad about bailing on Jerry.

Jerry and Janis must've been hit with the same salsa fever they'd been hit with earlier, because they were nowhere to be found. Not even in a dark corner. Damian hadn't even thought of checking his phone until they'd walked around the entire place. As soon as he saw the text from Jerry with a winky face saying he and Janis had made an early exit, he tugged Bethany toward the exit. "They're gone, babe. And so are we."

"What? They left without saying good-bye? How *rude*," she said, giggling.

He glanced back at her as he practically pushed his way through the crowd with a grin. "It had to be that dirty dancing."

"You taking me back to your place for some private dirty dancing now, Mr. Santiago?"

"You're damn straight."

Damian was glad now that Bethany had said no more surprises after tonight. Because as limited as their time together had been lately, he was done sharing her with his family, or anyone else for that matter. From here on whatever time he had with her, they'd be spending it at his place *alone*.

———

The buzzing under her arm had been going for a while. Bethany held her clutch tightly under her arm, not wanting Damian to hear it as they stood waiting for the valet attendant to bring their car around. The long buzzing meant one thing. It wasn't someone texting, it was someone calling. She was beginning to feel unnerved, because they'd called back-to-back. She thought of Max's earlier texts and wondered if her not responding had made him angry. Or maybe her sister was trying to warn her of something. Max obviously knew something.

Damian brought his arm around her and rubbed her shoulder. "You okay?"

She glanced up at him; until now she hadn't realized he'd been watching her. "Yeah." She smiled. "I'm fine."

Damian's car drove up, and the attendant opened her door for her. Bethany got in and took advantage of the moment it took Damian to tip him and walk around the car to check her phone. She had two missed calls. Both from Max, and just like the last time, her phone buzzed in her hand with a text from Max. Her heart thudded; could he be watching her?

Not just a Ferrari a classic. Impressive.

Her heart nearly stopped at the realization that he *was* watching her. He was there in Vegas. Probably just a few feet away. Had he watched them all night? She felt the air sucked out of her when she looked up and saw him across the parking lot, leaning against a motorcycle.

The driver's-side door opened, and Bethany looked down at her phone, clutching it so her shaking hands wouldn't be so visible. The second her eyes met Damian's, she knew he knew something was wrong.

He glanced down at her phone. "What happened now?"

Shaking her head slowly, she couldn't even speak, afraid her voice would squeak or break. "N-nothing," she said, almost breathless.

Looking completely exasperated, Damian started out of the parking lot. They passed Max as she stared straight ahead. "Look, Bethany." She could see him grab the steering wheel a little tighter. "I won't say you're lying, but obviously there's something you're not telling me. If this is about your family's financial situation, *please* let me help you. I hate seeing you like this."

She glanced casually at the passenger-side window, swallowing back the dread. As far as she could tell, Max wasn't following them, but she was glad Damian was way off. Still feeling enormously guilty, she decided to come clean at least about one thing. "I knew things were bad, Damian. I just didn't realize we might lose the house."

"How much do you need?" he said immediately. "I can write you a check or if you need it wired I—"

"*No.*" She turned back to him, feeling such blinding guilt that she couldn't tell this amazing man the whole truth that it nearly choked her.

"Why not?" He sounded as adamant as she felt about taking money from him. "I can guarantee you I can afford it." He glanced at her, and seeing the tears in her eyes only heightened the urgency in his words. He reached over and squeezed her thigh. "Baby, if this is such a burden on you, why won't you let me help you? I *want* to. It'd be so easy for me to do this for you, and I hate to see you like this."

She lifted his hand away from her thigh and brought it to her cheek, leaning against it as the tears leaked from the corners of her eyes. How had she been so blessed to find him?

"*Please* let me help you with this." His tone was less urgent now, but she felt the sincere need to make this better for her.

"I don't know how much it is exactly. I have to call the bank and find out." Feeling such a weight suddenly lifted, she turned to him, needing to make one thing clear. "But this would be a loan. I need you to promise to let me pay you back *every* penny."

He turned his attention back to the road with a smile. "Of course."

"I mean it, Damian." She squeezed his hand.

He smiled even more widely, staring straight ahead. "We'll work something out."

———

Though she had feared for a moment that it could end horrendously, tonight had turned out to be one of the most wonderful nights Bethany had spent so far with Damian. Every moment with him felt special, but tonight was extra special.

After over an hour of lovemaking in the bedroom, first so hot and frantic they'd barely made it to his bed, Damian slowed it down significantly, savoring every inch of her body, tormenting her with his tongue and leisurely kissing up and down her entire naked body.

Now she sat on the island counter of his enormous kitchen. She couldn't even imagine calling this place home. It still felt so surreal how dramatically her life would be changing, and in such a short time. But she had her siblings and aunt to think of first. Most important, before she'd even think of moving in with Damian, she needed things settled with Max. It would be the only way she'd even consider it.

She smiled as Damian set the tray of fruit down next to her. "I think this is yogurt," he said, pointing at the white creamy stuff in the middle of the fruit assortment.

Dipping a strawberry into it, he licked the white stuff. "Yeah, definitely yogurt." He dipped it again, then brought it to Bethany's lips, but instead of putting it in her open mouth, he traced her lips with it, smearing the yogurt all over them, then kissed her, licking it off slowly. She sucked the yogurt off his tongue, suddenly aroused again, and sat up straighter.

"Damian," she said against his lips. "We're supposed to be taking a snack break."

"We are," he said, putting the strawberry in his mouth, and she bit it.

Some of the juice dripped down her chin, and he licked it clean, moving farther down her neck. The tingling down her middle was already starting up again as he slipped his hand in her robe, cupping her bare breast.

They wore matching half-thigh spa robes he'd surprised her with last week. Damian's robe said "Hers" and Bethany's read "His." But he made her promise if his brothers, Mace, or even sappy Jerry ever saw them, she'd tell them *she* got them and wouldn't mention whose robe was whose. "I'll never live it down," he said as she'd giggled, stripping out of her clothes just to try hers on.

Undoing the belt of her robe, he opened it up, pushing the robe off her shoulders so she now sat there on his center island completely naked. Trembling as his hand made its way down her belly and between her legs, he paused for a moment. "You cold?"

"No," she whispered, kissing him feverishly in reaction to his slipping two fingers in her.

He pulled his fingers out and brought them to her mouth. She loved the way he watched her in awe as she licked and sucked them clean. "*God*, that's such a turn-on." Devouring her mouth, he picked her up and set her down on the lower part of the center island and threw off his own robe.

Staring at all his beautiful exposed muscles, she spread her legs for him anxiously, as if it'd been too long since she had him in her. With breathless pants against his lips, she ran her hands through his hair, then gasped as he drove into her with a grunt. "I'm not wearing a condom," he said, gulping, as he slid in and out slowly. "But you're on birth control now, so it's okay, right?"

Technically the doctor at the clinic she'd gone to to get the shot just days ago had told her she needed to wait at least seven days before having unprotected sex to be completely on the safe side. But there was no way she wanted him to stop now, so she nodded, moaning loudly as he slid even deeper now—harder.

Lifting her behind off the counter, Damian held her up,

holding her thighs on either side of his hips, and she wrapped them around him, allowing for even deeper penetration. He sped up, the noise of their bodies slapping against each other echoing against the stark kitchen walls.

Both her moans and his grunts grew louder as he drove into her harder and harder until . . .

His carnal groan as he came inside her, and her crying out at the same time, were louder than she'd ever heard them, and they echoed all around the kitchen. He swayed his hips as he continued to empty into her, her warm insides still enjoying the waves of pleasure.

"I love you, baby," she whispered when she was finally able to catch her breath enough to speak.

She felt the familiar emptiness that came with his pulling out, and his strong arm held her as he bent over and lifted his robe, wiping himself clean. Leaning against her between her legs, he kissed her gently as he cleaned her, too. "I love you, too." She sighed against his mouth, and he added, "so much," then picked her up and carried her back to his bedroom.

Lying there watching her beautiful boyfriend sleep, she glanced at the clock. It was nearly midnight now, and she'd have to wake him soon so he could take her home. Hating to leave his bed, his house, his side was all the motivation she needed. Settling things with Max was her number-one priority now.

CHAPTER 20

Staring out the bus window, Bethany thought of what her Tia Lupe always used to say: *La vida es un carnival.* Until now Bethany had never really agreed. If life were really a carnival, for years Bethany had been stuck on a roller coaster with far more plunging falls and sharp turns than ups. She'd never gotten off to enjoy the rest of the park, taste sweet treats, or bask in the slow-moving chairlift enjoying the view for a while. Every time she thought it was finally her turn to exit that dreaded roller coaster, it'd take another sharp turn or even an unbearable dive.

Now it seemed maybe, just maybe, she was closer than she'd ever been to boarding that magical boat ride in the sea of serenity and happiness. There was no doubt that even with all she'd been through in life, Damian held the key to her happiness. Being with him made everything better.

Lately she'd been doing her best to refrain from showing how deeply disappointed she was each time Damian had to cancel last minute on her in the last couple of weeks since their salsa night. There was no doubt he felt terrible about it, and he did so much to try to make it up to her when they did finally have time together. The case he was working on had heated up, keeping him working longer hours than normal, but he promised her as soon as he was done with this case, he'd take some time off just for her.

Done with her internship, Bethany, too, picked up more work. Amos had added a second night of her show to his lineup. But he'd also cut out her waitressing at his place. He said it was one or the other, and of course she chose an extra show over waitressing. That still left her with far more time for Damian than he'd had for her in the last few weeks. Regardless, she refused to complain. She knew he was already overwhelmed with guilt. His constant apologizing only made her feel worse about not being able to come clean yet.

She used the downtime to get some extra rehearsals in with Simon. Knowing Damian wasn't thrilled about that, she kept any talk of Simon to a minimum. It didn't help that he'd begun to insist she use one of his cars to get to and from work. But she wasn't having it. Even the one car he owned that wasn't a classic was a brand-new luxury car. Any of them parked in her neighborhood overnight would be stripped down and left on cinder blocks by morning. So when she tried to persuade him not to worry about her walking or taking the bus home after her late rehearsals, because Simon was more than happy to give her a ride home, it hadn't gone over too well. Ever since she had avoided the topic at all costs.

To her surprise, the only reaction Max had had to the revelation that not only was she not in Mexico, but she now had a boyfriend was to tell her he was no idiot and he'd known all along. He claimed he'd made a trip out to Vegas, and since he was in town decided it'd be fun to check it out for himself. She didn't ask how he knew where she'd be that night, because she knew he was full of it. When she tried to explain that Damian had only been in her life for a couple of months, not the entire time she'd been gone, he'd scoffed, saying *that* was bullshit. But she didn't argue, especially when he'd told her there'd be no more delays.

Another surprise was that he didn't do anything to try to make her life miserable, as she'd been certain he would. The texts and calls, however, still continued with all his non-updates.

The night they'd gone salsa dancing after Damian had snapped about her shoving her phone in her bag, she'd decided at first that until this was all over she just wouldn't check her phone at all when she was around Damian. She thought it safer, and going a few hours without looking at her phone wouldn't kill her. Then Max had shown up. Ever since, she'd hear the jaws music whenever the text or missed-call indicator flashed on her phone. She needed to make sure he wouldn't surprise her again by popping up unannounced, so she'd been forced to continue checking her phone even around Damian.

Inevitably, there'd been a few moments when she'd flinched or bumbled her response to Damian's casual inquiry about who she was texting. Because of her second show now and the need for additional rehearsals, a few of those times she'd claimed she was responding to a text from Simon with something related to her show and rehearsals. Damian didn't even try hiding his annoyance at that, but it was better than the truth.

She exited the bus, and just a few blocks from her place she answered Damian's call, already smiling. "Hi, baby."

"God, I miss you," he said with that familiar exhilaration laced with a bit of remorse in his voice.

It had only been four days since she'd last gotten to spend more than a few stolen moments with him, but he was right. It felt like an eternity. She wouldn't make him feel worse.

He'd canceled on her again last night, and he'd sounded even more pissed about having to than usual. "I know, I miss you, too," she said, trying not to sound as desperate as her heart felt, praying that he wasn't canceling on her again. "You're off today, right?"

"Yes!" he said quickly. "But I do have to go in for one thing right now. I should be free by this afternoon. I can pick you up around two?"

Feeling excited already, she smiled hugely. "That's perfect. I have some errands to run in the meantime."

"Good. Just be ready by two, *please*." She smiled, knowing he felt as desperate as she did, but then he added, "How did it go last night, by the way? Whatcha end up doing all by yourself?"

That made her wince as she opened the door to her apartment. Because of her limited time with Damian, even though she did spend some of her downtime while he had to work rehearsing, she'd also flaked out on some of those rehearsals at the last minute if it meant she might get to see Damian, even if only for a few minutes. Sometimes he'd call her and let her know he'd be in her area following a lead in the case, and he could stop by for twenty or thirty minutes. She felt bad, but if she had to choose between a few minutes with Damian and going in to rehearse, Damian won hands down. Since she'd done that a couple of times in the last four days, last night when Damian canceled, she decided to text Simon and ask if he was free to rehearse.

"I wasn't alone, actually. I went in and made up for the rehearsals I'd canceled earlier this week."

He was quiet for a moment. She knew he wouldn't be thrilled. But this was work, and she'd been kind of flaky about it lately, something she'd never been before. It was all because of him, and it was worth being labeled a flake to see him. Still, she was glad she'd gotten the chance to make up for it last night.

"You took the bus at night?"

She shook her head as she dropped her bag on her bed. It figures that's the first thing he'd focus on. "No, Simon picked me up." Hearing him go quiet again, she added the reminder. "We had a lot to make up for."

"Do you talk to this guy about us?"

"What? No!" She shook her head. "The only thing he knows now, because it did come up, was that you're my boyfriend."

"Oh, I'm sure the subject of your love life came up. How late did you rehearse?"

"Late," she said, squeezing her eyes shut, because she could already sense this might turn into an argument. She just hoped it didn't get ugly. "The show's a little longer now and—"

"How late?"

Taking a deep breath, she stood her ground. This *was* work, and he *had* to know he had nothing to be worried about. They'd been over this more than once. "Late, Simon, it was—"

"What did you just call me?"

Hearing his murderous tone and realizing what she'd just done, she brought her hand to her face, practically slapping her forehead. "I'm sorry. I'm sorry. I was just thinking about—"

"How late were you with him last night, Bethany?"

"First of all I wasn't *with him* . . . Damian," her conviction waned a little after catching herself before calling him Simon again. What the hell was wrong with her? "Second, this is *work*. I'd flaked out on rehearsal for *work* twice this week for a chance to be with *you*. And it was totally worth it, but we had a lot of lost rehearsal time to make up for. I wish you knew how almost the entire time I thought of *you*. Every song about love that I sing now means so much more than it ever did before. The whole time I'm singing, all I think of is *you*."

He said nothing for a moment, and she held her breath. "How late?"

Letting out an exasperated breath, she ran her fingers through her hair, deciding to try to see this from his perspective. She'd never even thought to ask him if some of the other detectives he'd been spending so much time with lately were women. Would she be uncomfortable if one were a good-looking woman who she *knew* was interested in him? Absolutely. But he had to know she was crazy about him and would never do anything to hurt him. "Baby, did you hear what I just said."

"Yeah, I heard," he said, his voice calmer, almost somber. "I'm just curious."

She sat down on her bed, feeling defeated. "Until almost midnight. Rehearsals running that late in this business is not unheard of, Damian. Ask your brother."

"I don't have to," he said. "I remember." She heard him take a deep breath, and she hated that he'd gone from being so happy to talk to her to sounding so down now. "Be ready for me at two, babe. I can hardly wait to see you."

"I will. I love you, baby. I really, *really* do."

"I love you, too." He sighed. "*Too* much."

She hung up feeling bittersweet. Thinking back to her earlier mental comparison, she frowned. What if she found out now that all this time Damian had been working late, he'd been doing so side by side with a woman? One he admitted had a thing for him. How would she feel even if he assured her their relationship was purely a professional one?

She closed her eyes tightly, because it suddenly dawned on her—she'd *hate* it. Damian was being far more patient about this than she'd ever be. She made up her mind right then and there. Replaying the entire conversation now, if the tables had been turned, it probably would've ended with her in tears. They wouldn't have even gotten past his calling her another girl's name, especially one she was already suspicious about, because she would've gone ape shit on him and most likely hung up.

No more. If she could just get past this one last hurdle, she'd never again behave suspiciously with Damian about anything. Because once it was over, she was telling him *everything*.

———

The whole time Damian had been at the station he'd opened and slammed drawers a little too hard. He tried to concentrate on his work so he could get the hell out of there faster, but he kept getting slammed with the same thought. It was happening again. While he was working long hours, someone else was keeping his girl company. As much as she had tried last night not to sound too disappointed and assured him she understood, the fact remained that the first thing she'd done when she got off the phone with him was call Simon. And of course the guy had come running.

He finished putting away the final piece of evidence needed to get a warrant for the arrest of the male victim's wife, Jessica Mahoney. An email had been brought forward in which Mrs. Mahoney vented to a friend about her cheating husband. In it she said he'd confessed to the affair, and she admitted feeling so betrayed she wanted to kill them both, even described how she'd do it. It was too close to how they'd been murdered and enough to nail her, but they wanted to charge her with two counts of premeditated murder, so everything in this report had to be meticulously put together. It'd taken longer than anticipated, and he'd already had to text Bethany, letting her know he'd be a little late, but he'd assured her he'd be there. His only consolation was it appeared they had their murderer, and this case was finally over.

Nearly ready to wrap it up, Damian reread a part of the email he'd already read a few times once again.

> He said we'd been drifting apart. He was lonely and she helped fill the void. That he never meant for it to become what it had but his bitch was going through the same thing in her own marriage. The more time they spent together the more their feelings grew and they fell in love. They hadn't planned it. It was something that just happened.

Startled by a folder being dropped on his desk, Damian flinched. "There's the rest of it, Santiago."

Damian looked up at Murphy, one of the two original detectives who had been handling this case until it turned into this giant clusterfuck that it had. "What's this?" He turned his attention back to the two-inch file on his desk.

"That's my part of the Mahoney evidence," Murphy said, pulling his sports jacket on.

"What am I supposed to do with it?"

Murphy shrugged. "Finish getting it prepped to take to the judge. Bates wants it by today. My wife went into labor last night. I came in to do as much as I could, but I just got the call." He grinned. "It's showtime." He opened the top cabinet and pulled out his wallet and keys in a hurry. "I missed the first one two years ago, and I still ain't done hearing 'bout it yet," he said, shaking his head. "She's warned me for nine months now if I miss this one, she's gon' leave my ass."

Damian glanced back at the file, his stomach taking a dive. "There's no one else who can finish this? I had to be somewhere at two." Feeling the irritation begin to overwhelm him, Damian glanced at the time on the corner of his monitor: 2:48.

"Bates said he wanted you on it. Talk to him if you want. I gotta go." Murphy rushed off before Damian could protest further.

"Fuck!" He threw his pen down on his desk and sat back in his chair, running both his hands through his hair.

Of course Bates would want him on it. He'd been so determined to prove he was good enough for this that he'd always gone above and beyond when it came to preparing evidence to present to the judge.

For a good five minutes he sat there trying to calm himself. Finally he reached over to the file and opened it. Scanning through it, he saw that Murphy had finished more than half. The rest wasn't too complicated; he could probably get it done in an hour or so. It wouldn't be his best work, but he didn't give a shit at that point.

He sent Bethany the dreaded text that he'd be there in under an hour and began plowing through the file. By the time he was near the end, he realized he was doing a half-ass job; it just didn't matter anymore. Once he passed the four o'clock hour, all he could think of was that Bethany had been waiting for him all day and how he had to fight thoughts of Bethany *filling a void* with Simon.

After this case was closed and in the hands of the prosecutors, he was taking some much-needed time off. He'd get everything set. Bethany said she had finally gotten the information she needed about her aunt's mortgage. The incompetent idiots down at the bank had given her the runaround on the exact figures needed to bring the account current. Damian was certain they were buying time in the hope that they could foreclose, since her aunt owed a fraction of what the house was worth. He told her he could just pay it off, but of course she refused.

Tonight he'd tell her about getting her moved into his place and how easily he could set up her siblings, either with them at his place—he certainly had extra rooms—or at one of his other properties nearby. He needed to get this straightened out already. This would be different than it had been with Lana. This time he wasn't going to blow it, because, unlike with Lana, there was no way in hell he thought he could get over losing Bethany.

Finally done, he rushed into Bates's office and dropped the files on his desk. Bates began to question him, but Damian was quick to shut him up. "I gotta go. I missed an appointment at two, and they're still waiting for me. Call me if you have any questions."

Not that he planned on answering, but it sounded good. Rushing out of his chief's office, he didn't bother to call or text Bethany. The extra hour he promised her it would take him to finish had only gone over by fifteen minutes. He'd filled her phone with enough disappointing texts. The next one he wanted her to see was one that said he was right outside her door.

He jumped into his '84 Ford Mustang. It was by far the least expensive of his collection, and he'd been hoping to talk her into keeping it. It was one of the first he'd ever restored almost all by himself, when he was just a teen, and that was the only reason he still had it. He knew she was worried about its being stolen or stripped in her neighborhood, so when he told her this one was worth less than ten grand, he hoped she'd agree.

His phone rang just as he turned onto her street. It was Bethany. He tapped his headpiece. "Hey, babe,"

"Damian," she sounded a bit out of breath. "Amos needs me to come in and wait some tables for him because someone called in. But it's only for a few hours."

As enormously disappointed as he felt, he dare not complain. He'd canceled on her way too many times, and at the last minute, too. Then he had a thought. He'd at least get to be with her for a few minutes. "I can give you a ride. I'm just—"

"No! I'm already on the bus."

He banged his steering wheel, biting his tongue so she wouldn't hear him cuss. He'd been so damn close, damn it! If he'd only called her when he left the station he might've caught her, because he was only a couple of buildings away from hers.

Glancing up at the still-open window of her apartment, he wondered why she hadn't closed it as she always did when she left. Then he saw someone close it. He sat up straight, suddenly relieved she wasn't home. His first thought was a burglar, and he was glad he hadn't taken his holster off yet. Looking around, he made sure he had the right window. It was hers all right.

"You said you're already on the bus, right?"

"Yeah," she said, sounding even more out of breath.

He was about to warn her not to go back to her apartment until he let her know it was okay when someone running out the front door of her building caught his eye. It was Bethany. Stunned, he watched as she waited at the curb to cross. "I gotta go," she said before stepping off the curb. "I'm at my stop. I'll call you when I'm done. Love you!"

She didn't even give him a chance to respond before she hung up. He watched her walk across the street to where a guy sitting on a Harley wearing a helmet handed her a helmet. She slipped it on, hopping on the bike, and wrapped her arms around his waist.

Feeling his insides light up instantly, he wondered now why he had never once bothered to ask Bethany what Simon drove. Racking his brain, he thought back to all the times she'd mentioned Simon's giving her a ride. He didn't remember her ever mentioning a bike, but then she'd never actually said car either.

As pissed as he suddenly felt seeing her wrapped around this guy, he wasn't sure if he should be more worried. The huge brick in his stomach decided he was both. Had his little outburst today on the phone about Simon caused her to think it was best not to mention Simon's picking her up? Was this what she was going to do from here on? Lie because his insecure ass couldn't take knowing she was getting a ride from her coworker, even though it was better than taking the bus? Either way, she'd lied, and regardless of why, it pissed him off.

The heat was now peaking, as he followed them, watching as she leaned against Simon's back. He quickly realized they weren't even going to City Lights when they jumped on the highway, and his heart sped up. Did she get tired of waiting for Damian and decide to call Simon—spend more time with him, because being with him until midnight hadn't been enough? Had something happened last night between them that had her needing to see him again?

A million things ran through Damian's mind as he made sure he kept up. Glad he'd brought the Mustang today, a car she'd only seen once and probably didn't even remember, he stayed close behind them.

They got off the highway and headed toward the strip. Not even sure if he had good reason to yet, he felt compelled to bang his steering wheel again. Only this time he did so a lot harder than he had the first time.

For weeks now he'd felt something like this coming—building. Every time she responded to another one of Simon's many texts to her, every time she'd *turn* to Simon whenever Damian left her hanging, but he kept telling himself he was comparing her to someone for whom he'd never felt even close to what he felt for Bethany.

Then he thought of her calling him Simon today. He squeezed the steering wheel, keeping his eye on the bike as he got closer to them in the lane next over. Even then his heart insisted it was just a slip—nothing more. His eyes could've burned a hole through her back. He didn't even care that he wasn't a few cars behind anymore; he was right behind them. Damian was this close to honking his fucking horn and making them pull over, because he wanted answers now. He hadn't planned on confronting them if they'd gone straight to the theater, where she said she had to be. He'd blamed himself for her feeling the need to lie about her ride if that had been the case. But now he sure as fuck was going to, because this was a boldfaced lie, and he wanted her to look at him in the eyes when she explained why she'd said it.

His heartbeat doubled as the bike pulled into the valet parking lane of the Crown Hotel Casino. The flashing sign for the big show here, *Imagine*, reminded him that she'd once taken on the lead in it. His heart was grasping here, but there had to be a reasonable explanation for her being here now with Simon. Maybe they'd called her back, and she was planning on surprising him.

If that's what this was, he was forbidding her to *ever* surprise him again, because she was about to give him a heart attack. He slowed, falling one car behind them now, and watched as they pulled up to the front door of the hotel casino and parked in what looked like a loading-zone-only space. They started getting off the bike as an attendant came over and greeted Simon with a big smile. They obviously had no qualms about his leaving his bike there.

The guy pulled off his helmet, and Damian saw now it wasn't Simon. "What the—?"

Damian stared as Bethany pulled off her helmet as well. It suddenly made sense. Damian knew enough about motorcycles to know this one was expensive. As far as he knew, like Bethany, Simon was barely getting by. And this guy was getting the VIP treatment here.

Just knowing she'd be walking into a hotel with another guy stabbed at his heart. He squeezed his eyes shut for a second, clenching his teeth. *This is not just a hotel. It's a huge resort.* Opening his eyes, he saw the guy tip the parking attendant.

Breathing a sigh of relief when neither reached out for the other's hand, Damian tried in vain to calm his anxious heart. There *was* an explanation for this. There *had* to be.

He reached the parking attendees just as Bethany and this guy walked through the casino entrance doors. Damian jumped out of his car, handing the attendee his keys and a couple of bucks. The guy started to say something to him as he ripped the ticket off the booklet he held and handed it to Damian. "Sorry, I'm in a hurry," he said, grabbing the ticket out of his hand and rushing up the steps of the casino's entrance.

He spotted them walking alongside the casino. Relieved that they hadn't gone to check in, he followed cautiously behind them, watching them closely. They were talking, and if he had to go by body language and the way Bethany walked with her arms crossed in front of her, he'd say she was tense. Nervous about an audition maybe?

They turned into a hallway off the side, and Damian looked up to read where the hallway led to.

ROYAL TOWER A ELEVATORS
Executive suites
Penthouse suites
Lucky 7 suites
Bachelor pad

"What?" Damian practically sprinted now. He was done guessing. He turned the corner in time to see the guy hit the elevator button. "Bethany!"

They both turned, startled to see him. The guy turned to Bethany with obvious disdain. "Why's he here?"

Damian didn't recognize the guy. He was dressed in full Harley gear from top to bottom, leather chaps and all, and though it all looked expensive, and he could see that under the chaps and leather vest he wore business attire, there was something sleazy-looking about him. He turned to Bethany. She looked terrified. If he hadn't seen her get on his bike of her own free will, he might think she had been brought there against it.

"What's going on? You said you had to work. Why are you here?" He turned and glared at the guy. "And who's this?"

"Damian." She shook her head. "I can explain all of it to you *later*."

The elevator doors opened, and the guy gave Damian a once-over, then began to walk in. "Let's go, Bethany. I don't have time for this."

Damian stepped in front of her. "What the fuck's going on? You're not really going up there with this guy, are you?"

"I have to," she said, almost in a whisper.

"You heard her. She has to," the guy barked from inside the luxurious elevator.

Feeling his insides set ablaze, he didn't even try to stay calm now. This was bullshit. "What do you mean you have to?" He looked up at the sign, jabbing his finger toward it. "What? To his hotel room?"

The elevator started beeping as the guy, looking even more impatient, continued to hold it open with his hand. "It's a bachelor pad, and why wouldn't she be coming with me?"

Taking a step toward the elevator, he felt Bethany touch his arm. "Because *I'm* her boyfriend, asshole, and I say she's not."

The scowl on the guy's face softened into a sneer, and he began to laugh. With the urge to charge in there and beat the asshole off every wall in that elevator, he took another step. "Damian, don't." Bethany squeezed his arm, lowering her voice. "His name is Max. He's a long story. I can explain all this later, baby, and I know you'll understand."

"Why don't you tell him now?" Max asked, forcing a laugh, but Damian could see he was losing his cool. "Tell him the cold, hard truth?" He laughed again. "Let's see how understanding your *baby* is about it."

He was taunting her now, and Damian readied his fist, taking another step forward, ready to beat the shit out of him. Bethany jumped in front of Damian now, her hands flat against his chest. "No, please."

Max banged his hand against the outside of the elevator. "Let's go, Bethany. I told you, I don't have time for this shit."

"And *I* told *you*, she's not going anywhere with you."

The guy smirked. "Oh, yeah," he chuckled into his fist. "That's right, because you're her boyfriend, right?"

"Exactly."

"Well, maybe," he said a little louder, stepping out of the elevator, "your *girlfriend* should've mentioned she's married!"

It didn't even register at first, and Damian heard himself ask, "What?"

"Awe!" Max pouted, walking around to try to get a glimpse of Bethany's face. "You didn't tell your boyfriend about your *husband*, Bethany?" He turned to Damian with a gleam in his eye. "How's it feel now, you clueless idiot? *I'm* her husband, and *I* say she is coming with me."

Stunned and feeling as if the air had been sucked out of him, Damian looked down at Bethany, whose eyes were closed now. Max was cackling, and Damian didn't want to give him the satisfaction of knowing he'd just dropped a monster grenade on him. One he never saw coming.

It was a struggle, but he managed to at least appear composed. He stepped back from her as she opened her eyes. "Is it true?"

"I can explain it all, Damian." Her eyes began to flood. "I swear."

He stared at her; the tightness in his chest making it hard to breathe, and all his shattering heart could think was she wasn't saying no.

CHAPTER 21

THE TRUTH

"Just tell me one thing. One fucking thing, Bethany. It's all I need to know. Is it true?"

Her pinched brows over her pained and flooding eyes said it all. The very weak nod was the final confirmation. Just as with everything else that had happened between him and Bethany—at lightning-fast speed—the lava in his veins was instantly frozen, and the murderous rage he had felt just moments ago was replaced by something so numbing he could barely breathe. His heart was still fighting it, but there was no way around this. No reasonable explanation, as he kept telling himself the whole way there. Not anymore. Damian had no choice but to accept it now. The relationship he'd dived into so impulsively, never imagining he'd fall as profoundly in love as he had, or so quickly, had been viciously pulled from under him like a rug, flipping him over on his back and knocking the wind completely out of him.

He began to make words out of the sound coming from

her mouth as the blood thrumming in his ears calmed slowly. Over Max's obnoxious cackling, he heard two sentences that enraged him now.

"I love you, Damian. You have to believe that."

"You're fucking married, Bethany!" Damian's voice boomed in reaction to hearing those words from her. She flinched, backing away. He hated that even for a moment he'd scared her, but he couldn't help himself. There was no way he was going to go along with this. "This whole thing's been a lie! Why?"

"It was *not* a lie. I was gonna tell you!" She cried openly, trying to reach for him, but he backed up.

"When!" he demanded loudly, feeling like he was about to lose it. "When were you gonna tell me you belonged to someone else!" A couple that had started toward them turned around and walked away when they saw the commotion.

Unable to take Max's cackling anymore and needing to unload on someone, he charged at him, slamming him against the marble wall, his head bouncing against it. He buried his fist in his face twice, but seeing the blood splatter, even through his rage, he knew he'd be hauled away in cuffs if he didn't stop and get out of there soon. So he settled for lifting Max away from the wall and slamming his head into it again. "Did your *wife* tell you this clueless idiot has been fucking her for weeks?" Max's eyes widened, and he heard Bethany gasp. "Oh, yeah, she'd spread those pretty little legs for me so wide again and again and *begged* for it." He turned to Bethany now, wondering if she'd actually been with Simon last night or here in Max's bachelor pad. Feeling like a complete idiot, he let go of Max with a shove. "Take your wife back. I'm done with her now."

Whatever she said to him as he blew by her in a mad rush to get the fuck out of there, he didn't hear it. He didn't want

to hear anything anymore. He'd been had. If she hadn't confirmed this herself, he probably still wouldn't believe it. His
heart *still* didn't want to. But the truth was this entire time,
he'd been the other man. Bethany, the girl he was so desperately in love with, was a married woman.

CHAPTER 22

———

One month later . . .

Damian took that much-needed break from work, as he'd planned to after the Mahoney case was handed over to the prosecutors. He was now on a personal leave, and he wasn't sure if he'd ever go back. He knew he didn't have to. The money coming in from his real estate investments and the family business was more than enough for him to keep up his lifestyle. A lifestyle that didn't mean anything anymore.

He'd just as soon sell the big empty house he lived in and move into one of the small condos he owned near the strip. He'd refused to sleep in his bed ever since . . .

It hadn't even been a few days after the blowup when his weak ass had gone running back to Bethany's apartment. At first he'd been furious and overwhelmingly hurt that she'd played him for such a fool. He'd been certain that she and Max were con artists and had planned the whole thing from day one to try to extort money from him and his family. He'd almost given her the money for her aunt's mortgage, and he wondered, after the fact, if the aunt even existed. Did she even have siblings, or was that Max she'd been so jumpy about his catching her on the phone with all the time?

What had him running back to see her only days after the big blowup was a couple of things that had kept him hopeful. His mind kept going back to that first night he'd been with her, when he had to stop and confirm it wasn't her first time. She was *so* tight. No married woman engaging in regular sex would feel that way. The other thing that haunted him those first few days, and still did, was that in the midst of his dazed reaction, trying to take in what had just been dropped on him—that Bethany was married—she'd said something he still couldn't get out of his head: "It's not at all like what you're thinking."

What did that mean? his wretched and hopeful heart begged to know. After almost a week of lying on his sofa sulking and feeling like the biggest fucking schmuck on the planet, it was suddenly something he *needed* to know. The tiniest bit of hope had resurfaced that maybe there was a valid explanation. Maybe she wasn't a cunning barracuda who'd played him so hard that he'd been sucked in to an extent he never would've believed possible if he hadn't lived it. His heart was grasping, but it kept asking. Why would she still beg him to believe that she loved him even after the truth was out? Words that had enraged him that day, just days later loudly challenged him to find out!

He'd practically raced to her apartment, only to find out she was gone. There was a "For Rent" sign on her window he'd seen before he even got out of his car. The slimy landlord, who'd finally come to the office door after Damian had banged on it for too long, said she'd paid up her last month's rent a few days before and left, leaving no forwarding address. When he asked about her lease, the landlord cackled annoyingly, reminding him of Max. "No one signs a lease to live in this paradise," he'd said, cackling even louder. And the lies were mounting.

Still, in his desperation, he'd knocked on Trinity's door and even gone to City Lights and spoken to Amos and Simon. None had answers about why she left, nor were any of them aware she was married. All were stunned when he told them, and the only one who'd shed even the slightest bit of information was Amos, when he mentioned her leaving him a forwarding address to her family's home—in California, not Arizona as she'd told him—throwing more water on the already tiny spark of hope that she wasn't a complete fraud and there was an explanation for this.

Out of respect for Bethany's privacy and because it was illegal to give Damian any more detailed information, such as a specific address, Amos couldn't tell him more.

Her phone number was no longer a working number. Just as on the very day he met her, she'd once again dismissed him unceremoniously, and Damian was left to wonder. Had she planned on doing this from the very beginning? Or had something happened to make her just up and vanish from his life as if their entire incredible experience had meant nothing to her?

Sure, he'd said some harsh things that day. But he was pissed, damn it. She had to know what an unexpected blow her betrayal had been. There was no graceful way to handle it. He'd been beyond furious but even more hurt.

Any normal person would've cut his losses and walked away at that point. And he did try to do just that and move on for almost another week, but nothing in Damian's life had been normal in weeks. Not since he'd met Bethany. The way their relationship had unfolded had been exceptional, to say the least. His gut told him he'd never feel normal again. Bethany had come into his life, and in just a few months changed him forever.

That's when he decided. He might never work another case for the LVPD, but he had one more case he needed to solve before he left the department. He'd use every resource available to him to figure this out. He needed peace of mind, no matter how painful the truth might be.

He sat in his home office now strumming his guitar as he waited for a call. He rarely used the office, but it was also one of the rooms in his home visitors never entered. It's where he'd set up his investigation headquarters; if anyone came over he could lock the door so no one would be witness to the madness he'd become obsessed with. He'd even rolled in the giant dry-erase board from the garage. Usually, it had the layout of the most current restoration he was working on, or planning on working on. Now it was full of notes dating back to the day he met Bethany. He'd written down all the clues he could remember about her odd behavior and things he should've picked up on.

He'd begun to build on a hopeful theory based on her statement: "It's not at all like what you're thinking."

So he'd written down at the top of the board what he *was* thinking. He had a ton of theories, but he narrowed it down to the two most likely. She was a married woman who decided to have an affair with Damian on her own. Or she and Max had been in on this together, something that began as a scam, but Bethany became emotionally involved, and when Max found out the truth, he took her away. His mission now was to come up with a reason that would prove it wouldn't—couldn't—be either of those two scenarios.

Putting all the facts together, the most telling was that she was living alone in an apartment she had no qualms about inviting him into. They'd even been intimate on more than one occasion in that little apartment. Damian followed up with another visit to Trinity to find out if in fact Bethany lived there full-time or if this was a side apartment she kept, as some married men were known to do for their affairs. But Trinity had confirmed that as far as she knew, Bethany slept there every night.

With his theory coming together, he was beginning to really get his hopes up that perhaps Bethany had married that crazy bastard on a whim or maybe in exchange for something—money, perhaps—and had moved out here to try to get out of it. Hell, maybe she was drunk when she did it. Who knew? Bottom line was Damian had done the math; she hadn't been living with the guy for over ten months now. The marriage *had* to be some kind of sham. It's what she'd been trying to tell him.

He'd been staring so hard at all the clues on the board that when his phone rang, he literally jumped. Putting the guitar down, he picked it up. Seeing who it was, he prayed he had good news. The guy working on the background he'd ordered for Bethany didn't know why Damian needed it run. But Damian wanted specifics on her marriage, mostly, so he told the guy he was doing this as a favor for his insecure cousin in California who was looking to hire Bethany as an assistant. Based on Bethany's looks and age, her cousin wanted to know how solid Bethany's marriage was before she brought her into her home to work alongside her and her husband. Damian was hoping for a slam dunk "The marriage is a sham" finding.

He hit speaker on his cell and answered, laying it back down on his desk. "Pierce, whatta ya got?"

"Well I got some good news, then some bad news, and then maybe some hope for your cousin about this girl."

Damian sat back in his seat. "Just give it to me. Is their marriage shaky?"

"It is," Pierce said, and Damian let out a relieved breath.

"But that's only because she filed for an annulment last year."

Damian sat up. That explained why she'd been living alone for eight months when he met her. But last year? "How long have they been married? And what do you mean only?" Damian's adrenaline was already pumping, but he was still nervous. "What could be shakier than a marriage on the verge of being annulled?"

"They've been married over a year and had a huge wedding, then a very romantic honeymoon in Maui."

"What?" Damian stared at the phone. So much for marrying the guy on a whim.

"Yeah, and these two looked to be really in love for a minute there. Aside from Maui, in the short time they lived together, they had lots of romantic vacations she documented on her Facebook page. Seems every damn photo she ever posted on her wall is of the two of them doing something romantic."

Damian didn't know which was the harder blow, finding out she was married or this. At least when he had found out she was married to this sleaze, his gut screamed there was something missing. There was no way she would've ever seriously married this guy, but who could argue with this?

"Are you sure this is the same girl?"

"Yeah, Maximiliano and Bethany Amaya. They share a beautiful home just outside Los Angeles. They go horseback riding on the weekends, do picnics in the park—"

"All right, I get it. They're romantic, okay?" Damian rested his elbows on the desk and sank his face in his hands. "What's this about hope? Hope for what?"

"Well, she'd been AWOL for a while now. No Facebook updates for months. They stopped around the time I'm assuming they separated. But the reason cited for the annulment is duress, meaning one or both were not of sound mind. They were under the influence of something. But typically that means they have a quickie wedding like the tons that happen here in Vegas every day. These two had a huge wedding, then a honeymoon to boot, followed by all that romantic shit on her Facebook page. How you gonna claim being under duress after all that shit? I mean, seriously, after sifting through photo after photo of their romantic outings, even I was kind of bummed to find out things had gone sour. And get this. Even though they're getting an annulment, not a divorce, under California law, she's still entitled to a lot of his loot, and homeboy's loaded. Yet she's asking for nothing. Nada. Zero. Zilch. That to me says she may be looking to keep this amicable because ya know maybe she's changed her mind and maybe she's hoping to work things out. You gotta see the pictures, Santiago, to know what I'm talking about. That's some deep love right there."

Damian was tired of hearing this shit already. He took a deep, irritated breath but felt no desire to lift his face from his hands. He'd probably stay that way even after he hung up with Pierce. "So that's it? That's the hope you were talking about that maybe things aren't so bad because she's not taking his ass to the cleaners?"

"Well there's that and the fact that she's back in town now, and they've been seen together."

Now Damian lifted his face away from his hands, feeling that familiar heat. "They have? Doing romantic stuff again?"

"Not so much. She hasn't posted anything on her Facebook page anyway, but there's this, and usually I'm not supposed to dig this deep, so don't say anything, okay? But it's not even digging, they make this shit so easy, it's a joke." Damian listened intently as Pierce shuffled more papers. "She went to a gynecologist just after she got here, and I'm thinking bingo. She's back and maybe things are looking so good she's getting back on birth control." Pierce chuckled. "Even better, man. She's pregnant."

Shooting to his feet instantly, Damian grabbed his phone, taking it off speaker and bringing it to his ear. "You sure about that?"

"Yeah." This seemed to please Pierce, because he chuckled again. "So even though they've been separated, apparently that hasn't stopped them from getting it on, and nothing will halt an annulment faster than a baby. So tell your cousin—"

"Text me the address where she's staying," Damian said, already rushing out of his office. "She's not staying with him, right?"

"No, she's somewhere else. I believe at an aunt's. But—"

"Text it to me," Damian said, his heart beating harder than it had in a while, and that said a lot, because the past month had been hell. "And thanks, man. I owe you."

He hung up and headed to his room to pack a bag. The memory of his first night with her jumped at him again. His gut had never been more sure about anything in his life. That baby Bethany was carrying was not Max's. And he didn't give a shit about all the other stuff Pierce had just told him. Romantic marriage or not, something had to give. Damian was still holding on to that sliver of hope in his heart. *It's not at all like what you're thinking.*

"I don't want you to do this." Tia Lupe crossed her arms in front of her.

"Yeah." Stella shook her head. "I don't think it's worth it either."

Bethany closed the kitchen door behind her, the frustration mounting. "I've already agreed, and he paid up the mortgage," she said, turning to face her aunt. "I was not about to let you lose this house."

"I care more about you than I do this house."

"It's not just the house he's helping me with," Bethany reminded her aunt with a knowing look.

"But you'll be miserable," Stella insisted. "You hated having to live with him."

"I know," Bethany agreed, the dread in her belly mounting, not to mention the very thought added to her already nauseated insides. "But he's agreed to all my stipulations. I've promised him nothing, and he accepts that. Six months and I'm out of there."

"This is ridiculous," her aunt huffed. "The man is delusional if he thinks he can make you fall in love with him."

"I've already told him it'll never happen," Bethany said, lowering her voice and motioning with her hand to remind her aunt that Max was on the back patio just a few doors down. "He wanted a year; I said no more than six months, and he said he's up for the challenge. I still need this money, and six months will fly by before you know it."

She'd need the money now more than her aunt and Stella could know, but she couldn't tell them about that yet. They were already against her agreeing to stop the annulment; if she told them about her pregnancy, they'd be even more against it. But she'd been upfront with Max about it, and he still wanted to do this, even knowing the baby wasn't his. The man truly was delusional.

Feeling a wave of nausea come over her again, she walked to the sink, afraid she might be sick. It began to pass as she took in long, slow breaths. "Are you okay?" her aunt asked, coming around and placing her hand on Bethany's back.

"I'm fine, I ju—" her jaw dropped midsentence at the sight of Damian getting out of his car in their driveway.

The nausea was quickly replaced with a mixture of excitement and pain. She'd missed him so much, seeing him now choked her up. Then she remembered Max was out back.

"Who's that?" her aunt asked, looking out the window.

Bethany quickly walked away. "I'll be back."

With her heart beating erratically, she rushed through the house to get to the front door before Damian rang the doorbell. She opened the door just as he made it to the top of the porch stairs. They stared at each other for a moment without saying anything. He was more beautiful than she remembered him. But his wounded eyes reminded her that she'd hurt him badly, and he probably hated her now. "We need to talk," he said simply.

"I can't now." She glanced back. "Max is here."

"I don't care," he said, those wounded eyes going hard. "I think I deserve answers. At the very least an explanation."

"You do," she agreed quickly. "But it's a long story, and I don't have time—"

"Then talk fast, because I'm not going anywhere."

She could see it in his eyes. He was serious. Without a choice, she decided to give him the quick and dirty version. "I'm not a citizen, Damian. I was born in Mexico. My aunt was diagnosed with cancer last year. The doctors said she might die, and if she did, my brother and sister would be put in foster care because I couldn't be their legal guardian, since I wasn't a citizen. I tried applying, but they said it could take years, and I didn't have years. Max was my director down at the theater I worked at, and he offered to marry me so I could get my papers quicker." She glanced back again to make sure Max wasn't coming. "He said it would be strictly business, and we could divorce after the two years I needed to stay married to keep my citizenship, but after only a few months he admitted he was in love with me and that he wanted to try to make the marriage work." She lowered her voice now. "I've never even slept with him, and I was miserable the entire time I had to live with him. My aunt's cancer went into remission, and when she found out what I'd done, she begged me to leave him—get an annulment. She hated to see me so miserable, so I did, but he said I owed him."

"Owed him what?" Damian asked, taking a few steps closer to her.

"For the wedding. For all the expenses he paid for to make the marriage look real. Like the honeymoon and all the other trips." She shook her head, feeling disgusted suddenly that she'd be back in that nightmare soon. "Trips *he* insisted were necessary because the Department of Immigration was watching us closely, and if they got wind that our marriage was a fraud, I'd be deported, and he'd go to jail."

"That's bullshit. You didn't have to pay him back. He did all that romantic crap for his own reasons."

Bethany nodded, agreeing. "But he held on to some things of mine. Things he knew I'd do anything to get back, jewelry that belonged to my mother. Until I could come up with this ridiculous sum of money I owed him."

The wounded look in his eyes was back. "Why didn't you just tell me?"

"I couldn't, Damian. I'd committed a federal offense. And there's other stuff I didn't want you involved in either." Taking a deep breath, she willed the emotion away. "I shouldn't have got involved with you in the first place, and I'm sorry that I hurt you. But everything happened so fast, and before I knew it, I'd fallen so hard for you I couldn't stay away from you no matter how much my head said I should. At least until the annulment was final."

He brought his fingers to her face, and she closed her eyes.

She'd yearned to feel his touch again for weeks, and even something this simple felt good. "So you weren't lying when you said you loved me?"

With her eyes still closed, she placed her hand over his and tilted her head into it. "God, no. I love you like I've never loved anyone in my life."

"Then why'd you come back?"

She opened her eyes slowly and looked into his, so full of questions still. "I had to."

A car pulled up in front of the house, and they both turned to look. A woman in a pantsuit holding a briefcase got out and began walking toward the house; Damian looked back at Bethany, but she offered no explanation. Instead she waited for the woman to near.

"Good afternoon. I'm Jennifer Allen. I'm here to see Max and Bethany Amaya?"

"Good afternoon." Bethany smiled, moving aside. "I'm Bethany, and, yes, we've been expecting you. Go on in." Stella walked into the front room. "Will you show her out to the patio, please?" Stella nodded, and Bethany smiled at Jennifer. "I'll join you in just a few minutes."

As soon as Jennifer was gone, she turned to Damian. "I have to go."

Damian took a step closer to her. "Why did you have to come back?"

Bethany fidgeted with her hands, feeling the knot in her stomach tightening. It was just a matter of time before Max came looking for her. "That day you confronted us at the Crown. He called me to tell me that he had my mother's jewelry for me, and he'd give it to me if I would just listen to a proposition he wanted to make me. He said even if I didn't agree to it, he'd still give me the jewelry. I knew no matter what, I wouldn't be agreeing to anything, but I'd worked my ass off to get the money to pay him so I could get my mom's jewelry back. It's all I cared about, so I agreed to meet with him. The jewelry was in the safe in his suite, and he said we should go there to talk. That's when you showed up."

She paused momentarily as the horrific images of that night came back to her. The sickened expression on Damian's face when she had to confirm that Max *was* her husband.

"If you remember, that was the day I finally got the exact amount I needed to bring the mortgage current, and we had very little time to do it."

Damian's eyes took on that iciness she'd only seen in them a few times, most memorably on the night of the horrible confrontation. "And what exactly was that proposition?"

"That he'd help me with my aunt's mortgage and some . . . *other* debt I owe if I agreed to cancel the annulment."

His eyes opened wide now. "And you did?"

Because of his raised voice, Bethany turned to check on Max again, but the front room was still clear. "I had no choice, Damian. Especially after that night, I knew there was no way I could expect you to want to still help me nor would I dare take your money knowing how much I'd hurt you. He was my only hope, and I was desperate."

"You canceled it?"

"Not yet. But that's why she's here," she motioned with her hand. "That woman is an attorney and notary public. She's here to make sure it's all done correctly and will be notarizing the paperwork."

His eyes opened wider now. "Does he know you're pregnant?"

Stunned and in a panic, Bethany reached for the wooden front door and closed it, stepping out onto the porch with him. "How did you—"

"Does he, Bethany?" He moved closer, so close to her

face that even at a tense moment like this she thought, even hoped, maybe he'd kiss her. "Does he know you're still in love with me?"

"He knows *everything*, Damian."

His brows came together as she'd seen them do so many times with his suspicious glare. "Then why'd you close the door?"

"Because I haven't told my aunt or sister, but he knows."

That seemed to surprise him, and he took a step back. "And he still wants the annulment canceled?" Then his eyes shot wide again. "He *does* know that's not *his* baby, right?"

Once again he'd managed to completely stun her. He said that with such certainty, but at the same time it warmed her that he had such faith in her even after everything. Holding back the emotion and the urge to jump into his arms, she nodded. "He knows it's yours," she said, lowering her hand to her still-flat belly.

His eyes followed her hand and stayed there for a moment before looking up at her again. "And when were you planning on telling me? *After* you canceled the annulment?"

"It's only for six more months, and then I'll file for divorce."

"But why? Why the hell would you wanna stay married to this guy for even another day?"

"He brought my aunt's mortgage back to current, and it was the agreement. And he got his lawyers to delay this for so long now that in six months it'll be two years, and I'll be able to keep my citizenship. It'll make it worth all the hell and sacrifice I've gone through."

Damian reached for her hand, and she took it willingly. But the pain in his eyes was worse than she'd ever seen in them, even on the night he'd confronted them. "Really? It'll be worth losing what we have?"

What we have? Even after everything she'd just told him. All that she'd put him through, he was telling her they still had something? "You'd forgive me?"

Pulling her to him, he brought his big arms around her and hugged her tight. Words couldn't begin to describe the bliss she felt being in his arms again, and she was instantly choked up. With a long, deep breath, he kissed the top of her head. "Sweetheart, this entire time my heart never accepted that there was ever anything real to forgive."

The door opened suddenly, and Bethany pulled away from Damian, but he slid his hand in hers and held it firmly.

"Get your hands off my wife," Max demanded, stepping out onto the porch.

Damian tightened his grip on her hand, but took a step forward. "I see your face healed, Max. Ready for round two?"

"It's healed now, but I have plenty of photos, and the hotel was gracious enough to supply me with footage of that night's incident in case I change my mind about pressing charges."

"You promised you wouldn't," Bethany reminded him anxiously.

Tilting his head, he glanced down at her and Damian's still-entwined hands. "Yeah, well, I suppose people change their minds. And if you're considering changing your mind about our agreement, then—"

"She is," Damian said, taking another step in front of her. "So if part of your agreement was not to press charges, go ahead. I'll pay the fine. It was worth every bruised knuckle. And I'll pay you whatever she owes you, but you're out of your mind if you think she's gonna stay even another day trapped in that hell of a marriage with you."

Bethany watched as Damian's words, which were news to

her as well, sank in, and Max's expression went from angry to suddenly smug. "Really? You gonna pay her pimp off, too?"

Her heart dropped, and with Damian standing in front of her, she couldn't see the expression on his face, but she could only imagine. Already that firm hold he had on her hand was weakening. So she gripped it tighter. "I've never had a pimp, and you know it."

Max scoffed, "I'm sorry. Let me rephrase that. Are you gonna pay the guy that paid her to have sex with strangers who she owes money to?" He cackled loudly, as he had that awful night. "Wait, did she make you think she was hiding in Vegas from *me* all this time?"

Damian turned to her, his expression once again broken. He didn't have to ask, but she knew exactly what his unspoken question was. Was this the truth? She nodded, her eyes instantly blurring. He let go of her hand and started down the stairs. "Wait!" she gasped, going after him. She wouldn't let him leave again thinking the worst of her. "He's twisting it, Damian, making it sound like something it's not."

"Bethany," Max called after her. "I think your little boyfriend is forgetting the penalty for assault is more than just a fine. You saw the footage and said it yourself. This could ruin him."

She stopped halfway down the walkway just as Damian reached his car. It was the main reason she'd agreed to leave Vegas with Max. Agreed to the proposition. Max would have made sure he ruined Damian if she hadn't, and would surely ruin him if she went after him now.

Opening his car door, Damian turned to Bethany, stunning her once again. "Get in the car."

"You leave with him, Bethany," Max sounded more panicked now than smug, "and not only are all bets off, I'll go straight to the police with that video."

She stood there, feet still firmly, frozen to the ground.

"Get in, Bethany," Damian urged.

She turned to Max. He wasn't bluffing. If she didn't leave with Damian, this would really be the end of any hope with him. But if she did, she was certain Max would press assault charges against Damian. She'd already hurt Damian so badly. She'd never forgive herself for ruining his career, too.

CHAPTER 23

Waiting for what felt like an eternity to see what Bethany would decide, Damian's heart thudded. He was terrified that she'd turn around and walk back to Max. At first he'd been pissed that she looked torn. How the fuck could she be torn? But he realized what that asshole was doing.

To his enormous relief, she finally rushed around the car toward the passenger seat. Max yelled out more shit about how he would ruin him. Damian turned to glare at him with a purpose one last time, and Max suddenly shut up. *That's right, you stupid motherfucker. Did you really think I'd let you take what was mine so easily?*

Too wound up and afraid he'd give in to the urge to run back up the porch steps and beat the living shit out of him, Damian jumped into the car. He prayed she wouldn't believe Max and change her mind at the last second. As soon as she was in the car, he skidded out of there. He needed to talk to Bethany somewhere where he could think straight without Max's mouth running.

Even for this he knew there had to be a reasonable explanation. He hadn't even made it halfway down the walkway of her aunt's house when it hit him. It was for that very reason he never for an instant questioned whether the baby she was carrying was his. If she was really a liar, she could've easily passed off that first night they made love as her very first because it might as well have been, as pure as she felt. Even if it wasn't her first time, it was obvious it was her first time in a very long time. And one thing he knew for damn sure was this girl he'd given his heart to so willingly and fallen so desperately in love with was *not* a whore.

"Maybe you should take me back," she said, glancing back at her aunt's house. "He's gonna press charges, Damian."

Like hell he was taking her back. "Don't worry about that. First of all he's full of shit if he thinks he's gonna *ruin* me."

"But your image as a detective can be ruined if you're arrested!"

"No one's getting arrested," he assured her. "And I'm leaving the force, so I couldn't give a shit about my image as a detective anymore."

"What?" she gasped.

"I'll explain later, just tell me about this guy you owe."

She brought her hands to her face and shook her head. "Oh, my God. I can't believe I've been so desperate for money for so long."

Okay, that wasn't a good start. She was scaring him now. "What do you mean? What did you do?"

"Long story short: Last year an escort service paid me good money up front for *services* I was naïve enough to believe would not involve sexual favors." She shook her head again, still holding her face in her hands. "I paid all the bills we were behind on. Including some of my aunt's medical bills that were piling up. Then they called me for my first job. It started off fine. It was my first time at the opera, then he took me to a really nice restaurant."

Damian squeezed the wheel. Afraid of where this was

going and in no mood to hear the details of her date with another man, he pressed, "Did you sleep with him?"

"No!" She turned to him. "I didn't even make it out of the restaurant with him. He was pleasant and respectful enough at first, but after a few drinks he started telling me about all the stuff he wanted to do to me when we went back to his place. He was very graphic, and that's when I knew how wrong I was about feeling relieved that his 'turn-on,' according to the profile they sent me, was *talking*."

For the first time in weeks all the tension that had built up, leaving every muscle in Damian's body completely stiff, finally eased a bit, and he actually laughed. Bethany turned to him, looking a bit appalled, which only made him laugh more. "He was a talker, huh? So what happened?"

She crossed her arms in front of her in an attempt to appear annoyed by his laughter, but he could see the tug at the corner of her lips. "After hearing about what he planned to do to me in *vivid detail* for over twenty minutes, I excused myself to the ladies' room and called a cab."

Damian laughed even more, holding out his hand. She undid her mulishly crossed arms and slid her hand in his. "I take it you didn't go on any more *jobs*?"

"No, and I promised I'd pay them back every penny, but with bills still hurtling at me from every direction, it was impossible. Then word got back to them that I'd married Max just a few weeks later. Since Max is a pretty big name in Hollywood, they figured he'd pay them off to keep it on the down low that his wife had worked for an escort service, and he was going to until I started talking about getting an annulment."

Damian pulled into the parking lot of a park, feeling the relief begin to flood his body. This whole past month had been absolute hell, and after hearing her explanation about the escort thing, he was even more relieved he'd gone with his gut when he decided that asshole was probably making it sound a lot worse than it really was.

He shut the engine off and turned to her cautiously. "So, you owe Max, this escort service," he paused looking into those tense eyes that at closer examination looked very drawn and even a bit sunken, "and you're not canceling the annulment, right?"

"Damian, he's already paid for—"

"I'll pay his ass. I'll pay whatever else you owe. Fuck Max. You don't have to stay married to him."

She shook her head, her eyes widening. "No, I don't want you to pay!"

"Why the hell not?"

"You can't be serious. After everything I've put you through, you'd still be willing to pay for all—"

"Yes! Yes! Are you kidding me? I'd be willing to pay for *anything* if it means you're done with that asshole for good. Hell, I'll get lawyers involved if it'll speed the annulment up." He reached for her hand, feeling the very desperation that had weighed so heavily on him this past month. "I won't live without you again, Bethany. And if you don't wanna move back to Vegas with me, then I'll move out here." He choked up now, remembering all those painful sleepless nights he'd had since that night he found out about her marriage. "I can't do that again."

She smiled, bringing his hand to her mouth, and kissed his knuckles one by one slowly. He watched as the tears slid down either side of her face. She finally looked up at him as he wiped the tears away. "I'm *so* sorry for what I put you through, baby. I don't want you to think all this was for just any jewelry." She looked at him, her eyes full of regret and sorrow. "When my mom died so suddenly, the wedding ring my stepdad had given her was automatically slated to my sister because it represented my mother's marriage to Stella's father. Then just a few days after her death my stepdad hung himself."

Damian stared at her pained expression and squeezed her hand. "Sweetheart, you don't have to explain—"

"No," she shook her head. "I want you to understand why I *had* to get that jewelry back." She took a deep breath and composed herself. "My stepdad was a good man. He loved my mom more than life. It's why he took his own. He left a note asking us to forgive him, but he just couldn't take another day without her. In a separate note to me, he explained how much he always loved me like his own and told me about the bracelet my mother said would be mine one day. It's been passed on to her down through the family, and as her oldest daughter it was rightfully mine." She sat up, bringing her arms around him, and he wrapped his arms around her, breathing in the mixture of her hair, the lotion she wore, and everything that made up the amazing feminine fragrance of Bethany, something he didn't even realize he'd missed so much. "I'm so, *so* sorry," she cried.

"It's okay," he whispered, massaging her head with his fingertips as she continued to cry against his shoulder. "You don't have to explain any more about that. Just tell me right now if there's anything more I *need* to know."

She pulled away, shaking her head, her face a beautiful crying mess. "That's all of it. And I swear I'll never keep anything from you again."

He smiled, attempting to wipe some of her tears away with his thumbs. "Do you wanna come back to Vegas, or should I start house-hunting here?"

She bit her bottom lip, a smile breaking through even past the fading tears. "Is this really happening?" Her eyes welled up all over again, and her bottom lip quivered. "I was so sure I'd lost you for good. Am I really getting you back?"

He took her face in his hands and kissed that quivering lip softly. "I'll be honest with you. You scared the hell out of me for a minute there. I had no idea how I was *ever* gonna get over you. But let me tell you something, not for a day, or an hour, or even a fucking minute did my heart believe it was really over. You *never* lost me." He laughed suddenly, kissing her again. "I never realized what a stubborn heart I have. I guess my sister hit it on the nose before she'd even met you."

Bethany's brows pinched suddenly, and already Damian could feel that permanent smile making itself comfortable on his face again. The one only Bethany brought out in him. "You're the one," he said, as her eyes brightened. "I don't give a shit anymore about how fast things happened or how much time is a reasonable enough time to know. I think my heart knew it from day one." He reached down and touched her belly gently. "You're the one, sweetheart, and as soon as this annulment is canceled, I wanna look into *really* locking things down. Okay?"

She took a deep breath, smiling, then sighed in that way that always made his heart swell. "Okay."

"God, I love you," he said, kissing her again.

"I love you, too."

EPILOGUE

The annulment was wrapped up faster and more easily than any of them had imagined. Damian's obsessive detective work about Max and Bethany proved to have been worth it in more ways than one. It uncovered some interesting findings Max had failed to mention to Bethany. Like that he had a three-year-old love child with a woman in northern California. Though he claimed he'd mentioned it *once* to Bethany, she was certain he never had, and even though she couldn't care less, it gave her reason to claim fraud. This was something Max didn't want his name tarnished with, so he agreed to speed up the process in exchange for Bethany's not filing fraud as her reason for the annulment.

Among the other things Damian had uncovered about Max was the clever ways he'd evaded paying his full taxes. Damian let him know his taxes weren't any of his business, but if Max insisted on pressing charges, he'd be forced to give the IRS a heads up. They hadn't heard from Max since.

Exchanging glances and silly smiles, Damian and Bethany signed the marriage license papers, thanking the clerk behind the counter, and walked out of the courthouse. Bethany had already told Damian that, being almost seven months pregnant, she was in no mood to plan a big wedding. So when she said something small and quick would be fine with her, he knew just the thing.

He opened the door to one of Desert Heat's latest restorations, a '53 convertible Corvette. He'd told Bethany he borrowed it for the day, but he had a few surprises for her.

"I'm hungry again," she said with a remorseful little smile as she sat down.

He laughed, closing her door, then leaned over and kissed her. "We'll stop somewhere on our way home. Whatever you want, sweetheart. Your wish is my command."

"My feet are a little swollen. Maybe we can just go through a drive-thru somewhere and head straight home."

He walked around the car, smiling to himself. "A drive-thru it is."

They drove a couple of blocks as Bethany decided what she wanted, then he pulled into the parking lot of a drive-thru where Fina, Carey, and all his brothers, with the exception of Dominic, of course, sat in an old Cadillac convertible waiting for them. Carey lifted her basket full of rose petals.

Bethany looked around and spotted the other convertible in the parking lot, the one with Mace at the wheel, her aunt next to him, and her siblings in the backseat. Bringing her hands to her mouth, she looked up and read the sign to the "drive-thru."

Tunnel of Love Wedding Chapel

Through her tears she laughed, then turned to him. "A drive-thru wedding?"

He nodded, bringing her hand to his lips, and kissed it. "Why not? I figured as fast as things happened with us a quickie four-minute ceremony through a drive-thru would be the perfect way to do this."

He drove through the tunnel, and the other two convertibles followed. The four-minute thing was no lie. In the time it would've taken them to order a cheeseburger, they were married and out of there. Bethany laughed gleefully the whole time, even afterward when they all pulled over in the parking lot and exchanged hugs and kisses with their families. "I can't believe you did this," she said as Damian hugged his pregnant wife.

"When do you go again to find out if my cousin is a boy or a girl?" Carey asked, tugging on Damian's pants.

He glanced down, then back at Bethany.

"Tomorrow," Bethany said, looking just as excited as Carey.

They'd tried several times, but each time the young sonographer said the baby was in a very uncooperative position, and she dared not give them wrong information. Their appointment to try again was tomorrow, and he knew Bethany, like his niece, was dying to know. Damian didn't mind waiting until the day the baby came, but as he'd told Bethany earlier, whatever she wanted she got. As far as he was concerned he now had everything he wanted—this thing with Bethany locked down permanently.

Remembering her swollen feet, he wrapped it up, and they all jumped back into their cars. "One more drive-thru to make, and then we'll meet you all back at the house."

They decided on rotisserie chicken from one of Damian's favorite places. Just as his beautiful wife had asked, they drove through the drive-thru, bought enough for everyone, and headed home.

"So how does it feel to be officially part of the Santiago clan?" he asked, squeezing her hand.

Smiling the huge, excited smile that had stolen his heart

the very first time he'd been witness to it, she sat up straighter. Her face fell suddenly. "What?" he asked, a bit worried.

"I just realized my initials will now be B.S." Damian thought about it for a second, and about the fact that almost the entire time they'd dated she had kept something so huge from him, and couldn't help laughing. She lifted that cute little eyebrow with a frown. "Maybe I won't change my name after all."

He stopped laughing and glanced back at her. She couldn't be serious. Just because of the initials? The corner of her lips inched up slowly with that evil little smirk of hers. Then *she* suddenly laughed. "You are too easy, Damian Santiago."

He smirked, glancing back at the road. "And you're not funny, Bethany *Santiago*."

"Ooh, I like that!"

Now he laughed, shaking his head, and looked back at her. He'd never tire of her quick mood changes. "Good, because it's what you'll be going by for the rest of your life."

"I like that even better." She leaned over and kissed his cheek. "Mrs. Santiago for the rest of my life."

Damian put his arm around her shoulders and leaned his cheek against the top of her head for a moment. Oh, yeah, he had everything he could ever ask for right there.

———

Carey ran out of Damian's front door as soon as the car pulled up the circular driveway. Fina and Dimitri followed. The second Bethany opened her door she heard it. "What is it, Auntie Bethany! Boy or a girl?"

Bethany exchanged glances with Damian, who tilted his head with a smile, letting her know it was up to her. They'd stopped at her aunt's new town house to give her family the news, so she knew Damian's family would be anxiously waiting. "Looks like we're gonna have another little girl asking lots and lots of questions around here."

Carey squealed, while Dimitri groaned! Fina elbowed Dimitri. "What's wrong with little girls?"

"Nothing, if you like getting your toes painted. I don't. Yet . . ." He looked down and wiggled his multicolored painted toes.

They all laughed. "They're pretty, Uncle Mitri."

"Yeah, having pretty toes is not what I'm going for, baby girl." He picked her up and kissed her on the nose.

"Congrats," Fina said, hugging Bethany, then Damian as they reached her at the front entrance. "And yay for more girls in the family! There've been too many stinky boys for too long."

They made their way into the house. "Okay, Carey," Fina said, grabbing her purse. "Now you know. You heard it first-hand. Can we go now? I gotta lot of things to do."

Bethany smiled at Carey. Fina had told her that morning how Carey just had to be there when they got home to hear the news. A text or a phone call wouldn't do. She was dying to know if her cousin was going to be a girl or a boy, and of course she was keeping all her fingers, toes, and eyes crossed that it was a girl.

"But I didn't get to see the pictures yet," Carey reminded her mom.

"That's right," Bethany said, pulling the sonogram photos out of her purse and handing one to Carey and another to Fina.

"Wow," Dimitri said, squatting to look over Carey's shoulder as she stared at the sonogram. "That's crazy how you can see the face so clearly."

"She looks like me," Carey said with a big smile. "What are you gonna name her?"

Bethany turned back to Damian. They'd discussed a few names in the car but were far from decided. Though with all the D names, Bethany's mind kept going back to what Trinity had referred to Damian as once—a daisy. She'd let it simmer for a while.

"We're not sure yet," Damian said, leaning against the back of the sofa and pulling Bethany into his arms.

Making herself comfortable between his legs, she placed her hands over his on her belly as they all discussed baby girl names for a few minutes, until Fina said they really had to go. Not long after she and Carey had gone, Dimitri began to make his exit, but not before mentioning whom he was giving a ride to—Ashlynn.

They were now in the kitchen, and Bethany glanced at Damian's already frowning face. "Why are *you* giving her a ride?"

"Because she posted on her Facebook page that she and her friend were hitching a ride to the Suns game today. I commented back, thinking she was joking, but she was serious. So since I was gonna be over here today, I offered to drop her off on my way home."

"She was hitching a ride?" Damian asked, looking as disgusted as he always seemed whenever Dimitri spoke of Ashlynn.

Bethany tiptoed out of the kitchen to the living room, but both men followed.

"Yeah, she said she does it all the time." Dimitri reached for his baseball cap on the sofa's middle sectional just as Bethany plopped down on the sofa and lifted her feet onto it.

"Does her dad know about this?"

"I don't know. She didn't ask me not to say anything, and it's right there on Facebook," Dimitri said, slipping his baseball cap on. "So if you're gonna rat her out, tell Jerry to just say he saw it on her Facebook page. Don't go throwing me under the bus."

Dimitri kissed Bethany on the forehead and said good-bye to them both before walking out.

Over the past few months Bethany had come to the conclusion that Dimitri enjoyed riling Damian about any time he spent with Ashlynn. It's why he always made comments like today's. He could've walked out without mentioning it, but he had.

Glancing at her still-frowning husband, she smiled, opening her arms. "C'mere, my grumpy bear." One glance at her, and his expression softened. "Why do you let it get to you?"

"Because," he said, lying down next to her with his head on her lap, "he's young and dumb and a girl like her'll eat him up and spit him out. Even as young as she is, if he spends too much time around her it's just a matter of time before that happens. Not that that'd be such a bad thing. The way he blows through girls, a bruised ego is just what he may need to get him to feel what I'm sure a few of those many girls he's discarded must've felt. I still think she's trouble, and I don't want her dragging him down with her. Did I tell you she got a tattoo?"

She ran her fingers through his hair, looking down at him with a smile. "Yes, you did, baby. It says *Loca*, and I told you it's different from the three dots that stand for *Mi vida loca*. Doesn't mean she's in a gang. It's just a word."

He frowned. "It's still a reflection of what she's very proud of. That's she's a crazy girl who's hitching rides from strangers." He turned his head and kissed her belly. "If Jerry weren't on his honeymoon, I'd call him right now to tell him."

"I'm sure you would." She laughed, leaning over and kissing him.

She wouldn't remind him again that she'd gotten a chance

to get to know Ashlynn a little better in the past few months when they'd been over at Jerry's a few times, and the girl wasn't as bad as they both initially thought she was. Bethany actually felt for her. She'd detected a sort of sadness about her, and it tugged at her heart. From what Damian had told her about Ashlynn's mom, and the fact that Ashlynn had chosen to leave her mom to live with a father she hardly knew, Bethany was certain the girl was carrying some heavy baggage. But she wouldn't go there again. The last time she'd brought it up, Damian had dismissed it, saying that after years of being in the force he knew Ashlynn's kind and Bethany's sweet heart was just too untainted to see it.

Instead she went back to thoughts of Damian's best friend. After only a few months of dating, Jerry and Janis had gotten hitched. Damian said he couldn't believe Jerry had called it. He'd told her about the day he went to take Bethany her hair clip, how Jerry had mentioned the speed date had possibly landed the two of them future wife prospects, and Damian had thought him crazy. Now here they both were married less than a year later. Damian even had a child on the way.

Damian pulled her down and kissed her again. As usual the kiss turned into more. "Speaking of honeymoons, Mrs. Santiago," Damian said, sitting up suddenly. "We really should get to bed early." He stood up and held out his hand. "We have a long day tomorrow."

Bethany took his hand, smiling excitedly. Because she was too far along to really travel anywhere comfortably, and now that they knew what they were having, she had asked Damian if they could spend what they would've on a trip shopping for the nursery. Of course he had agreed, and starting tomorrow they'd go on their honeymoon shopping spree.

But Damian assured her this was just the beginning of their honeymoon. He hadn't quit the force, but he had taken an extended leave, and urged her to do the same. With her inflated belly, she really couldn't argue about it. Zumba and her sexy one-woman act would have to wait until long after the baby was born. Even then the temptation to take a few years off and raise her baby as Damian had suggested was growing with every precious kick she felt.

Her new husband was very generous. As soon as Bethany told him she'd prefer to move back to Vegas with him and be near his family, because she already knew her family was more than willing to move here, he had a plan. Within weeks they'd situated her aunt and siblings in one of Damian's townhomes, for which he was refusing to take any rent from them. If that wasn't bad enough, he was also paying all the utilities, and someone had *anonymously* paid off what her aunt owed on her California house. Since the rent in the Los Angeles area was astronomical, they'd rent it, and her aunt and siblings would now be living off the rent from that house. Not that Damian wasn't still insisting on paying any other expenses they had.

Once up, Bethany peered at Damian. "But it's not even seven, we don't need to go to sleep this early."

"Who said anything about sleeping?" Those sexy bedroom eyes burned through her, igniting her insides instantly, because she knew that look—knew exactly what he had in mind.

Glancing down at his bulging crotch, she stifled a giggle. Her being pregnant hadn't in any way impeded his insatiable hunger for her. If anything it heightened it. "Aren't you even gonna try and adjust that? Have you no shame anymore?"

Pulling her to him abruptly, he smirked sinfully. "Absolutely none." He licked her bottom lip. "Besides, with the visual I have going of your beautiful thighs over my shoulders, no amount of adjusting is gonna help me now."

Moaning shamelessly at the very thought, she kissed him back feverishly. "Just don't make me beg, Damian."

"Are you kidding me?" He lifted her, cradling her in his arms. "That's the best part. And this is technically just the beginning of our honeymoon." He grinned scandalously. "So start begging."

Bethany laughed. "Baby, please make love to me until I'm screaming your name," she murmured, then laughed out loud, holding on for dear life when Damian broke into a sprint.